Keeper Of Reign

EMMA RIGHT

KEEPER OF REIGN

Book cover design by Lisa Hainline at www.lionsgatebookdesign.com

Published by Emma Right Books

Visit emma at www.emmaright.com

ISBN 978-0-9892672-3-6 (paperback)

Library of Congress: 2013917901

Version 2013.10.25

Printed in the United States of America

10 9 8 7 6 5 4 3 2 1

Table of Contents

ACKNOWLEDGMENTS

Words of Gratitude.

I am grateful for the sixty-six true Ancient Books that have guided my very step and shown me the light. Too many quotes to be thankful for. One that I hold onto and believe wholeheartedly, from Philippians 4, "I can do all things through Christ who strengthens me."* And these words are so true. Believe it and see your miracle.

"I am with you always, *even* to the end of the age." Matthew 28:20 *NKJV

PRAISES!

Read more on Amazon
KINDLE BEST SELLER
AWARD WINNER
Keeper of Reign is a **Finalist in the 2013 Readers' Choice Award**!
INDIE BOOK OF THE DAY AWARD WINNER.

"Exciting new author, Emma Right, ignites an electrifying new series with spine-tingling action and thrilling suspense!"
Lisa Vanderbilt - LVCMinistries.com, co-author of "Living Victoriously in Christ"

***

Keeper of Reign is a book in the rich traditions of fantasy novels of Lord of the Rings. The novel has cliffhangers at the end of each chapter which makes it impossible to stop reading. Young adult readers who are fans of Lord of the Rings should make this book an addition to their reading lists. I would recommend Emma Right's "Keeper of Reign Book 1" to people who like adventure and fans of C.S. Lewis' novels will also enjoy this book.
Pacific Book Reviews

***

For fantasy book lovers. The book, though it seemed long (340 pages), was actually a very quick read. This was the first in the "Reign Fantasy" series. I enjoyed this book and look forward to reading the next one.
Reviewed by Ben Weldon (age 16)

***

"I loved all the characters. The story has many twists and turns, but is not hard to follow. The plot is great. An easy read for all ages. The story teller did a great job."
D Taylor

***

The story is well-written with characters who are complicated and often conflicted about their choices in considering the consequences of their actions. From page one, the story leaps into action never resting until the end with definite foresight of a possible sequel. Keeper of Reign is a wonderful story for all ages as they join Jules on his quest to save his people.
Midwest Book Review

CHARACTER LIST

Jules Blaze, age sixteen, and heir of a Keeper, who suspects his family hides a forgotten secret. And hates the idea that he has to care for his four (yes, so many,) younger siblings. So uncool.

The other Blaze siblings:
Ralston, thirteen years old and a budding artist who can invent just about anything. If he can overcome his slowness!

Bitha, ten-year-old sister, with flowing jet black hair, and a caring personality, and definitely not keen on adventures.

Tst Tst, pronounced Sit Sit, and also known as Miss Big Words due to her profuse vocabulary which she uses freely unless her life is in danger, which is about almost all the time in Reign these days. She is eight.

Tippy, three years old, lisps and nothing much escapes her sharp eyes. Much to Jules's annoyance.

Neighbors:
Miranda, daughter of Saul Turpentine, and closest neighbor of the Blazes. Also a subject of much interest for both Holden and Jules.

Holden Lacework, age sixteen, and his mother, Jessie Lacework, are also close neighbors of the Blazes.

The Evil Lord, Gehzurolle (pronounced as Geh-zoo-rawl) and his army of Scorpents. Their headquarters is in Euruliaf across the River, Brooke Beginning, in the Handover side of the territory.

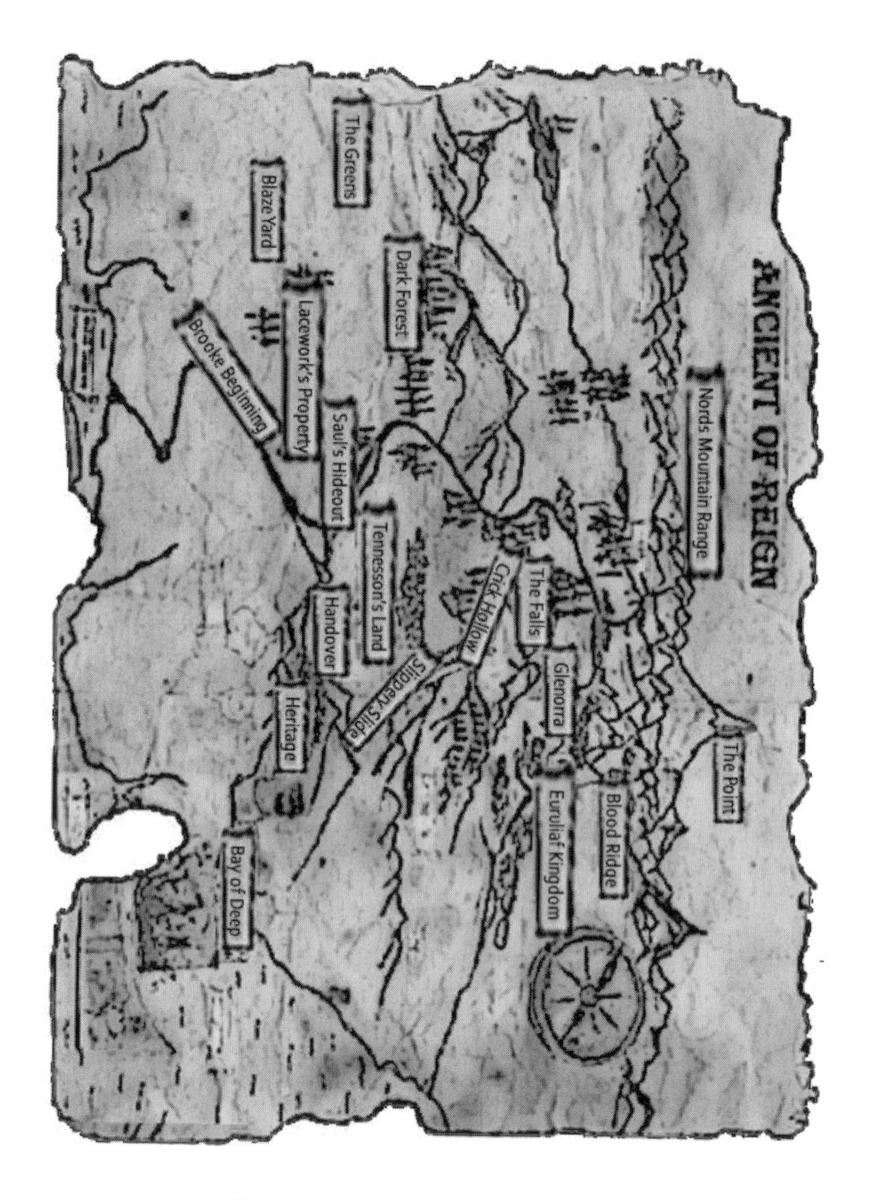

The old map Jules found.

Keeper Of Reign

Prologue: Beginning

"SIRE, YOU'RE RUNNING out of blood." Eleazer's voice quivered as he addressed the only other occupant in the royal chamber. He tried to veer his eyes from the King's bruised arm but could not pull his gaze away.

The young King grunted a response, his attention focused on the red words whispering out of his plumed pen.

Glancing at his cupbearer, he said, "I am aware, Eleazer." His velvet lapels caught the golden gleam flickering from the lanterns hung on the columns, giving it a rich burgundy sheen.

"Perhaps the wine will help?" Eleazer poured scarlet juice into a goblet and held the fluted stem out, his eyes drawn to his Highness' pale wrist. His Master's pallid face sent a shiver up his spine, and a knot of worry formed above Eleazer's brows. Palm clammy, he set the goblet next to his Master's arm.

The room was dim despite the golden sparkle of the dragonfly lanterns hooked to the four columns of alabaster that flanked the two draped windows. Books, their golden spines atop each other, were stacked on the mahogany table. Copper wires forming two "X"s upon each spine bound the leaves of the magnificent Books.

"The new star," the King said, "will be birthed tomorrow, so I must finish writing the Sacred Tomes." He paused and shot Eleazer a smile. "Why don't you bind this remaining stack? You can include this end page I am finishing later." He waited for Eleazer to reply, but the servant only stared at the floor. "My instructions are in the Master Books, but you must inform the others to keep the matter to yourselves."

"I know—Gehzurolle must not find out."

"More importantly, do not let him deceive you."

"I promise."

"You are a most faithful servant—friend, Eleazer. Thank you."

"It has been my honor, Your Highness. *I* should thank you." Eleazer wanted to say more but his throat strangled the words. He swallowed hard a few times and bowed, as a sigh slipped from his lips.

"Do you comprehend my wishes?" The King's eyes rested on Eleazer's face.

"Completely." Eleazer dared not add anything further lest his voice break entirely. His hands busied with the binding of the closing chapters, whilst his Master penned the final paragraphs.

All those books, yet not a single ink pot on that writing desk or on any other furniture in that library. Too soon Eleazer would have to bid his Master adieu. What if he failed the King?

"Master, I wish you didn't have to d—"

"Don't start this again, Eleazer—no other way exists. You must trust me. If *all of you* heed the words, you *will* end up better off."

Without looking up, the King said, "Once you've completed the binding you must leave me alone. I am almost finished."

Afraid he might forget the Majesty's visage, Eleazer's eyes flitted to the King's face and drank in the dark brows, the high cheekbones, the soft lips. He opened his mouth to say something, but only shook his head, bowed a fraction, and exited through the double doors.

Alone in the chamber, the King pierced his bruised vein a last time and completed the closing paragraph.

1.
ONE NIGHT

THE LAST THING Jules Blaze thought of before he closed his eyes was how he, how anyone, could undo the curse his people were under. He was in the middle of a dream, a nightmare as far as he was concerned, begging Grandpa Leroy and Grandma Bonnie not to leave, when someone banged on their front door, shaking their entire tree house.

Who'd be crazy enough to disturb them at this hour? He sat up on his bed and cocked his head. His mother's soft tread tap-tapped on the wood floor.

"Who's there?" her muffled voice asked, harsh and whispery from sleep.

The banging stopped.

"Erin, open up." Saul's voice, gruff and loud, jolted the last fog of sleepiness from Jules. He peered over at his brother sleeping noiselessly in the bunk below him, and quietly slipped down the ladder. On tiptoe he sneaked to the trapdoor opening that led down to the living room where Saul stood dripping from the rain.

"Is everything okay?" Erin said.

"Would I visit now if it were?" Saul said. Then in a gentler voice he added, "I'm sorry. Please, let's take a seat, Erin." He nodded at Jules who'd slipped down the pull-down ladder to join them. "Jules."

Jules thought about his father at the war front and swallowed a lump in his throat. Was this why Dad hadn't sent any word to them for the last months? Because he couldn't?

Saul held Erin by the arm. He led her to the dining room chairs behind the sofa covered with knitted shawls and afghan throws.

Jules trudged to the window and peered at the branches outside. The arm of the oak tree grew so thick they could easily live in it, although getting up there could be a problem, especially since he was afraid of heights. These days they didn't even live in stone houses, or even wooden ones, unless living under a tree counted as a wooden home. Elfies lived in trees, or burrowed under rocks, in the forest of Reign.

"Take a seat, Jules." Saul locked eyes on him for an instant. "I just received word from the riverfront patrol—Leroy and Bonnie's boat capsized in the storm. They're searching for the bodies, but it doesn't look good."

Erin let out a gasp and brought a fist to her mouth. "No!"

"Boat? How can they be sure it was them?" Jules leaned forward in his chair.

"Some of their belongings floated to shore, and I identified the wreck—the pieces drifted to the bank."

Erin looked at him blankly.

Saul said, again, "The boat…was a wreck."

"Boat?" Erin said.

"I'd loaned it to them."

"Why?"

Saul looked at the ceiling. "They'd wanted to get across to Handover."

"Handover? That's preposterous. After telling us never to cross the river and saying how dangerous Handover is?" Erin's voice sounded angry amidst her sobs.

Saul pushed his chair back and stood. He reached into the cloak of his pocket, brought out a few items and laid them on the dining table. "Some things to remember your folks by." And with that he turned and stalked back out into the dripping night.

Jules stared at his grandpa's pocket watch, the green felt hat the old man always wore, especially on damp days, and his grandma's silk scarf she donned when the wind ruffled her snowy white hair. Erin sobbed more violently, and Jules stood behind his mother's back, leaned over and hugged her trembling shoulders.

2.
TWO WEEKS LATER

WHEN JULES BLAZE peered out his living room window, the sky was still dotted with a million stars. He craned his neck out farther and stared at the branches that cast dark shadows upon each other like black bones crisscrossing. Out of the corner of his eye a shadow passed, but it swooped so fast he couldn't say what it was.

He'd planned this too carefully to let anything spoil it. He couldn't believe Grandpa had died. Just like that. Swept away, some Elfie neighbors had said. Or maybe they were on the Handover bank. Surely a sixteen-year-old could go to Handover to seek answers?

But should he leave his mother and his younger siblings? Like this? Without him could they fend for themselves? Especially with the rumors he'd heard? But he wouldn't go for long, he promised himself.

Between the foliage, tearing the darkness, a bright line whizzed in the inky sky. It was as if someone had drawn a silver line across the expanse.

Was it lightning?

But when he strained to hear the rumble of thunder that should follow only the whispers of the forest came. Jules blinked several times and rubbed his eyes with the back of his hands. Had drowsiness made him see things?

Without another thought he whisked his cloak off the peg by the front entryway, grabbed his pouch of jeweled stones by his feet and headed for the outdoors. Before he crossed the threshold he glanced at the closed door to his mother's room. What would she say when she found him missing? Ralston would have to take charge, at least until he got back.

Jules was about to step off the porch when the whole sky lit up and a golden glow brightened the deep forest. And then everything darkened again, as if nothing extraordinary had happened.

What was that? Jules's heart quickened, and he steadied his breathing as he sprinted down the pebbled path away from his home, one hand clutching the pouch of stones over his shoulders. When he rounded the corner of the last spruce, the one that had burned into a charred stump and marked the beginning of the meadow, crunching footsteps stopped him in his tracks. Who was awake this late? Following him?

He crouched and, hiding between the blades of grass, slowly turned to face the sound. The steps hurried toward him, quick and frantic, as if unafraid of detection. Jules was sure his pursuer had circled to get behind him, but just as he readied to spin around and hurl a rock, two arms pounced upon his shoulder and grabbed his neck.

"Jules!" his captor shrieked.

"Tippy?" He swung around and dragged his two-year-old sister from behind his back, relieved he had not flung the stone. "What are you doing here?"

"What are *you* doing here?" Tippy's brown eyes were round with fear.

He had a strong urge to smack her little arm, but bit down on his tongue instead. "Tippy, you shouldn't be out here."

"Like you?"

"Don't be sassy."

"I was following you."

"You can't. Go back. Now."

"Are you running away, Jules?"

"It's none of your beeswax." He stood, straightened his cloak, grabbed his pouch, and took a step forward. But something made him turn around. Tippy still crouched where he'd placed her. Even in the dark he could sense her pout. Her outline in the dimness looked small, even vulnerable.

He stared beyond her dark form and noticed from where they stood he could hardly see the oak tree that held their home.

"Come on, now." He pulled Tippy to her feet and half dragged her home.

On the walk home, his little sister in one hand, Jules wondered about that bright flash. But as they were about to enter their front porch an acorn fell, missing his head by a hair's breadth. He leapt back and turned to check on Tippy.

"That was close," she said. The acorn was of normal size, yet it measured about half of Jules's height and weighed probably twice as much.

Jules always found issue with his inconvenient stature. And even though those of his race, the Fairy Elves, or Elfies as they were more commonly called, had suffered the effects of the curse for centuries and had adapted to their surroundings, he always regretted his size more than anyone he knew. *If only I could reverse this curse!*

Inside his home Jules quietly shut the front door and placed his cloak exactly as he'd found them on the peg. Reaching into one of his pockets he brought out a tattered booklet, the size of his palm. The thought of placing it back where he'd found it earlier crossed his mind, but he felt Tippy's eyes watching his every move. It wouldn't do if his mother found it.

"Bed now, Tippy." He pointed to the narrow staircase that led to her attic bedroom, where his two other younger sisters slept. But Tippy just blinked at him. So, he slid the booklet back into the cloak pocket. He trudged to the hearth and hid his pouch of stones behind a loose brick to the right of the hearth. "And don't tell Mom about me, either, or I'll snitch on how you went out all by yourself."

Tippy yawned and slunk up to the attic room she shared with her two slightly older sisters. Before she climbed the first rung, she turned and faced Jules. "Will you be here tomorrow?"

"Go—to—sleep," Jules said.

"Promise?" She padded up the spindly steps.

"Go." But he smiled at her.

As he stood by the window and watched the night sky, the blonde hair on the nape of his neck suddenly prickled. A shadow sifted past the bough above his window and a soft whoosh made him step back.

What was that light? That glow in the sky? A bomb? Lightning?

He gripped the rough window sill and leaned out to see what could have caused the shadows to move, but he saw nothing suspicious. If Grandpa was here he could've asked the old man, but that was out of the question now. And his mother never had the right answers. Even his father could have helped him, but that too was out of the question.

Jules climbed the stairs to the attic and to his bed on the upper bunk, cautious not to rouse his brother, Ralston, below, who, fortunately for Jules, could sleep through a tornado.

If I can convince Mom to let us outside tomorrow, I can find answers to that strange light. Some had rumored that the war was coming closer.

****

Outside in the cool, breezy night a pair of eyes spied on the Blaze home. Through the open window he saw the candle flickering on the dining table but no boy. Whisperer glided from branch to branch, a swirl of darkness hiding a face with a beaked nose and twisted lips, and landed on the lowest branch on Jules's tree.

"If you can lure them out I can check out the place," a muffled voice said.

"Beta, you'd better pass this test." Whisperer weaved himself in and out of the foliage around Beta, but Beta didn't move or show signs of fear.

"I'll get it one way or another, but you must be patient."

The leaves on the oak rustled softly and a couple of late fall acorns already loosened by the season dropped as Beta swung from the tip of the branch to an adjacent tree.

3.
THE SOUND OF TROUBLE

NEXT MORNING, JULES couldn't have thanked his lucky stars more when his mother agreed—after much arguing on his part—to allow him and his four siblings to play in the backyard.

"Since you're already going out, watch for more precious stones. I need those aquamarines so I can buy some trout from Mr. Saul."

Tippy jumped up and down and clapped her hands. "Fish!"

The thought of flaky white fish melting in his mouth made Jules's stomach rumble. He'd almost forgotten the texture of fresh trout, baked with butter and sprinkled with chopped cilantro. A whole fish would mean a feast for at least three days. This was one advantage of their size, since practically every other animal had not altered with the curse.

"Daydreaming again?" His mother's sharp voice rose.

"The blue stones seemed pretty scarce there. But I can get embers and moonstones easy enough."

"Whatever you can get your hands on. But be back before supper. I'm making potato soup and hazel cream butter." She nodded at him and he rushed toward the front door, his mind on the flash that ripped the sky.

Was it a stray bomb from the war? Since his father had left for the war, he was expected to be man of the house. Take care of his four younger siblings.

Bitha, his ten-year-old sister, yelled from behind. "Wait up, Jules." She pushed her jet-black hair away from her pixie face.

Their home under the oak was narrow but long, the kitchen situated at the back end, the dining room sandwiched in the middle and the living room to the front where the only entrance to the home stood. Supposedly his father's ancestors who built the home considered this a necessary security feature.

Jules turned and waved at Bitha as he stepped off the porch and shrugged into his cloak. It still smelled fresh from the pine soap Mother used and didn't give her clues that he'd sweated in it trying to run away the night before. He heard his mother's muffled voice from the kitchen and wanted to say good-bye but reconsidered. She might change her mind and keep them in again. Paranoia.

Behind him Bitha said, "Don't worry, Mom. Jules is with us." She flicked her long black hair over her shoulders, and winked at Jules, her emerald eyes sparkling.

Jules scowled and rushed down the path, pine needles crunching under his swift feet. Just then several acorns dropped, narrowly missing his head.

"Whoa!" *What's with the acorns? Death by acorn will not look good in my obituary.*

He scanned the branches above. For a split second he considered warning his mother, but what if she stopped them from leaving? So he brushed aside the urge.

His three sisters, Bitha, Tst Tst, which sounded like Sit Sit, (she's otherwise, also known as "Miss Big Words!") and Tippy, scrambled to keep up, but he just turned and gestured with his head for them to hurry, his dark blonde hair flopping on his forehead with each quick jerk.

Jules had just rounded the corner where the marker spruce stood tall when another acorn dropped close to him and he hopped back. *What the…?* Was someone up there?

"Wait up, Jules!" Ralston, his thirteen-year-old brother, hollered as he tucked a sheath of papers he'd meticulously handbound into a sketch pad into his khaki green cloak.

Jules couldn't help but shake his head when Ralston finally caught up. Mr. Slow himself. "If you keep lugging your sketch pad everywhere, you'll *always* be last."

"You have your stone collections, and I have my art."

"You can buy things with my gems. Grandpa said it's a worthy pastime." He nudged Ralston and rushed down the pebbled path pushing stray grass that had encroached onto the pathway with his arms.

Jules looked at the patch of blue between the foliage above, seeking signs of a pending storm, but even though there were clouds sailing by he didn't think it looked like rain. Was it possible the bright rip in the night sky was just lightning? Maybe it had burned a tree?

He wasn't sure what he was looking for exactly but he meant to get to the bottom of things. A burnt patch of grass or a toppled tree trunk might tell a story. Something. He noticed a piece of ametrine by his foot and slipped the quartz of purple and yellow into his pocket. He hoped Mr. Saul might accept it in exchange for fish, though he doubted it. The old man was enamored with aquamarines. Before he could search further, an ear splitting howl broke his concentration. "Tippy!" In trouble? Already?

Weaving between the tall blades of grass swaying in the breeze, he ran toward the screaming. Behind him, Bitha's panting came in short bursts, her steps quick and short.

Thud, thud, thud.

"What's happening?" She flicked her jet-black hair out of her eyes and kept up with Jules.

A few steps ahead Tippy stood stamping her feet. Through the criss-cross of her leather strapped sandal Jules saw the side of Tippy's foot had turned red.

"You're bleeding!" He squinted at a projecting object Tippy kept pointing at with her hurt toe. A colored pebble stuck out from the mossy ground.

Bitha pushed her hair behind her ears, and pulled Tippy away. "Stop. You're hurting yourself."

But the little girl kept digging at the reddish stone with her foot.

Before Jules could assert himself, Tst Tst plopped herself next to Tippy.

"What, perchance, are you doing?" Tst Tst's bobbed hair looked darker than its usual brown, possibly because it was matted with sweat.

"*Perchance?*" Jules tried not to roll his eyes but couldn't help himself. Where was she learning these words? Miss Big Words! He shook his head in disbelief and knelt next to Tippy.

With the palm of his hand, he rubbed off the caked dirt on the bit of the red stone sticking out. "It's a common sardius, a crystal some call carnelian. I have enough in my collection, so you can have this one, Tippy." He thought about his precious stones behind the hearth and hoped he'd hidden them well enough. His grandpa and he had spent hours picking those stones.

Jules was about to stalk off when their pet dragonfly, Fiesty, whizzed by, pitching its head back and forth. "Watch out! Why's Fiesty trying to bite us?"

Tst Tst had found Fiesty when it was a wee of a nymph, and the children had nursed it till it was grown. Attempts to free Fiesty always failed for it simply came back, and so the children considered it a family member.

As the dragonfly somersaulted and spun in the air, like a kite caught in a whirlwind, Bitha tilted her head, her pixie face in obvious confusion. "Has Fiesty gone mad?"

When Fiesty came toward her she reached out at it, but it jerked violently and she toppled backward. It kept flying to a distance toward the forest and returning. Back and forth, like the needle of a metronome. Its wings buzzed a hundred beats a second. But, finally, as if giving up, the pet whizzed off into the woods.

"He's gone," Tst Tst cried.

"Let him be." Jules frowned at the pet as it disappeared between the tall blades of grass. Things were getting more and more bizarre, and he couldn't understand why the nape of his neck prickled.

Better get them home. If he could persuade his mother to show him the Book he might find some sort of explanation. His mind wondered about the acorns. Should he have warned her?

"Are you hurt, Bitha?" He reached for his sister's hand and glanced up.

The sky held a bright glare, which meant the sun was setting, almost faster than he'd expected. "Mom wants us back before supper. And where's—where's Ralston?"

"What's wrong?" Breathless, Ralston poked his head from behind a tall dandelion, his brown eyes in a squint.

"We have to leave, Rals," Bitha said. She grasped Tippy's elbow but the little girl twisted free and plopped herself next to her new found sardius.

Tippy said, "I—want—my—gem!"

Before Jules could give her a piece of his mind a shadow swept over them. The air felt still and the usual swishing of the blades of grass stopped. Something about the shadow seemed familiar, and it sent chills up his spine.

"I vote," Jules said, "we leave this crystal here. It's too embedded." The fine blonde hair on his arms stood on ends for reasons he couldn't understand. He hated it when these feelings overcame him.

"I'm—not—leaving—without—it." Tippy wailed, again. "It's not fair."

Ralston yanked Tippy by the arm. "Tippy, do you want to be grounded for life?"

"I'll give you one of mine," Jules pleaded. "One of the rare ones Grandpa found."

But she glared at him and the corners of her mouth drooped dangerously.

"Let's just dig it out," Bitha said.

But that was easier said than done. To get the sardius out, the boys struggled long. A dark shadow flitted past them again. It was only a slight shift of the light upon the vast lawn but Jules's senses told him to beware, and now his heart pounded wildly.

Stuffing his pad into his cloak pocket, Ralston said, "Was that a passing cloud?" He shielded his eyes with one hand and peered in the direction of the dark forest some hundred feet ahead.

A blood-curdling scream pierced through the cold evening air and all five children jerked and stared at each other. The scream appeared to have come from the dark forest. Was someone in trouble? Or was it just someone trying to scare them?

"*Wh—at* was that?" Bitha grabbed Tippy's hand and tugged at her, but the little girl, her face indignant, squirmed and pulled away.

"No–o!" A series of ear splitting protests came from Tippy and she shook her head vigorously. Her eyes, the rims red, locked with Jules. "I want the gem! It's *mine*!"

Arms on her hips, Tst Tst said, in a sinister whisper, "If we don't leave now, *Gehzurolle will kill us*!"

Tippy slumped her shoulders, let out a sob and opened her mouth as if wanting to protest but at the last minute she only stepped aside. "All wight!"

"We'll give the stone another try. Ralston, you wedge it with that stick and I'll pull." Jules glanced at the sky and thought he saw a dark blob in the blue far away. *Must get away quickly. The meadow is too bare for a good hiding spot.*

Nausea swelled up from the pit of his stomach and a shiver crept up his back. The last time he had such a feeling was right before his grandpa left on that trip. "Rals, hurry! Pull!"

How to get this useless stone out?

4.
HUNTERS

"RALS, YOU CARRY Tippy." Jules tucked the sardius inside his green cloak, relieved it finally broke free from the mossy ground, but he couldn't help the uneasy feeling.

Somebody's watching. But who? And why? Must bring them to safety. Jules glimpsed at his sisters. He tiptoed to peer over the tall grasses. Nothing but the dark blob far away. How was he to plan for his secret getaway to look for Grandpa like this?

Horrifying pictures of Scorpents invaded his mind. He joggled his head a few times to dispel the images. But even as he quickened his steps something told him his troubles had just begun.

What was that verse from the Book about fear Grandpa taught him? "Perfect love casts out all fear." He repeated it several times under his breath hoping the feeling would disappear.

But when he gazed at the sky again he spied something else: the blob had turned to four patches, as black as the night, contrasting against the blue background. He stopped and pointed, his eyes in narrow slits as he tried to understand the meaning of this latest mystery.

The others halted, too, and stared at the objects until the four dark blobs came close enough.

"A flock of birds with impressive wingspans." Tst Tst pointed at the fowls.

"Mrs. Lacework warned Mom," Bitha said, "about the rise of savage birds."

"She claimed," Tst Tst lowered her voice, nodding a few times, her hazel eyes wide. "They're after Elfies."

As the birds came closer the sheen of the dark bluish feathers glistened in the sun.

"They're just ravens." Jules tried to sound convincing. "Hunting for food."

"We," Tst Tst said, and gulped, "*could* qualify as food."

Jules glared at her and gestured at his brother, some twenty steps behind. "Hurry, Rals."

The ravens circled directly above them now. When the black birds flapped their massive wings, gusts of wind billowed the children's cloaks.

Jules, standing ahead of everyone, noticed the dirty talons on one of the ravens opening, as if the bird had already decided on its prey. Then it hit him.

"Ralston! Duck! Duck—" he yelled. He's so slow!

Still battling with Tippy's weight in his arms, Ralston, brown hair disheveled, looked up and Wham! The talons dug into his shoulders and he dropped Tippy.

Within seconds, Bitha and Tst Tst, screaming, dodged the onslaught of other talons swooping at them. The girls dived behind a large mushroom in a nick of time. At first, Jules just stared at the bird, eyes round, mouth open like an O.

"Rroankk-rroankk." Ralston's captor seemed to signal to his accomplices. Within seconds, the murder of ravens thrashed their four feet span of wings and headed for the blue sky, with the very still Ralston as their ransom.

"Ralston! Ralston!" the girls screeched at the top of their lungs, their arms waving in frantic motions above their heads.

"We must get Ralston back," Jules shouted to Bitha, wondering, the moment he said this, why he'd used the word "we" when he knew he'd have to try alone. He ran to a large boulder and clambered to the top.

Tippy was nowhere to be seen but Bitha and Tst Tst shadowed him. For a fleeting second he worried about Tippy, but he had to save his brother before it was too late. Once on the rock, the children swung their hands above their heads and screamed at the ravens.

Then Jules groped for Tippy's sardius he'd concealed within his cloak and waved it above his head. He angled the stone this way and that in the direction of the ravens. The crystal caught the sun's rays and shimmered bright and red.

"Come back! Come back!" Jules and his sisters cried.

Their voices may have dissipated in the wind, but the glint from the red stone burned bright and must have attracted the birds, since they did return. Their scraping rasps intensified as they descended toward the three children on the big rock.

"Oh, no! They're going to attack again." Bitha jerked Jules's arm back and forth.

"What do we do?" Tst Tst shook her fists as if she was shivering.

"Hide, girls! Hide!" *Now what?*

They slid from their perch and lay prone on the ground, panting heavily. Tippy, who must have been hiding behind the boulder, slipped herself between Bitha and Tst Tst.

Steadily, the deafening screams from the approaching flock heightened as the hunting party swooped toward the boulder again. Jules could hear their cries, but he also thought—although he couldn't be sure—the wind whispered, "It's the other boy, you stupid fowl." He looked over his shoulder but saw no one except his sisters.

"Let's stick together," Bitha pleaded, and she tugged at his cloak. Her eyes shone with tears, and she wiped the sweat upon her brows.

More than anything Jules wanted to hide with them. He swallowed the sour taste rising up his throat a few times and placed his forefinger to his lips. With his free hand he motioned for the girls to stay put, and he crawled on scraped knees and elbows to another rock.

Two ravens now roosted on the boulder. The birds' beady eyes flitted from spot to spot on the ground, as if searching. A third hovered nearby, flapping its large wings vigorously.

When Jules spotted Ralston his fist shot to his mouth involuntarily and he shuddered. He wanted to scream, but his voice snagged in his throat. The lifeless body of his brother lay in the grip of the fourth bird circling close to the mossy spot where Tippy had stubbed her toe. Jules racked his brain for a plan.

Is Ralston alive? Can I save him?

Slowly, he stood and dashed in and out of the sweeping blades of grass toward the mossy plot. Quiet at first, his lips pressed into a determined line, he made sure not to snap a twig as he threaded through the tall grasses. He ran so fast that the edge of a blade cut his forehead. As he neared the fowls he yelled at the fourth crow in hoarse madness.

The bird's yellow eyes flitted to him. It squawked and in three big flaps its beak honed in on him, talons still clenched onto Ralston.

Staring the bird in the eye, Jules flung the red stone at the black bird's beak but the stone struck its eye instead. Better than he'd expected.

"Yes!" Jules shouted and beat his fist in the air in triumph.

The raven dropped Ralston, almost on top of Jules, who swerved away just in time.

The other three birds swooped to the mossy spot and made a ruckus, as if scolding the fourth. Jules braced himself for another attack but something else caught his eye.

A cloud of dark mass was flying in their direction. The droning hum the dark mass made reverberated and filled the air.

Jules clapped his ears shut. What was happening?

He'd heard of mutated insects the Handovers had experimented with, but they were supposed to only inhabit Handover. Not here in Reign. Could they be invading now? After all, the Scorpents had started coming. But when one from the mass broke away he saw he'd been mistaken.

Fiesty!

As Fiesty flew over Jules's head the mass became identifiable: a swarm of dragonflies. More than a hundred of them whizzed in and out, targeting the ravens' eyes and nostrils. In obvious fury the afflicted ravens thrashed their massive wings at each other.

Kneeling beside Ralston, Jules sucked in his breath, hardly daring to breathe. "Ralston," he whispered at last.

Getting no response, he shook Ralston vigorously. "Hey, wake up!"

But still, his brother didn't stir. He pounded on Ralston's chest, hard. "Breathe, Ralston! Breathe!"

5.
HURRY

WHEN RALSTON'S ARMS twitched and his eyelids fluttered, Jules heaved a sigh of relief. "Ralston! Get up, up." He prodded Ralston's rib some more and tugged at his brother's arm to get him to sit up, but failed.

Whap! Whap! Whap! The beating wings were approaching.

Jules's heart skipped as the flapping of the ravens' wings became threateningly loud. They only had so much time before the ravens broke free from the dragonflies and hunted them again.

"Where's my sardius?" Tippy materialized next to them in her demanding voice.

Jules had a mind to smack her. Perhaps if they hadn't dawdled trying to get that sardius out they could've avoided trouble. But tears welled in Tippy's eyes and her mouth quivered. The crows were not visible but the flapping of their wings meant they were still hunting. He could try to carry Ralston but his brother was almost as heavy as he was.

"I only have one," Tippy said.

Before he could answer, Bitha and Tst Tst slid down next to him, their faces wet with tears. "Ralston!" they said in unison.

"You girls stay here with Rals."

And just like that he ran off in the direction of the flapping wings. If he didn't retrieve the sardius Tippy might not leave, and if he carried her she might make a commotion a crow a mile away would hear. There were plenty of colored stones in the area. He might even stumble upon another one. When his eye caught a reddish glint lying beside a boulder he dashed to it and pocketed his find.

"Here," he said presenting it to Tippy, although his eyes were on the lifeless Ralston. But as he brought it across Ralston the stone dropped out of his hand and hit Ralston on the nose.

"Ouch!" Ralston yelled. He bolted to a sitting position and rubbed his nose. He stared at Jules blankly. "Where am I?"

Jules jerked Ralston to his feet and propped him up with one arm.

For a moment Ralston stood, tottering.

"We must get away." Jules hoped the worry would rouse Ralston out of his stupor. He didn't seem too hurt even though his eyes looked glazed.

Bitha hugged the pale Ralston, then quickly touched his head, neck and shoulders. "Did you break any bones?"

Jules said, "Can you run?"

Ralston nodded, even though he still swayed like a blade of grass.

"C'mon, Rals." He gestured and then grabbed Tippy's wrist and asked her, "Can you run fast?"

She rolled her eyes at him, both hands clutching her precious sardius in front of her chest. But Jules caught sight of her bleeding foot and shook his head. "Hop on my back."

"All-wight."

As they scrambled home, the five siblings kept glancing at the sky, afraid the ravens might reappear, but by the time they neared the oak that held their home the flapping had ceased.

"I hope Fiesty's all right." Tst Tst's upper lip quivered as she spoke. "I don't know what I'd do without him. The ravens could have eaten him."

"Have more faith in Fiesty." But Jules didn't sound confident. "If it weren't for him we'd be dead meat. At least, Ralston would've been. I never knew Fiesty had friends."

"I never knew I could survive a bird attack." Ralston looked at his bruised elbows and rubbed his knees. "I didn't even tear my cloak. No broken bones, nothing. I can hardly believe it happened to me. I must have passed out. I think I'm allergic to heights, just like you, Jules." This was more than anything Ralston had said in a single breath his entire life.

Jules just glared at him.

"What was that horrible scream?"

"Maybe someone trying to scare us."

Ralston's eyes widened. "What happened to the ravens?"

Jules shrugged. "We'd better try to stay inside as much as possible."

Ralston said, "But what about food?"

"I'll sneak out. Or you can." And he grinned at Ralston, finally relieved that no great harm was done.

"Jules," Bitha said in a worried tone, "what should we tell Mom?"

"Just that it was a misfortune. Mrs. Lacework said some neighbors had seen bird aggressions. Maybe Mom will know why the ravens invaded our land." He stared at the ground and felt his heart sink. He looked up at the branches and remembered the acorns and shuddered. What if his mother was in danger?

"Hurry!" Then he said, "Ouch!" He rubbed his forehead. "Someone pelted a stone at me."

Bitha and Tst Tst stared at the welt that had already started to bulge. The leaves rustled overhead and a lithe figure wearing a black cape landed next to Jules. It was quite a feat for an Elfie as even the lowest branch was a few heads higher than the tall Jules.

"Miranda!" Jules said. His eyes lit up.

"Sorry, I didn't mean to hit that hard." The girl with hair of flaming gold who'd jumped down covered her mouth as if she was shocked and stepped closer to peer at Jules's bruise. She brushed her golden strands away from her smooth, high forehead, her blue eyes locking with Jules's green ones.

Such riveting eyes the color of the heavens. Jules thought her flowing golden hair smelled of roses and honey and everything good. He noticed the ear clip she had on. "What's with that thing on your ear?"

"Like it?"

Jules frowned. "Interesting. Hey, were you pelting acorns at me?"

"Acorns? I meant to scare you. Not kill you." She smiled up at Jules sweetly.

"Could have fooled me." Jules fingered the emerging welt above his brow and eased Tippy down.

Miranda said, "You in a hurry?" She eyed Ralston and then Bitha, who was shaking her head slightly at Jules.

"What are you doing out so late?" Jules said.

"Maybe I was spying on my favorite friend?" She lifted an eyebrow at him.

Jules reddened and stared at her. "Would your grandpa mind if you joined us? For supper, I mean."

"He won't notice I was gone. But only if it's my favorite—potato soup?"

The boughs above them trembled and some oak leaves floated down like giant flakes. Jules scanned the foliage wondering if some ravens had rested on the branches. "Come on, it's getting dark."

Miranda pulled at his cloak. "No need to be so edgy."

Jules said, "You're in luck, hazelnut butter *and* potato soup." Should he have warned Mom about the acorn incidents? But with Miranda beside him he pushed any worry away.

****

In the yonder forest, perched on a cypress, Whisperer watched the group with what could qualify as disappointment on his crooked face with his crooked lips. His efforts had failed. This sort of fowl tactics worked umpteen times before when his master ordered him on some mission.

Now he considered other prongs of attacks. The ifs and what-ifs, the whisperings, he could float in the wind. Whisperings that wafted down and instilled fear to all who heard him. This was one assignment he could not afford to blunder. Too much was at stake.

He debated over his options, his heavily lidded eyes darting from tree to tree. For a second he determined to strike the bumbling boy again, but he decided against this. He would wait for Beta and re-evaluate the problem with the latest update.

Whisperer pursed his crooked lips, his breath a gray tube of smoke that swirled toward its goal: the clouds. First softly, then more intensely, he blew. But his gaze never wavered from the struggling, lanky lad with his sister on his back.

Beta had better find that Book, or he would find a suitable punishment for the servant.

6.
HIDE!

WHEN THEY APPROACHED their home Jules noticed their front door ajar, tottering on a hinge.

Creak-creak, the door seemed to say, as the wind blew on it gently.

"Something's wrong." He barred the entrance with his back, his elbows spread out to prevent Tippy from sailing in. He poked his head through the doorway and was about to step over the threshold when Tst Tst pushed past him, and he stumbled forward.

"Tst Tst, no!" he whispered, hoarsely. "What if someone's in—?"

"Mama? Mama!" Tst Tst stood in the middle of the living room and wrung her hands.

The others cautiously followed her in.

As Jules took another step something cracked under his feet. He glanced down. It was the spout of his mother's favorite china teapot, and a foot away, remnants of the teapot lay strewn in bits and pieces.

Debris littered the dwelling they'd left three hours ago. Pieces of broken furniture scattered over the floor in the dining room, some smashed to smithereens. Crockery lay broken. Even the breakfast dishes of that morning lay strewn on the sink counter. And the pot of potato soup lay on its side on the kitchen floor. Jules had smelled the herb from it when they first stepped into that kitchen. The smell of buttered garlic still hung in the air. The doors of cupboards, armoires, and commodes teetered on hinges as if some force had wrenched them off in a rage.

Jules's mahogany desk Grandpa Leroy had fashioned for him for his eighth birthday lay on its side, one splintered leg broken and swinging slightly from the break, and Tippy's miniaturized collection of dolls Grandma Bonnie had woven together out of multi-colored blades of grass lay crushed at the bottom of the stepladder that led to the girls' attic bedroom.

The children tiptoed about to avoid tramping over their things, as their eyes drank in the mess.

"Who'd do this?" Ralston looked around, blinking several times, and wiped his wet eyes with the back of his hand.

Tst Tst said, "They destroyed everything. What did they take from us? And where's…where's Mom?" Her breathing grew louder and she clutched her chest, as if in pain.

"What are we going to do?" Bitha's tone was barely audible. "Mama should be here—where else could she be?"

"Maybe she's hurt." Jules peered behind a toppled table, afraid he'd find her unconscious.

"Do you think—do you think someone—took her? Maybe they…." Bitha said.

Bile crept up from the pit of Jules's stomach, and he quickly avoided Bitha's red rimmed eyes. What if something happened to Mom? Maybe he should have warned her about the acorns? Or that bright flash? Whoever plundered their house was no ordinary scoundrel. He was only ten when his grandpa warned him about Gehzurolle, yet he remembered as if it was only yesterday.

7.
DESTROYER

THE WARNING GRANDPA gave had frightened Jules then, as it did now.

"Jules, the days are coming," Grandpa Leroy had said, that bleak day as they sat before the fireplace. "One day, Gehzurolle will intensify his efforts against us. Beware of that day."

Picking up his Ancient Book, Grandpa read, "Suspecting the lives of the now insignificant Fairy Elves will be restored to the former glories they once enjoyed, the Scorpents and their leader, Gehzurolle, the Lord of Shadows, will be driven to distraction. After many failed attempts to annihilate the Race throughout the centuries, Gehzurolle will scheme to extinguish every inhabitant of the land because finally a Keeper has invited him into our Kingdom. He will spare no Elfie. Not even those who work for him.'"

"But which Keeper would do something like that?"

"One who's desperate. When you see the signs, Jules, you must flee. You and everyone in our family. Immediately!"

"But why, Grandpa?"

"Because it means he's close to succeeding. He will seek us Keeper families first because without the Keepers and our Books our Kingdom cannot survive. I entrust this knowledge to you for you will take over from your mother as Keeper of the Book, just as she'd taken over from me." His grandfather's gentle blue eyes locked with Jules's own green ones.

"But how will I know when this will happen?"

"The Ancient Book says thieves will come to steal—so beware. But these are no ordinary burglars, Jules. They *will* destroy everything in their path. Whatever happens they mustn't get our Book."

****

That was what Jules recalled of that conversation.

"We must locate Mom's Ancient Book," he quickly said. "Rals, you–" Then he noticed Miranda staring at him. It wasn't like her not to voice an opinion. "Don't be afraid," he said to her. He wondered if Saul ever told her they were a Keeper family. He scanned the top of the mantel where his mother's Book usually sat, but nothing was on it. Or on the strewn floor, either.

Before he could utter another word a tap tap tap on the window sill, followed by soft footsteps as if inching closer to the open front door alarmed him further. A rustling outside sent shivers up his spine. Jules put a finger to his lips and gestured to everyone to stay quiet.

Had the intruders returned? How many were they?

Soon the scrunching of dried leaves outside grew louder. Who were these shifting below the front windows?

Bitha said. "Where to hide?" Her eyes flitted from one overturned piece of furniture to another.

Tippy, clutching her red stone, scrambled to the kitchen table, the only furniture still upright in the room, and sat beneath it, hugging her knees. She rocked herself back and forth, her lips ashen gray. Tst Tst and Bitha looked at her pale face and crawled after her. They sat flanking her and hugged her, each with an arm about her thin shoulders.

"Where to hide?" Ralston whispered and tugged at Jules, his nails digging into Jules's arm.

Jules gestured to follow him but Tippy didn't budge. She kept shaking her head and pointing at the window. "Tippy, quick." He kept his voice calm.

"I want Mama!" Tippy cried, too loudly.

"I want Mama, too," Jules said, quietly. "But Mama would want you to hide. Ralston, help her." To himself he muttered, "They're after Mom's Book."

A faint smell had wafted into the room. Sweet, almost too sweet, but masking a pungent fragrance. He breathed in deeply and the pungent fragrance cut into his nostrils like acrid acid seeking to lodge itself inside his brain. *Strange!*

He pushed the small of Tst Tst's back to get her to move quicker. "I know where to go."

"The attic's too small," Ralston whispered back.

8.
SECRET CELLAR

"NOT THE ATTIC." Jules rushed to the dining room wall and unhitched two dragonfly lanterns from their hangers. The burglars seemed to have missed them. For an instant, he worried about his pouch of stones behind the hearth brick. His grandfather and he had collected many of the stones together, a last vestige of a token of Grandpa. "I know a secret hideout." He pointed at the cloak closet.

Miranda said, "We can't all fit in there!"

Just then, whoever, or whatever, skulking outside, scraped at the bark that acted as the shingles of their tree home. The grating made Jules's teeth tingle, and he clenched them tighter to stop the discomfort. It sounded like metal claws upon wood.

The window shutters rattled as if a strong wind wanted to pry the wooden slats loose and slip in. Maybe whoever ransacked their home didn't find Mom's Book and had come back for a second try. He scanned the room for any sign of the Book—nothing. Should he hide and leave the skulker to find it? No time.

Jules opened the closet door and shoved Tippy. The others followed suit.

Once inside the cramped closet, Jules stooped and cleared away the mountainous pile of apparel on the floor. (These cloaks had fallen off their twig hangers.) Tumbled clothes obscured a trap door. Lifting the insert with some difficulty, as the panel appeared jammed, Jules jerked the board to the left to make room for his siblings and Miranda to rally on ahead into the gaping hole in the floor. Steps hewn out of rough wood greeted them. Save for the light from the dragonfly-shaped lanterns in Jules's grasp, the passage wound into darkness. Steps corkscrewed round and round to somewhere deep beneath the house.

"Here." He shoved a lantern into Bitha's hand. "Hold it higher."

Once Miranda entered, Jules stepped down into the passage, ducked and slid the trap door back into place. He squeezed past the rest and led them down the winding stony steps. Some of the stones came loose as they edged their way in a single file down, down the narrow tunnel. The air smelled hot and musty as if moths had once lived there. Miranda, who was last in line, slipped once and almost pulled Ralston down with her as she grabbed his arm.

Ralston said, "How far down does this go?"

But Jules didn't answer him. The dragonfly lanterns made diagonal patterns of light on the rough wooden walls on both sides of the crusading party.

"Where are you taking us?" Bitha's voice quivered, and her words echoed in the darkness.

"Grandpa showed me this place before he left."

"Why didn't you inform *us* about this?" Tst Tst said.

"I said 'secret' hide-out."

Suddenly Jules's outstretched hand hit a wall. He groped on it and found a rusty ring like a knocker in the middle of the expansive wall.

"I saw Grandpa do this." He twisted the ring round and round a few times till a click echoed in the tunnel. He slid the creaky slider of a hidden latch and pushed the wall open.

When Jules stepped onto the stony floor of the cellar the cold traveled from the ground through his strapped sandals and bit the soles of his feet. The cold air enveloped him, and his nose started to run. He tilted his head into his shoulder and wiped his nose into his cloak. With the dragonfly lantern held above his head he saw books lined from floor to ceiling in rows and rows of bookcases, some against the four walls and others back to back in the middle of the cellar with its high ceiling. Just as he'd seen them last. The bookcases themselves looked like giant buildings at least thirty or forty times taller than Jules.

The others stood by the doorway and gaped.

"Why didn't Grandpa tell *us* of this—this library?" Tst Tst's eyes stared accusingly at Jules.

He shrugged. "Maybe you were too young—I don't know. We shouldn't argue about this, we don't even know where Mom is."

On hearing this, Tst Tst and Bitha cried, "They took her!"

Tst Tst whimpered between sobs.

"Do you think the intruders are inside our living room, now?" Ralston's voice quaked.

Miranda said, "These books are made for giants! There's no way a normal Elfie can handle them."

Jules had never heard her so surprised. "They were for normal people. Once. Elfies were normal, *once*."

She took the lantern from Bitha and moved toward the nearest bookcase. "Where did your grandpa get all these books?"

"It's a family thing. An inheritance. You wouldn't find it interesting."

"Like jipsy I wouldn't? How'd they even bring these giant books through your tiny doors?" She faced Jules squarely, her blue eyes burning like emeralds. "Tell me your secrets."

Jules felt Ralston nudging the small of his back with an elbow. "It's common knowledge we all shrank, right?"

"So these bookcases and books didn't? What's so special about them?"

"My grandpa said they belonged to the King."

"Wait." Miranda stretched her arm and shoved his chest. "How are you related to this exactly? To the King? Jules, we've been friends since forever and you kept this from me?"

"There's a lot you don't know about me."

"Explain."

"If you help me find our Book maybe I'll tell you." *Could Mom have kept it down here, and that's why it was not on the mantel?*

"Making contracts, are we? And what Book? This place is books galore—take your pick—which one do you want? Ha! If you can lift even the smallest." And she doubled over and broke out laughing, the lantern in the other hand swinging wildly.

Jules had never seen her like this.

Miranda strode to one of the shelves and ran her hand on a book's spine. "They're all in alphabetical order. What's the Book like? The one we're supposed to look for?"

"It's about this big." Jules held a span about double his hand's width for the height and one hand length for the book's width. "And it has a double 'X' on its spine."

Miranda glanced at the looming bookcases. "Nothing's that small here unless it's behind one of these giants, which means you can forget about finding it unless we have ten years."

Miranda was right. How could they even move these giants, as she'd termed them? Maybe if they had days—which they didn't. Jules glimpsed at Tippy squatting in a dark corner, small and forlorn, cupping her stone and sobbing into it.

"Maybe we should stay quiet." He walked over to Tippy and was about to sit with her when a tapping sound jerked him upright and he turned around.

"Shh!" he said.

Everyone stared at the doorway. No one had slid the oaken door shut. Someone must have found the trap door in the closet! Jules wanted to kick himself as he realized he hadn't pulled the fallen clothes back over the entry as his mother always had. His eyes scanned the library.

This had seemed like a safe place, but where could they hide amongst the books? They couldn't possibly climb the shelves. Before he could summon them to maybe squeeze between some of the books the sound of metal squeaking and a loud click sounded.

"Quick!" Jules pulled Tippy to her feet while gesturing to the others, who were staring at him with fear on their faces, as if he had answers to every trouble.

They followed him as he ran down the hallway of bookcases, his lantern lighting the path only a few feet at a time.

"Turn the lantern off once you hide." He shoved Tippy into a slight gap between two books to get behind them.

A much smaller book fell, a rare Elfie-sized one, and he quickly picked it up and shoved it back so no one could guess Tippy stood behind the tall ones. He was just about to slip behind another book when the door creaked open. His last thought before light spilled into the room was, at least the others were safely hidden.

9.
ANCIENT BOOK

JULES PEEKED. THE intruder had a walking stick and was tap-tapping the stone floor as his feet shuffled across the library ground. Except for the light from his lantern, a rusty can with a stumpy candle within, the old library was as dark as a cave. He kept his lantern low, making it impossible to see his face.

He and Miranda turned their dragonfly lanterns off just as they'd heard the door creak open as it slid on its tracks. From behind a particularly dusty book, Jules peered at the dark form shuffling and waving his stick as though testing every bit of stone on the floor. Jules felt his nose tingle as the moments wore on.

Then it happened. He sneezed. The muffled explosion wasn't loud, but in the dead silence of the library with only the intruder's shuffling feet and the distinct tapping of the stick, it might as well have been a blast.

Instantly, the tapping and shuffling ceased. From almost nowhere the metal tip of a stick rapped Jules gently on the crown of his head.

"Come out," the intruder demanded, voice stern and angry.

Jules could hardly believe it.

"Mr. Saul?" What was Miranda's grandfather doing there? He slipped out from his hiding spot above a not-so-tall book and landed next to the old man's lantern, as he turned his own on.

"Where's Miranda?" His usual gruff voice sounded fiercer than ever.

Behind one of the books Miranda said, "How'd you find me?"

"It's irrelevant."

Jules said, "Mr. Saul, how'd you know about this place?"

"I know more than you think, boy."

"Did you see anyone upstairs?"

"Your place's a wreck, that's for sure. Where's Erin? I need to speak with your mother about you kidnapping Miranda."

"My mother isn't here and I never kidnapped Miranda. Tell him, Miranda."

Saul Turpentine peeked over his silver-rimmed glasses and peered at Jules's face. His smooth bald head seemed to pick up the glow of the lantern and radiate strangely. "If I ever catch you taking my granddaughter for a secret rendezvous like this I'll make sure your mother grounds you. Indefinitely."

Jules hated asking Saul for help, but what choice did he have? And how'd Saul know about the secret cellar? "I wish *you'd* find Mother for us."

"She's not here?"

Jules shook his head. "We think whoever wrecked our home kidnapped her."

Tst Tst blurted, "Jules thinks they stole Mom's Book."

Jules may have forgotten many stories from the Ancients but who could forget the warning against Keepers losing their Books? It was the fear most Keepers dreaded. If Mom's Book was lost, her days, and theirs, too, were numbered.

Even in the dim light Jules saw Saul's face turn ashen.

"Are you sure?" Saul asked.

By now the other kids were hiding behind Jules, looking curious and afraid. They'd heard of Saul Turpentine's bad temper and his even worse mouth. When he started spewing darts the best defense was to run. Or hide.

Jules said, "I'm not sure about anything. Mom's not here—*that's* for sure. And I don't remember when I last saw her Book. But Mom should have been home—she made potato soup."

"Maybe she ran off when she heard the burglars?" Saul didn't sound convincing.

"Or Scorpents?" Jules said.

"You heard about them prowling around, too?"

Jules nodded. "Holden swore he saw one, and Mrs. Lacework also warned Mom about birds and we almost—but, but how'd you know about this place?"

Saul turned his gaze toward the bookcases around him. "Your grandpa. Brought me here once or twice, way back, before—"

Miranda said, "Before your fight?"

"It's irrelevant. What's important is finding Erin. Let's hope she had the sense to hide."

Tippy's sob startled Jules and he turned to reach for her hand. "It's okay. We'll find Mom."

Jules glanced at Miranda. "Mr. Saul, we need to find my mother's Book."

"Book?" Saul said, as if hearing it for the first time.

Gehzurolle was always on the lookout for Keepers and their Books. He made it his life's mission to destroy Keepers, and those without their Books ran vulnerable. Rumor had it at least one Keeper family was lost forever. No one recalled the lineage, nor the Book they once were ordained to keep.

Jules drew a deep breath and forged on even though his mother had warned him not to advertise they were a Keeper family. But Saul knew, even if Miranda didn't, and this wasn't the time to keep secrets from neighbors. "Her Ancient Book. Maybe Grandpa told you?"

"Let's look for your mother first." Saul looked hesitant.

10.
KEEPER

THE MESS IN the living room still upset Jules and his company as they came tiptoeing out of the closet door.

"We can't," Saul said, brusquely, "lose any more time. Without her Book your mother cannot hide from Gehzurolle. Would you have any clue as to where she might hide such a Book?"

"But I'm hungry and thirsty," Tst Tst announced.

"A little hunger never killed anyone." Saul said, as he dragged Miranda by her arm out of the home.

"But where could Mom be?" Tst Tst asked.

"I'll go ask the Laceworks if they've seen your mother." Saul shook his head and tsk-tsked all the way to the tottering door.

"Miranda can stay here with us," Jules quickly added.

Saul cast him a murderous stare. "Miranda comes with me. You stay here and wait. Don't go out—it's dangerous." He stalked out the door dragging Miranda behind him. She seemed helpless in the old man's grip.

Jules wanted to ask why he'd leave since danger lurked outdoors, but the old man stomped out with much speed and slammed the tottering door behind him.

"What are we going to do if Mr. Saul doesn't find Mom?" Ralston asked.

Tst Tst and Tippy started crying, and Jules shot him a glare and pulled him aside. "I think we should look for Mom's Book. We might find answers."

Ralston said, "Answers to what?"

"To what's happened. I know Mom's been very careful not to let anyone know she's the Keeper."

"But you told Mr. Saul."

"Mr. Saul already knew. He and Grandpa were buddies before their fallout. Besides, the last time I saw that Book was when Grandpa showed it to Mr. Saul and they sat right there." He pointed to the chairs near the fireplace.

"You think Mr. Saul ratted on us? Told spies and they told the Scorpents, and they—"

"Stop! I have to think." Jules rummaged within his cloak and came upon his grandpa's old contact journal he'd found.

He rubbed his fingers over the dark brown leather cover, smooth from constant touch, and even though two or three cracks ran across the leather, it still felt supple and exuded a leathery smell. Typical of most contact journals, Leroy's contained names of hundreds of Elfies he'd known in his long life.

Jules showed Ralston the journal. "I found this the day after Grandpa disappeared, under my pouch in that hearth hiding spot. Maybe he meant for me to have it. But I wonder why."

Ralston took the journal, leafed through the pages and handed it back to Jules. "But there's a gazillion names in there."

"But only one is circled." He shoved the page for Ralston to see. "And in red, too."

"Mosche Falstaff? Who's he?"

"Can't you remember anything? *Falstaff.* That's the name of the last Keeper who disappeared with Petra, the gift, centuries ago."

"So? That Falstaff can't possibly be alive."

"Maybe this Falstaff's related to that *other* Falstaff. Also, Mom said Grandpa wanted to look for Mosche Falstaff but he wouldn't elaborate—just that it was better for us not to know details."

"But why would Grandpa want to visit him?"

Jules drew a deep breath. "It was my fault."

"What?"

"Never mind. Grandpa wouldn't have gone if it hadn't been for me. And I know he wanted to visit Mosche—I overheard something."

"What?"

"Tell you later—now, we have to figure what to do, in case we don't find Mom."

"Could we look for Dad?"

"He could be anywhere. But that's a possibility."

"If Mosche Falstaff's from the 'accursed' family, was it safe for Grandpa to visit him?"

Jules nodded. "That's what Mom said. But Grandpa said we're all affected anyway."

"I hate to break up your party," Bitha said, joining the two. "But we need to feed Tippy. She's eating the floor."

Tippy and Tst Tst both sat cross-legged under the kitchen table, having successfully scooped the potato chunks from somewhere and placed these in the walnut dishes.

"Stop!" Jules smacked the dish in Tippy's clutch and the contents spilled onto the floor. "If Scorpents stepped on these they could be toxic."

11.
STRANGE CLUES

TST TST SET her walnut bowl on her lap. "But we got these from the pot." She pointed to another soup pot that was still on the stove. Jules and Bitha went to inspect and there the pot stood half filled with the thick chunks of potatoes and leeks peeking amongst the creamy base.

Bitha said, "That's odd. Somebody definitely spilled soup on the floor. How is it that only *some* of the soup spilled—look there's the other pot under the chair." She looked confusedly from the overturned pot to the one on the stove.

Jules said, "We need a plan. Let's check what's missing." He rushed to the hearth and pried the loose brick to the side. He reached his arm deep and thought he felt the soft nap of the pouch but then he jerked his hand back out and sucked on his finger." Ouch!"

Ralston said, "We can't afford to lose your pouch—maybe the only way to buy things if we have to look for Mom or Dad."

Jules glared at him.

Ralston said, "What's wrong?"

Jules reached back into the hole, this time less enthusiastically. "Something sharp." When he pulled it out he stared at the shard of glass in his hand. "Hold this, Rals."

Ralston held the sharp edge gingerly. "Is it yours?"

"Would I put something sharp like that to cut myself up?" Jules then brought out his pouch, and sighed. He gave its contents a quick peek and slipped the soft pouch into his cloak pocket.

"It's a good thing the burglars missed that," Ralston said. "Should we toss this?" He passed the shard to Jules who turned it over.

"Some words here." He read, "'—ook within.' What's that mean?"

Bitha came over. "You never noticed it before?" She shone the dragonfly lamp into the hole. "It's a lot deeper than I thought."

Jules peered in as well. "Nothing else in there."

Ralston said, "'—ook within'? Look within?"

Bitha said, "Book within?"

Tst Tst said, "Cook within would be good. Or maybe it's supposed to be a warning like, 'crook within.'"

Jules wrapped the sharp mirrored glass with an old rag lying on the floor and placed it back in the hiding hole. "It's too sharp to take with us. But it could mean something. Only we know of this hiding spot, so either Mom placed it there or Grandpa. But why?"

"Maybe the person who hid it, found it, and saw it's important. Like a clue."

"But what to?" Jules took the mirror out again, unwrapped it, and turned it over. It could have come from some antique since the back was tarnished.

Bitha said, "Is anything missing besides our Book?"

They went about and agreed nothing was taken.

Tst Tst said, "Maybe they only came for Mom." And she and Tippy wept again.

They waited for Saul but even when darkness completely swallowed the sky the old man still had not returned. First their dad left them for the war, then their grandparents drowned and now this? Could things get worse? Jules doubted.

"But if Mom had her Book, the Scorpents couldn't have taken her. The Book *should* have protected her. Unless she was separated from it. She didn't even use the dragonfly lamp, which means she couldn't have sighted Scorpents. She might be out there. Maybe hiding?"

"We should stay put," Ralston said.

Jules was polishing off the last of the potato soup in the pot with a spoon from the kitchen sink. The buttery smell of the savory garlic had made his stomach rumble. He scraped the bottom of the pot for the last drop of the thick creamy potage and licked the spoon. And that was when he saw it.

At the bottom of the pot. Written in black, with the permanent squid ink similar to the ink Ralston made. The writing was faint but Jules read it: "Lacework."

Ralston peered over Jules's shoulder and looked at the message. "Did Mom write it? Like a message she didn't want anyone else to see?"

Jules said, "That was risky. How'd she know I'd peer into the pot?"

Tst Tst came over and peered in too. "Everyone knows you'd die for potato soup."

Bitha dragged Tippy by the wrist and looked in, too. "But does this mean she'd gone to the Laceworks'? Or she wants us there? How do we even know Mom wrote it? She wouldn't leave us here to the burglars."

Jules traced the words with his forefinger. "Unless she didn't have a choice. Anyway, we can't stay here."

Ralston said, "Let's go to the Laceworks'. Maybe we can ask Holden."

Jules said, "I'd rather eat glass, but what choice do we have? We must look for Mom, or something."

"But it's dark outside," Bitha said. "Mr. Saul said to stay put."

Jules said, "We have our dragonfly lanterns."

Bitha said, "But what if we're not hiding from Scorpents? Besides, we only have two left. Miranda took one."

Jules said, "Maybe she saw the Scorpents and needs it. Two's enough."

"What if Mom isn't at the Laceworks'? Then what?"

"Stop it, Bitha!" Jules saw his sister's round eyes and softened his tone. "We go to the Laceworks' and if Mom's not there, we'll ask Mrs. L for help. You and the girls stay with her and Holden. Ralston and I can see if the Taylors or the Bradfords have seen her."

"And if they haven't?"

"Stop it!" Jules looked at the strewn room.

Tippy came over and handed him her sardius. "You can pay for things with it."

He smiled at Tippy. "You keep it. Let's pack some food and stuff in a couple of pillowcases, in case we need to stay away for a while."

He saw his sisters' eyes widen. "Worse come to worse, we will find Dad. Dad'll know what to do. Mrs. L might know where he could be. Mr. L's camp's not far from Dad's."

Bitha said, "But they're fighting in a war!"

12.
DRAGONFLY LANTERN

AS THEY WERE about to leave, a persistent thudding on the front window startled them.

The girls froze. Even Jules held his breath. Could it be Saul back and tapping with his cane? But the rapping sounded more like thudding, different from the sharp metallic *tap tap* the end of Saul's cane made.

"Shh!" He motioned with his arm toward the closet. Not again!

But Tippy ran to the window and squeaked, "Fiesty! Fiesty's back!"

When they flung open the shutters, Fiesty flitted about, just as good as new.

"I hate to say this," Jules said, and looked at the faces staring at him, "but we can't take Fiesty along. It'll be too—obvious." What if they had to hide in the undergrowth? Fiesty's presence might give them away.

After much argument, and since he was outnumbered, Jules gave in. Especially after Tst Tst reminded him, "Fiesty's of the breed found only in the King's garden centuries ago." Grandpa had said this.

When everyone was out, Jules turned to face the living room. "Good-bye," he whispered to the broken things on the floor, but, naturally, no one answered him.

"I wish we didn't have to leave." Bitha sighed as she looked back at the house.

"Would you rather wait here for them to come get you?" Jules asked.

Bitha rolled her eyes at him. "I just get the feeling we won't be back for a while."

He led them in a single file down the pebbled path with Ralston way in the back holding on to a blue ribbon they had harnessed over Fiesty to make sure he followed them.

Tippy clung to Jules's cloak and Tst Tst clung to Tippy's other hand, which still clutched onto her sardius. Jules shot a glance or two up at the branches. It had grown completely pitch dark but he felt comforted by the dragonfly lanterns. No Scorpent could see them with the lanterns' light but what about their other enemies? Who were they?

13.
WHISPERER

MIRANDA PULLED HER arm free from Saul's grip. "Why do you enjoy humiliating me?"

"Why do you insist on leaving the house without *my* permission?" Saul paced his breathing and placed a hand to his chest.

"I'm not a piece of furniture you can set in the corner and expect to stay put."

"I will not let history repeat itself. You know our situation. We must take extra precautions."

"*You* must take extra precaution. Me? I have a *nor-mal* life."

"There's nothing normal about what you're doing, Miranda." Saul's eyes locked with his granddaughter's. Blue like the seamless sky. How similar her eyes were to Chrystle's. It was as if his daughter had returned, been brought back to life, after all these years.

"What—what are you talking about?" Miranda stumbled over her words.

But Saul just turned and walked away, his head bowed low, shoulders drooped.

"Grandpa! Wait." Miranda kept pace with Saul's brisk steps. "You think Mrs. Blaze is at the Laceworks'?" She wrung her hands and looked at the branches.

"If she wasn't captured."

"We have to get there quickly."

"Why so nervous?" When Saul looked up he reached out, grabbed Miranda's arm again, and yanked her into the undergrowth.

****

Before them, hidden in a swirl of gray smoke, a white face materialized. Eyes of blue fire and twisted lips contorted into a smile. The being floated stirring the fallen leaves just an arm's length away from their hiding spot. The smoke drifted to where Saul had stood seconds ago and then wove its way in and out of the leaves and twigs in front of the briar rose where Saul and Miranda hid, as if teasing them to come out. Whispers swished through the foliage all around them.

Sweat dripped from Saul's temple but he didn't wipe at it. He stood still, his grip on Miranda firm as they watched Whisperer.

"Beta?" Whisperer whispered.

Can he smell Elfies, too? Saul never asked Whisperer before.

14.
GEHZUROLLE'S AGENTS

RALSTON HURRIED TOWARD Jules as they trudged the familiar pebbled path to the Laceworks' home. Despite the stars above, the grassy terrain below was pitch. A soft wind rippled the long grasses that towered over the tall Jules in some parts. Even with the lanterns the night seemed to rule. Their lantern glowed faintly between the swaying blades.

Ralston said, "How'd Gehzurolle even know we're Keepers? We were always so careful not to tell anyone."

Jules looked over his shoulders. "Gehzurolle's not supposed to be omniscient, but his spies lurk everywhere."

"You mean the Scorpents?"

Jules lowered his voice. "Not *just*. Could be Handoverans, or Elfies who've been bought with a price. Then there're three others. One looks like a red flame and his name is Rage. It's hard to notice him, especially during a fire, although some have seen him and lived!"

"So, he's in charge of fire?"

"Rage lives up to his name. He's in charge of anger. That's what Grandpa said."

"Who else?"

"Another resembles smoke: name is Whisperer. He whispers things in the air to influence people or the weather or such. He gives them suggestions. And the third is Sekt: he's rumored to roam in fogs and mists, but he hides well and not much is known of him. Gehzurolle'll do anything to make trouble for us. He can even manipulate birds for his end."

"Birds?" Ralston made a face.

"Not all kinds. Prey birds. That's why I think Gehzurolle's involved. Our raven attack seemed too coincidental, especially with this." He swept his arm about. "Did you hear anything last night?"

"Besides your snoring?"

"I saw a bright flash across the sky last night," Jules said. "At first I thought it was lightning, but then in the distance a glare brightened the night and the ground trembled."

"A bomb in the forest? Maybe the war's coming closer?"

Bitha came up from behind and said, "I hope Dad's okay."

"Maybe the glare came from an explosion." Jules hastened his steps, eyes skimming the thick branches above.

The trail brought them to the edge of a clearing leading to another moss-covered house under two twisted roots of a redwood, the home of Cori Lacework, his wife of eighteen years, Jessie, and their son, sixteen-year-old Holden.

"What do we tell Mrs. L?" Ralston said.

Jules shrugged. "Saul should be there and might have told her. We shouldn't scare her."

"What if," Ralston asked, "the burglars attacked the Laceworks, too?"

So many questions! Jules scanned the boughs above. "We'll find out soon enough."

15.
LACEWORKS'S HOME

WHEN THEY NEARED the Lacework home, Fiesty tugged at his leash as if unwilling to get any closer. Bitha nudge Jules. "Fiesty's acting weird again."

Tst Tst, struggling behind with the dragonfly, cast a worried glance at Jules.

"Let him go," Jules said.

Tst Tst released the blue ribbon, and Fiesty whizzed higher and higher up to the boughs. The children looked at each other, shrugged, and hurried toward the Lacework door.

****

For a second the shadow following them determined to strike Jules and his siblings again, but he stopped. They thought they were invincible with the dragonfly lantern, but direct attack wasn't the only way to exterminate Elfies. Whisperer should know. He'd been perfecting the art through the ages. The proper time would come. It always did.

He pursed his lips upward toward the clouds, first softly, then more intensely, his gaze never wavering from the siblings. His master had given him authority over the elements of the air. He could use it to his advantage, but this time he would use something that had worked before.

Beta had told him about the Laceworks, and it was a perfect plan, assuming Beta's trick had convinced the boy and his siblings to get inside. And once the Blaze kids were gone, he could finish his task and search the wreck left behind by the fire.

It should be on one of them.

Whisperer flew from the cypress he was perched upon, and several more pinecones dropped from the redwood tree.

16.
BEWARE

THE LACEWORK HOME stood under the niche of the tallest redwood in that part of the woods. The redwood poked above the rest in the canopy of green rivaling even some of the oldest spruces there.

"Look." Ralston pointed to a shred of green fabric on a branch, obviously torn by some brambles near a boulder.

"Someone was in a hurry." Jules picked the fabric and examined it. "Looks like Holden's cloak."

Ralston parted the brambles and slipped, cutting his hand as he righted himself. "There's a hole here in the ground."

"Stay away. Could be a gopher home. You don't want to end up being gopher food next."

Standing on the Lacework's front porch, a savory fragrance, maybe potato soup, wafted toward them. Which was an odd coincidence, Jules thought.

His stomach rumbled and he was about to knock on the door when Tippy let out one of her infamous shrieks. He turned and there she stood, tangled in Fiesty's blue ribbon as she and the dragonfly struggled to detangle themselves. Tst Tst and Bitha, in helping, only made things worse, so Jules strode over.

"Here, take my lantern," he instructed Bitha, who already had her hands full, what with their pillow-cased belongings.

Tst Tst was handling the other one. "Maybe Mrs. L has a pair of scissors to cut her loose."

Jules motioned for Bitha to place her lantern over Tippy's head. "Here's the problem—pass me your stone and squeeze your palm inward really tight." To free his hand he pocketed her stone. "Now, pass your hand through here." Finally he freed her and pocketed the ribbon. "It could've strangled you."

He strode to the door again but a roar above stopped him from knocking. Thunder? He hadn't noticed the lightning due to the canopy. Was this like the solitary flash last night, a single warning of a pending storm?

The hair on Jules's arms stood on ends. Static electricity. "Back away!" He pushed Ralston back and grabbed Tst Tst and Tippy's arms. "Quick! The boulder!"

Bitha and Ralston scrambled after him and dove under a groove beneath the boulder. The brambles cut their arms and legs and tore parts of their cloaks.

The crack shattered the night's quiet and sounded close. Jules had never heard thunder that close. But it was nothing compared to the explosion that turned the Lacework home and the redwood it was under into an inferno. Flames consumed the tree as if someone had doused the wood with alcohol. Even from behind the boulder the heat from the fire turned their faces red and the smell of singed shrubbery and smoke made their eyes tear.

"Get away," Jules shouted amidst the roar of the fire. He pushed them farther behind the boulder and they all fell into the gopher hole Ralston almost slipped into earlier. "Go, go!"

He shoved the girls in front of him deeper into the hole and pulled Ralston who was coughing and sputtering behind him.

"My eyes!" Ralston cried. "Help! I can't see. I'm blind!"

17.
UNKNOWN

JULES SLID UNCONTROLLABLY, deeper and deeper down the tunnel, gripping Tippy in one arm. He hoped the others were close behind him but he wasn't sure. It was dark and he was falling too fast. Screams from Bitha and Tst Tst echoed around him. Were they okay? Mustn't let go of the lantern, he reminded himself.

The bottom eventually came. Ralston smashed into Jules's back, somersaulted and landed with a thump into the side of the burrow, followed by Bitha and Tst Tst. Puffs of dust clouded the air and everyone choked and spluttered. Between hackings Jules said, "Stay put. Let the dust settle. Here, drink water." He passed Ralston a water pouch.

"I still can't see."

"Stop fidgeting and just blink," Jules said.

The burrow they stood in was large and, even though the air seemed cool, Jules didn't think they could stay down there indefinitely. Especially if gophers lived nearby.

"We need to stay alert," he said once everyone had calmed down. Tippy and Tst Tst looked dazed and drowsy beside him.

Ralston peered into one of the tunnels leading out of the burrow. The lantern high above his head lighted their dismal paths ahead. "There're too many ways branching out. Which one should we take?"

"One away from that fire."

Tst Tst and Tippy sobbed loudly. Jules felt like biting his tongue but he, himself, had to gulp down a sob. Were his mother and the Laceworks in there? He never liked Holden, but still, he felt bad for him. And what about Saul, and Miranda? He blinked at the shaft they'd just dropped from. Smoke drifted down in puffs from that shaft, as well as from some of the other tunnels next to it. He hoped the air was breathable. What if there were toxic fumes underground?

He brought a lantern close to the page in his grandpa's journal and studied the address and directions to Mosche Falstaff's home. "Mr. Mosche's home isn't too far from here—in fact, it's located by the river, about a mile from Saul's. We can go to Mosche's and ask him for help."

"What if he's not there?" Ralston said.

"Hand me the pillowcase. We need a compass."

Ralston took the journal and traced the route in the tiny map below the address with his finger. "But why don't we just look for Dad?"

Jules said, "Dad could be anywhere along the River front."

Bitha said, "But what about Mom? She might return to the house, and find us missing. Then what? We didn't even leave her a note."

"And let the Scorpents know where we are if *they* returned?" Jules sat on his haunches and wrapped his fingers around his temple.

"Do you think Mom was in the house with Mrs. L and Holden?" Ralston's voice shook.

Jules dared not think.

Tst Tst said, "And Fiesty? You think he's okay?"

Fiesty had flown up to the trees. Had he been caught in the fire? Would they never see him again?

18.
LOST

FINALLY, THEY OPTED for the tunnel directly opposite the one they'd dropped down. It should lead them farthest from the burning redwood, Jules explained.

Also the path up the tunnel ran gradual, and they could almost walk up the incline without having to grope up on hands and knees. Some sections were high enough to stand on; others had caved in and only allowed a crawl space. When they reached a large chamber they were all ready to catch their breaths.

"There are some rusty rungs that lead up." Ralston pointed to what could have been iron rungs spaced like a ladder up one side of the wall into a gaping hole above.

Jules said, "Maybe someone used this for a home or a secret path." But where to? And who were they? Handoveran spies? Scorpents?

Jules peered at the lowest rung. It was still a ways above and the little girls would not be able to climb, as some rungs appeared missing between the spaces. Were these just gopher tunnels or something else altogether?

They took a swig from their water pouches and were about to set off except that a glow from another shaft next to the one they had emerged from alerted Jules.

"Shh!" he motioned for the others to stay behind him. Gophers didn't carry lamps.

After some seconds the glow brightened. Jules glanced from one tunnel opening to another. Which one should they rush into to escape from whatever was heading their way? A part of him was curious to see who could be traveling in these parts with lamps. But if he stayed behind and it was an enemy, would he endanger his siblings? He shoved Tippy behind him and determined the direction to take. Hopefully toward the river. Hurry!

"Jules!" a whisper echoed in the chamber.

Jules swiveled toward the speaker.

It was a gopher, all right! With his back to the tunnel he'd edged out from, Holden stood, a crude jar lantern in hand and with a stunned face. Even in the dim light it was obvious Holden had bruises and cuts on his arms and face.

"Who pummeled you?" Jules rushed toward his neighbor, eyes wide.

"We must get away." Holden was still panting. His green cloak was in shreds.

"What happened? Did you see my mom?"

"Your mom?" Holden shook his head, eyes dazed. "But my mom…." He hung his head and slumped to the ground.

They consoled Holden as best they could and Jules briefed him on their plight, with Ralston and Tst Tst breaking in the story to remind him of details. Bitha was too busy keeping Tippy awake.

Holden said, "It started last night. My mother was reading during dinner. Someone knocked at our door. It was Miranda. Said we must hide and she didn't have time to explain. So we grabbed some things and told her we wanted to warn you, except Miranda said she'd go instead. Did she get to you? Warn you?"

"Miranda? Last night? No, no."

Holden took a deep breath. "That's odd. She told us to wait for her by the elm tree next to the Bradley home. And no matter what not to go home. But then—"

Holden rubbed his eyes.

"What?" Jules said.

"It happened so quickly. We were running past the arbor and one minute my mom was next to me, then a dark shadow swooped by and she—she vanished."

"Did you ask the Bradleys for help?"

"They weren't there. Not the Oakleys, Nor the Primroses. No one was in."

"Did you see Miranda again after that?" Jules said.

Holden shook his head. "I waited all night at the Bradleys' front steps and took their lantern." He held out the jar lamp which had a crude hook upon its cover. Two fireflies fluttered within the jar and their lighted back twinkled on and off.

Holden said, "I must have dozed off after. Then earlier this afternoon I went home, thought I could scrounge up some food, then head over to you, except I saw something enter my home. A swirl of smoke, and when it turned, I saw its red eyes. I ran and hid behind a boulder, but there was a rabbit or gopher hole and I fell in. I can't say I wasn't glad."

"Maybe Miranda somehow knew your house was going to be lightning struck," Jules said.

"But how? Like she has some hidden powers?"

Ralston said, "Maybe she *is* the hidden power." Both Jules and Holden shot him a glare.

Jules said, "It's a good thing you fell into the hole."

"Except I can't find my way out. It's useless. And I don't know what happened to my mom." He brushed his palm over his eyes.

Jules handed Holden a water pouch and the small morsel of food they'd packed in their pillowcases. "We figured on a system to get out. We're trying to always head east."

"Toward the river? Brooke Beginning?" Holden said between mouthfuls. "How'd you know where east is?"

Ralston shoved a small object toward Holden's chin. It was a tiny bowl of water with a thin piece of metal rod floating on the surface. "I made a compass with our dish and Bitha's hair pin."

Holden's eyes widened as he looked at the homemade compass.

Ralston said, "I magnetized the pin."

Holden nodded slowly with respect. "But why Brooke Beginning?"

"A Keeper lives near it."

"A Keeper? Then I'm not going with you."

"You have something against Keepers?"

Holden locked eyes with Jules, then Ralston.

"It's just that Miranda told us that night that they're after Keepers—"

Jules said, "And why'd she say that *to you*? It's not like you're a Keeper family."

"Why so touchy? It's just that, do we *want* to find a Keeper if Gehzurolle's after them?"

"Let's go, Rals. Bitha, get Tippy." Jules turned away.

"Hey, you can't leave me here." Holden yanked Jules's cloak. "I'm not prejudiced or anything—and why should that bother you?"

"We're going to Mosche's. He's our best bet to get answers. I have no idea where my mom is. Or my dad. Or what *really* happened to Gramps."

Holden held on to Jules's cloak. "We should go to Saul's. He knows stuff. Besides, Miranda might be there. They could be in danger, too."

Jules stared at Holden.

Holden said, "If you want to see a Keeper, I think Saul's a Keeper."

"Miranda told you this?"

"You jealous?"

"Of a pea?" Jules gathered some of their leftovers, shoved them into a pillowcase and passed it to Ralston. "Let's try Saul, then. And if he's not there we'll get to Mosche's."

19.
NO HIDING

AWAY FROM THE blazing redwood Whisperer scoured the grounds for any signs of movement. The children had hidden behind that annoying boulder. Had the fire singed them to a crisp? He sniffed the air but didn't detect burned skin or singed hair. Whirling down like a tornado he landed beside the boulder and sniffed at a burnt rag amidst the ashen twigs.

Whose was this? A hole beneath that boulder? Sneaky. Smoke still seeped out of the hole in gray wisps of spiral threads.

Whisperer floated about by the gopher tunnel and thought he heard steps far in the depth of the earth. One of the tunnels ran to the river, he was sure.

A plan popped into his mind. Keeper children with his prize. Keeper children who couldn't swim. Perfect.

20.
TUNNEL SYNDROME

JULES AND HIS company charged on deeper and deeper from one passageway to another with the meager light from their lanterns, the Blazes' dragonfly ones casting sparkles like cut diamonds on the rough tunnel walls, while Holden's firefly lamp glowed on and off yellow and muted.

Jules told Holden about the rungs. "My Grandpa said the older homes that belonged to Keepers have tunnels to help Keepers escape if needed. Maybe this was one of them."

"Jules, look!" Bitha traced her fingers against the wall. "Why's this all wet?"

"We must be close to the Brooke," Jules said. The air smelled damp. Mold. Mildew maybe. He strode over to her and fingered the droplets. "Water's seeping."

The wall on the entire left side ran moist into one of the tunnels ahead. Heading south the mouth of the tunnel coursed in the same direction as the river.

Ralston said, "Maybe the wall acts as a dam."

Bitha said, "The wall won't collapse, will it?"

Jules peered into the darkness even as his mind considered the moisture on the wall. He gestured to them to follow. "Let's hurry."

Ralston said, "You think Fiesty escaped the fire?"

"He must have sensed *something* since he wanted us to untie his ribbon."

Keeping a brisk pace, some hummed a ditty whilst others concentrated on their footwork.

If Saul was a Keeper he'd sure kept the secret well. It also meant Miranda was his heir since her mother was gone. But would Saul share his Book to help him find his mother? And Mrs. L? But what if he was too late? And what about that flash in the sky, or the earth shivering right after?

Jules clutched at his cloak pocket and fingered the stones in the pouch. Worse come to worse they could pay for information. His Grandpa would have wanted that.

Suddenly, without warning, the ground quaked as if angry. The rolling and vibration intensified; it became more violent, and they struggled to keep their balance, unable to walk.

Just when they thought the shaking couldn't grow worse, a growling noise echoed about them and the girls screamed even more.

"Lions don't live in forests—do they?" Tst Tst's shrill voice muted due to the rumblings.

"Uh oh!" Jules and Holden said simultaneously.

"Quick," Jules shouted. "We need to—run—flash flood!"

"Flood...?" someone said.

"Behind us!" Holden dashed forward, the dragonfly lantern swinging, its hinges creaking in the mad rush.

Jules gestured. "Up, this way!"

He grabbed Tippy's and Tst Tst's hands, one on each side. He whisked them away with giant steps, their feet barely grazing the ground. He dragged them on, never looking back. He ran to higher ground up the chosen tunnel hoping those behind kept his pace. Holden pushed the small of Tst Tst's back, and she half stumbled to keep up with Jules.

Ralston, carrying most of what was left of the supplies in one hand and Holden's firefly lamp in the other, sprinted faster than he'd ever done.

Only Bitha, last in tow, trailed farther and farther behind as the roar of the torrent growled, growing louder and closer. She tripped and groped in the dim pathway, the light of the lantern in front always rounding another corner and another as she struggled up the incline.

The dim glow from Ralston's firefly lamp was barely enough to keep her from avoiding the stumps and bumps that littered their path. She tripped, slipped, and almost fell on her face a few times.

Ralston, some twenty steps ahead of her, turned and saw Bitha faltering. His hands holding the hook of the firefly jar lamp shook even more when the rumbling of the roiling water grew. He wanted to shout to Jules but instinctively knew no one could hear him above the roar. He wanted to hasten his pace, wanted to follow the others, but he kept looking over his shoulder at Bitha.

"Bitha!" He breathed out his pant.

In minutes the torrent would engulf her. Ralston's eyes darted here and there searching for something. Already he couldn't see the flicker of the dragonfly lanterns ahead—Holden had rounded some bend ahead in one of the tunnels that climbed up. But which one?

The light from Ralston's firefly jar glowed dim and the rumbling from the roiling water roared loud, like angry lions. That was when he glanced up and saw something on the ceiling, a few steps away: what looked like a pocket as the ceiling bulged just in that section. And iron rungs similar to the ones before.

Ralston flung the sack in his grasp upon the ledge, a protruding bit of stone. He scrambled up the jutting precipice using the iron rungs, one hand still clutching the lighted jar. But his foot slipped and the jar fell. He wanted to jump back down to rescue the fireflies in the cracked jar, but it was too late.

21.
TRAPPED

BEHIND THE RUNNING Bitha, a roll of white foam gained speed. Ralston's panting came in short wheezing spurts. He clutched his chest. Something screamed in his ears. He wobbled as if about to faint. He covered his face with his hands, squeezed his lids tight.

But then he looked down at Bitha, saw her struggling.

"Grab my hands!" Ralston shouted above the grumble that surrounded them. He could barely make out her form with the glimmer from the lighted jar quivering on the ground below his niche.

Bitha glanced up. Ralston reached his hands out and waved at her frantically. He leaned over more, grabbed both her wrists, and jerked her up the precipice, then into the pocket, the cleft in the stone. Below, the torrent growled into the tunnel and flooded the channel up to the ceiling. Except for that tiny alcove, the cleft in the stony ceiling, the water filled the entire passageway and rushed toward the tunnels ahead.

It took several *long* minutes before the current ran its course and the water subsided. Not knowing if Jules, or any of the others, had escaped the flash flood, Bitha and Ralston waited in darkness, huddled and damp from the sprays of the passing waters.

Ralston rummaged in his cloak. "I have a light stick."

Several minutes and after much rustling of his cloak, a tiny, and almost ineffective, glow came from a wand in his hand

"I didn't make a very good one." Ralston's eyes searched the ground for the firefly jar but it was gone, borne away by the current.

"Good-bye, firefly," Ralston murmured. And Bitha held his hand.

When the water subsided, they clambered down the ledge. Careful not to slip on the sloppy mud, they groped and trudged up a tunnel that they hoped would lead to higher ground. Eventually, a glow grew brighter ahead. Jules and Holden!

Jules slapped Ralston's shoulder when they met. "You have to stop trying to get yourself killed."

"You have to see what Bitha and I found."

Ralston led them to the alcove and shone the lantern on the rough ceiling.

Jules said, "A strange marking."

He climbed up using the rungs, the rusty metal smell rising to his nose. He fingered the circular hole with seven sharp prongs jutting out, each prong no wider than Tippy's pinky, and all the prongs laid out in a circle within the shallow circular hole.

"Nothing happens even when I tug at these. Strange. But we have to hurry. The later we get help the slimmer our chances of finding Mom and Mrs. L."

They went back into the tunnel and continued east. When they reached an opening, they saw that it was light outside.

"We walked all night?" Tst Tst gave a deep sigh and yawned. "No wonder I'm so pooped!" She hopped up and down on one foot and somersaulted. "Maybe Fiesty's here."

Bitha shot Tst Tst a frown. "I can't walk another step."

"We can't stop till we get to Saul's. It's not safe here." Jules hoisted Holden up out of the shaft, grabbed a thin root protruding into the tunnel and yanked himself after Holden. The roar from the nearby river filled the air. Fewer trees grew here and the sky seemed to expand into a vastness he never thought possible. So this was where Miranda lived. She'd always visited them and for some reason Saul never wanted them near his home. He studied the branches. "Stick close together."

"Look, Tippy's asleep." Bitha pointed to the huddled form by her feet.

Jules studied his grandpa's contact journal and studied the direction for Saul's. Every conifer looked alike. How would they find Saul?

"I can get us there," Holden said.

Jules threw him a murderous glare. "You've been there?"

"Miranda showed me."

But before Jules could argue more a giant net plopped down upon them. Trapped, the net reduced them to a tangle of arms and legs. Someone had heard them.

"What's happening?" Tst Tst shrieked.

Jules said, "We're trapped." Obviously.

"What's that?" came one of the girl's confused mumbled cry.

Jules felt like kicking himself for talking loudly.

As they struggled the net tightened even more like a noose strangling a writhing neck.

"Stop fidgeting." Jules whispered. "Maybe one of us triggered the trap. If no one comes along we can try to cut our way out." He fingered Tippy's sardius in his pocket. Its sharp edges might cut through the net's twines. The mirror shard buried deep in a pocket could come in handy if he could get to it. Thank goodness he'd taken it.

But then shadows loomed from behind the nearest conifer and a dozen figures emerged and advanced toward them at a hasty pace. The Elfie children could have sworn they were blazing bushes of fire, so impressive was their camouflage. Some of the flaming figures checked the net, tightened the bundle of Elfies further and, circling them, heaved the strategic lines attached to the net upon their shoulders. Numerous steps later the aggressors dumped them in front of a large oak with a void at the bottom, a natural cave, where its twisted roots converged and looped upward. A glow flickered from within.

"Ouch! Ouch!" Bitha cried.

"Stop that!"

"Help!" The protests continued.

At the doorway of the opening, silhouetted against the backlight, an imposing form stood with arms akimbo. For a long while the trapped Elfies stared at the apparition. Then Jules recognized the figure and gasped.

"Why are you doing this?" Jules said when he could gather his wits.

"Mr. Saul!" Ralston said.

"Have you been tailing us? Where's my mother?" Jules struggled to upright himself, wiping dirt off his cloak.

"Where is Miranda?" Saul asked.

"She probably found out you were a crook and tried to save herself." Jules bit his lower lip and regretted his words.

"She ran away from me, and she was going to look for you."

"To tell us to get away from you, no doubt." Again Jules wanted to kick himself.

"Boy, you have no idea what or who you are up against."

"Then maybe someone should start spilling the beans." Jules felt Ralston behind him kick his ankle, and he was sure Tst Tst had pinched his arm.

But his words had a strange effect on Saul, who slumped on to the ground and wrapped his hands over his head. Next to Saul, five camouflaged figures with masked faces whispered to one another.

22.
DECEIVED

SAUL LOOKED AT Jules. "If I cut you loose will you promise not to run? Say you won't run away! Say it. There's something you need to know."

"We won't run away," Jules said.

The strange figures cut the children loose and the girls cowered behind Jules and Ralston.

"Come in." Saul moved away from the lighted doorway under the oak and gestured for them to step across the threshold. "We don't have time to lose."

"How do we know you don't have a Scorpent in there waiting to pounce on us?" Jules eyed one by one the strange camouflaged figures.

"Because I don't need Scorpents if I wanted you dead. Don't waste my time."

The room under the oak measured about ten steps by ten steps, with only a table at one end and four or five chairs arranged in a circle in the middle. But when they approached the table Jules noticed an open book upon the table. Was this an Ancient Book? Was Saul really a Keeper? As Holden said?

Saul sighed. "I meant to tell your mother. Warn her. But I was too late."

"Too late for what?"

The furrows above Saul's white brows deepened and his eyes glowed with moisture. "Your mother's in Handover."

"What? Was she kidnapped?"

Saul shrugged. "Word has it she's looking for your grandparents."

"So, they're not … dead?"

"But they could be in grave danger, at least that's what I'd heard."

"Who from?"

"Gehzurolle's forces? Handoverans?"

Jules stepped forward and leaned in toward Saul. Would his mother leave them just like that? Without a note, nothing?

Saul said, "I overheard someone, something. I fear Miranda's in grave danger. I can't afford to lose her. She doesn't realize what she's dealing with."

"What do you mean?" Jules stepped toward the old man. Was Saul going to confess that Miranda was somehow hooked up with evil as Holden suggested?

"I had suspected it for awhile but refused to acknowledge the signs. She's been deceived. My precious Miranda's been deceived."

"What are you saying?"

Holden stepped forward. "She really was the one who tricked us? She caused my mother to be abducted. But why?"

"They told her Chrystle, her mother, was still alive, living in Handover and that if she helped them gather the Keepers they would take her to Handover to get Chrystle. So possibly Erin ran away from her, too."

Was that why Miranda knew of the potato soup? Because she'd been there? "Where is Miranda now?"

Saul shook his head. "She went with them. I'm only guessing."

"Who's 'them'? Scorpents?"

"Enemies. Miranda invited them—Scorpents, Gehzurolle's agents—into our land. That explains the Scorpent sightings of late. For centuries they kept away, had to keep away, since none from a Keeper family had ever invited them over. None, till Miranda." The old man sighed and slid onto a chair.

Jules stared at the old man's bald head and regretted his feelings of hatred toward Saul. "I have an idea. But first some answers. What's this place? Your home?" He gestured about him.

Saul looked up. "I needed a secret place away from prying neighbors so no one would suspect I'm a Keeper."

"Not even my Grandpa?"

"Leroy found out, and that's why we had that tiff. He felt cheated I knew about him but I kept my Keeperhood a secret. Well, I had to. What with Chrystle gone. I couldn't risk Miranda."

"I have my grandpa's contact journal and there's an address for a Mosche Falstaff." Jules told Saul his thoughts on Mosche. Jules felt hopeful.

Saul shook his head. "For centuries our people have sought Falstaff's descendants, but none has ever succeeded."

23.
BROOKE BEGINNING

JULES TAPPED HIS forehead as his eyes scoured Saul's dim den. He refused to believe he'd reached a dead end. If he didn't find Mosche Falstaff, then what?

"There must be a way we can locate him. If we find this Falstaff, we'd have located another Keeper. That's a big plus for our Kingdom."

"'If', and that's a huge 'if.' Besides, we'd only have four Keepers accounted for. The fifth Keeper, some say, would never be found. He and his family were killed by Gehzurolle."

"And his Book?"

"Possibly lost forever. Maybe Gehzurolle has it. Or destroyed it. After all, without its Keeper, the Book is useless to Gehzurolle."

"Maybe the fifth Keeper left for Handover, too."

Saul shrugged. "The Ancients said *Falstaff* left for Handover afraid of the stigma his name had brought his family."

"But what about this address? Says here, Mosche Falstaff—by the River. See the map?"

Saul leaned over and peered at Leroy's journal. "That must be an old address. Or a fake one to throw off enemies. Or could be any number of so-called 'Rivers.'"

"Maybe my grandparents know where Mosche lives. Why else would Gramps have wanted to get to Handover? He must have guessed a storm was coming. Yet, he went. He must have had strong reasons to go despite the storm."

"I was never convinced your grandpa perished in that storm."

Jules's eyes lit up. "Before he left, Grandpa said he wanted to check on our family's secret but I don't know how that's related to Mosche."

"Did he say what the secret was?"

Jules avoided Saul's eyes and glumly shook his head.

"So this Mosche knows something about your family. Maybe your mother has gone to him, too."

Jules nodded. "I still can't believe she'd leave us like that."

"She must have had no choice. Things must have happened in a hurry."

Jules mentioned about the potato soup pot.

"We had potato soup when Miranda came," Holden said. "Maybe that wasn't a message from your mom. Maybe someone wanted to trick you."

Ralston said, "To trick us so we'd go to Holden's place before the lightning struck?"

Saul said, "That's irrelevant at this point. Get Mosche's Book to me so we can use it together with mine to find your mother. The Books must always work with another in synergy."

"But why can't you come with us?"

"I can't go to Handover in case Miranda returns, you understand, but I can help you cross the big river."

Also known as Brooke Beginning, Jules had heard tales of it. Tales of Elfies who'd lost their lives braving the fickle waters of the Brooke that sometimes swelled and swallowed up Elfie explorers even in the calmest of days. With the recent storms and lightning episodes these recent days hardly qualified as placid. Let alone safe.

"How will I get across? I don't even have a map of Handover."

"You saw my helpers? They're masters of disguises, and are from Handover. Half-breeds. They know ways and people there."

Jules looked uncomfortably at one of the guards at the door. The mask didn't allow anyone to see his face and having never even met a half-breed before he was curious. "I didn't know half-breeds were real."

"The real term is 'Hanfies.' It means half Handoveran, half Elfie. Just like how Elfie means half Elf, half fairy." Saul beckoned to the guard, who stepped into the lighted center. "Take off your mask."

Except for his high forehead, no one could have suspected the guard had Handover genes. And so easily the forehead could be hidden under a heavy fringe of hair, or a hat.

Saul dismissed the guard with a wave of his hand. "I have ideas where Mosche could be. But if Leroy isn't there, don't panic. Tell Mosche he must help Miranda. She's the grandchild of a Keeper and my sole heir. He'd understand the irreversible danger our Land is in if she's taken. Once we get her back we can convince her of her deception. She's still young, and the young always make mistakes. Make sure Mosche brings his Book to me. The more Books we collect the easier it'd be to find your mother."

"Provided she's not with Mosche," Jules said.

"Naturally. I am just assuming the worst scenario."

24.
HIDDEN BRIDGE

JULES AND HIS companions slept in Saul's room for the night with the promise that Saul would take them to a hidden bridge that spanned Brooke Beginning the next morning. He seemed to know of things about the Brooke Jules couldn't fathom.

They surmised the bridge must be how the gangly stick insects walked across the river and wreaked havoc in some parts of Reign. Where these carnivorous insects now resided the Elfies could not determine. They appeared and disappeared like ghosts, and some were called ghost insects.

The children waited for Fiesty but he didn't appear. Fiesty's presence might give them leverage if they met more bird attacks. Only Jules and Holden would go across the bridge to look for Mosche. They hoped Leroy would be with Mosche, and if not, Mosche might know where Erin, or maybe even Jessie Lacework, might be, having concluded that the two lady

Keepers, if imprisoned, must be in the same place. Saul felt certain Scorpents must have abducted Jessie. He regretted that Miranda might have played a part in Jessie's capture.

Before Jules and Holden left, Tippy tugged at the edge of Jules's cloak.

"I can help, too." She brought the sardius from her cloak and pressed it in Jules's palm. "You can use it to pay."

Jules stroked the top of her shiny hair and stared at the red stone in his palm. "I have plenty in my pouch. But thanks."

Saul stalked over and stared at the stone in Jules's outstretched palm.

"Where did you get that?" He took it from Jules and examined it, turning it this way and that, in the light of the dragonfly lantern. Without another word, Saul shuffled over to the table with the big Book and flipped the pages furiously.

"What's the matter?" Jules said. "It's just a sardius. We have plenty in our backyard. Grandpa and I used to collect them and other gems, too."

Jules patted about his cloak, and brought out the pouch filled with gems. "Here!" He poured out the contents of the pouch onto the table next to Saul's tome. Some stones fell off the table and clattered to the wooden floor.

"Leroy found all these?" Saul bent and picked up the fallen stones and arranged them on the table with the rest.

"Mostly. But I found some, too."

Saul nodded. "May I keep this one?" He pocketed Tippy's sardius.

Tippy shrieked. "No!"

"I'm sorry she's possessive. She only has one." But even as Jules offered Tippy others from his pouch she continued to wail, and Saul returned it to her.

Jules said, "Why are you interested in that one?"

"No particular reason except that I needed a sardius to complete my collection. As you know, I already have quite a display of aquamarines."

25.
INCANTATIONS

UP ON THE bough of a giant cypress a pair of eyes that never blinked stalked them. The pursuer peered from between the leaves, his body a thick black smoke that obscured him from the most observant creatures. His master bestowed this cloak upon him so he could go about his business in Reign without detection.

He floated like the clouds with only a dark, dense fog trailing him; his voice, the whisperings of the wind.

Most Elfies had forgotten about Whisperer, but his evil marred their lives often enough. Even if they were unaware of it, or unwilling to acknowledge his presence.

That evening Whisperer fixed his gaze from tree to lofty tree and spoke incantations beneath his breath that were too foul to repeat. Each tree scarred by his utterance, quaked and quivered as if struck by lightning.

He then pursed his sunken, twisted lips beneath the dark smoke and launched his phrases, like arrows, at the darkening sky. The words shot out and pierced the clouds that hung low. The sky roared and growled in agony at his command.

More and more thunderous crashes sounded as lightning struck tree after tree. The ground vibrated and rattled as though giants were stomping everywhere. Several of the conifers blasted into flames as the bolts shot down upon the forest in greater and greater fury. The affected trees instantly burst into flames and burned black before toppling with deafening booms. The fire swiftly consumed entire trees.

Whisperer was furious.

26.
THE GOING GETS TOUGH

MANY STREAMS ORIGINATED from Brooke Beginning. Some of these rivulets were unlabelled in most of Reign's maps although ancient inhabitants marked them with curious names like Lightning Rapids, Mammoth Burn, The Drowning Run, and Serpentine Crick.

But the present watercourse Jules, Holden, and Saul came to was the main river, the one that plagued Jules's dreams, and supposedly had taken the life of his grandparents. Brooke Beginning. Now Jules and Holden had to cross it.

Saul said, "Few know of this bridge, so let's keep it that way."

Jules wondered if he should have left the girls behind with Ralston at Saul's hide-out. But taking them to Handover could spell trouble, maybe even death, if they didn't find Mosche, or if enemy Handoverans found them. Whether the dragonfly lanterns would protect them totally no one knew since Handoverans were not Scorpents.

"Brooke Beginning," Holden focused his gaze on Jules, "and most of these tributaries have dark and mysterious tales linked to them."

Holden pointed to the white, foamy water venting its furor against tumbled logs and jutting boulders as it bubbled and gurgled furiously.

"Must we discuss this *now*?"Jules said.

"It makes little difference," Holden said, "if we speak or not. The fact remains: the water of the Brooke is tainted."

"But don't all these watercourses feed the lakes that are the very sources for our water supplies? How could it possibly be *tainted*?" Jules tried to gauge how far the other embankment was.

Some parts of the Brooke spanned wide and the other side could not even be glimpsed, but this portion of the river seemed narrower than what Jules imagined.

Saul gripped Jules's arm, "Don't trust the Handoverans. They tell many lies. I wouldn't put it past them to be in cahoots with Gehzurolle. They'd certainly want us doomed. But still you'd need to ask around. Someone's bound to have heard of a couple of Elfies living or traveling in Handover. They're a rare breed, and tongues wag. Remember, the lives of the mothers and your beloved grandparents rest in your hands."

"And Miranda, too," Holden said.

Saul cast him a look. "Naturally."

"And if she doesn't want to return?"

"Tell her I have news of her mother. That would motivate her to return. Now go. The clouds are moving rapidly. You need to hurry."

And just like that Saul scurried into the undergrowth and disappeared. Only Jules and Holden remained on the bank eyeing the toppled trunk that spanned the narrowest but, probably, deepest part of Brooke Beginning.

Holden said, "Maybe we should have agreed to have those Hanfies with us. At least they know the terrain."

"But you were so adamant they can't be trusted." Jules tugged at a branch and edged himself up slowly. He planted his feet on the log, but then slipped back down. "We need to secure the ropes here to help us get up."

They tied knots on the rope and used these as footholds to get up. Once on top they noticed branches ran at intervals along the span of the burnt trunk.

Jules said, "We'll study Saul's map once we get to the other side."

"*If* we get to the other side. How does Saul imagine we can get across those protrusions?"

Jules peered at the long stretch they must cross and consoled himself that the redwood at least had a thick trunk and the path across ran broad. Some sections held more branches and twigs poking out than others. Unless he wanted to suffer the fates of his grandparents, he'd have to tread extra careful, he reminded himself. Still, this must be safer than the boat Grandpa took. Saul must not have thought Grandma could climb such a structure.

"I don't like those clouds." Jules pointed upstream.

Jules and Holden wove in and out of the protrusions across the trunk, taking each step in deliberation, afraid to dislodge the fragile sections of bark from the damaged and precariously poised tree. They moved at a crawling pace. A careless moment could cause a slip and a fall into the swift waters, especially since they had to cling to twigs and tread close to the edge of one side in some sections because some protruding branches smelled singed.

The briskly rushing waters gushed against the underside of the trunk. Frosty splashes pierced through their cloaks like cold needles. They belabored protruding offshoots and kept glancing at the darkening sky when the first roll of thunder growled.

As Jules placed one foot before the other, Holden muttered strange words that sounded like mumbling. His utterances were barely audible. Jules made a mental note to ask for an explanation. Sounds like something his grandma would say. Was it like his grandpa's verse: Perfect love casts out fear?

Jules grabbed at burnt bark to steady himself as a strong wind rushed against him. The roar of the water below made his fear of heights small in comparison.

"What's that?" Holden asked.

Jules bent on to his knees and peered into the opening in the bark. With sandaled feet he punched at the frayed fragments of wood around the aperture and widened it so he could slide inside if needed. He placed his face near the hole and shone light into it.

"This trunk looks completely hollowed out. Lightning must have bored a fissure right through."

Holden said, "Should we get in there and see if the going's easier within the trunk?"

"Did you hear that?"

"You mean the water below?"

"Anyone can hear the water. I mean that echo inside the trunk—like someone talking?"

Holden shoved Jules aside and put his face inside the opening. "About two or three of them coming toward us. Should we ambush them?"

"Let them pass. The tree's several hundreds of feet long. They won't even know we're here. Unless they're Saul's Hanfies following us."

But when the voices passed right below them, Jules could hardly believe it. He dropped into the cavern of the trunk through the aperture, lantern in hand.

"Hey? Whatcha you doing?" Holden yelled from the top.

"Ralston!" Jules held his hand out and stopped his brother in his tracks.

"Jules!" Tippy said, shrieking.

"Hide from Jules," Tst Tst said.

"Why are you here?" Jules demanded.

So Bitha and Ralston told Jules their story. Jules had a good mind to make them walk all the way back to the opening they found at the uprooted side of the trunk and return to Saul.

"Please, no," Tst Tst said. "We saw a dark cloud, like smoke twirling outside the tree. That's why we rushed inside the hole in the root—to hide."

"You sure it wasn't a squirrel with a singed tail?" Holden said. "Cause I swear I saw a squirrel following us."

Bitha scowled at him. "What we saw had pursed lips blowing, blowing continuously. At the sky."

"You should have stayed with Saul." Jules said. "Some porcupine could have spiked you. You know how dangerous it is in Handover?"

"Saul said beware of mines," Holden said.

Jules touched Ralston's shoulder. "Where'd you get that lantern?"

"Miranda must have left it before she took off." Ralston said. "It's not like we're stealing. It's ours."

"I was hoping she took our lantern to Handover," Jules said. "She's an easy target without it. She's still a Keeper heir."

"Look!" Ralston pointed to the aperture Jules dropped in from. "It's raining."

Jules scratched his forehead. "We're already half-way across. We'll figure out what to do with you four when we get to the Handover side. I'm not saying you four come along further than that, or anything. It's too dangerous with Scorpents and Handoverans running around, and we can't even guess what sorts of wild animals await us." He shrugged. "Maybe we can hide you somewhere."

The trunk passage filled their nostrils with the odors of incinerated wood, which seemed unbearable at first, but staying inside was a drier choice even though puddles started to form where the ceiling leaked with the rain.

Later, Bitha tugged at Jules's cloak. "Isn't it strange Saul never advised Grandpa to get to Handover using this bridge?"

"Maybe the bridge just happened with the recent storms. Or maybe he thought it was too hard for them with branches sticking out."

"It's gotten pitch dark in here. We'd better stick closer together." Bitha groped the wall of the trunk with her fingertips, blind to the objects before them. "Rals, I need the lantern."

Ralston turned the lantern on and handed it to Bitha's free hand.

Outside the rain pummeled the tree trunk with conviction. The Elfies recognized its pattering even as they trudged on. But something else bugged Jules.

"Rals, do you hear that tapping noise?"

"I was hoping it was my imagination." Ralston's blue eyes grew wider as he searched Jules's face.

"I don't like how the trunk is wobbling."

"Let's get out soon," Holden said.

"If," Tst Tst said, one hand clutching Tippy's small one, "we hadn't lost our powers the King bestowed upon us—"

"We wouldn't be so annoyingly small!" Jules said, regretfully. At least this tunnel made going faster. He remained quiet the rest of the journey.

"Hey, daydreaming?" Holden said.

"With you around, Holden, it'll have to be a nightmare. What was that you were muttering up there?"

"Muttering?" Holden avoided Jules's gaze.

Suddenly, the trunk gave a violent roll and they lost their footing and fell.

"See that opening ahead." Jules said. "Let's get out and see what's up."

The rain seemed to have petered out, and they could see the Handover side clearly from where they stood. The tree's apex rested on two boulders. Maybe another half hour and they'd reach the rocky beach.

"What if we get separated?" Bitha said.

Tst Tst tugged at Jules's cloak. "Let's have a code. Like 'XYZ.'"

Jules scowled at her. "XYZ? What kind of code is that?"

"Something simple. So if you hear XYZ you know it's true."

Jules sniggered. "I don't plan for us to get separated, so stop overworking your gray cells."

They were parting stubborn sprigs, moving fast as they could hope, when a "whoosh-whoosh" cut their concentration. Initially the noise was imperceptible, but in two seconds Jules knew what it meant. As the noise intensified, it brought with it bursts of wind that roared in giant spurts.

"Hurry, Ralston, Bitha," Jules shouted to those behind him, his blonde hair caught in the gale swept to one side. Mustn't lose my footing, he reminded himself repeatedly, one hand grasping Tippy's arm.

Ralston was dodging the branches that whipped back and forth like the head of a mad cobra. Holden and Tst Tst, whom Holden was supposed to care for, were nowhere in sight. Jules hoped they hadn't slipped into the turbulent Brooke. Were they separated as Tst Tst had feared?

27.
SEPARATED

AS THE GALE gathered speed and force, the trunk shivered and trembled even more. Leaves and smaller branches thrust about, assaulting and slamming against the travelers. Jules wondered if the tall tree would soon dislodge and topple into the swelling Brooke. But they were close to the end of their crossing.

The whirr and whistle of the storm terrorized them as much as the wobbling of the bridge. Jules could hardly walk a step without tottering now. He focused on simply staying up and on the wobbly structure. Sprigs and offshoots tossed and jerked from side to side and battered him relentlessly. It was a feat to just hang on.

Then they heard it.

Louder than the fury of the wind, another sound was rushing their way. Jules felt it first. "Another storm's coming—from downstream."

The bridge vibrated even more. The southern tempest gushing in hit the northern wind smack where the toppled trunk lay. It created a pocket of stillness for a few minutes. The air around them quieted down unexpectedly.

"There's a lull," Jules said. "Hurry!"

Please! Where were Ralston and Bitha? Holden ran past him and leapt to the ground like a flying squirrel with Tst Tst trailing behind him. Jules literally threw Tippy in the air toward the rocky beach and hoped she wouldn't hit her head. He looked behind, but Bitha and Ralston were gone.

I have to go back.

His eye caught Holden on the ground scrambling to free Tippy from a branch she'd landed on. Tst Tst crawled on all fours up the sandy embankment.

The tree joggled and jolted violently, as though the two winds had settled their duel, and the tree became their sacrifice. The redwood quivered, jerked, and slid backwards into the roiling Brooke with a loud splash.

Jules stared in horror and he slipped on the trunk as it dislodged from the tangle of twigs and boulders on both banks. Free from spanning the Brooke's width, the tree was borne by the current. Jules clung to the end of the tree pointing down river, even as it dipped into the roiling waters. He swallowed gallons of river water and sputtered when the tip he clung to rose above the surge. *How long can I hang on to this?*

****

On the Handover bank, Holden, his mouth in an "O," stared at the trunk as it plunged downriver. Jules, Ralston and Bitha seemed to have disappeared, perhaps swallowed by the river.

How are we going to get back?" Holden whispered as he stared across to the Reign side.

And Tst Tst and Tippy cried, "We want Jules!"

28.
LOGS

THE REDWOOD TRUNK, battered by the gushing current, wobbled and Jules balanced himself by grabbing to this and that as he made his way to the opening they came out from. He hoped Ralston and Bitha had fallen in there. But what if water had seeped in and filled the hollow trunk? Then eventually the trunk would sink lower.

Water sloshed up to his ankle when he dropped in. He squinted into the dim tunnel. He'd passed his lantern to Holden, and now he regretted it.

"Rals! Bitha! You in there?"

He used the wall of the trunk to steady himself and took a few steps into the darkness. Sloshing sounds grew behind him.

"Jules!" Ralston panted as he tapped Jules on the shoulder. The glow from the lantern revealed worry lines on Ralston's forehead.

"Where's Bitha?"

"I'm here." Bitha poked her head over Ralston's shoulder.

Jules sighed. "The trunk's sinking."

He looked at his knees, already covered with river water.

They climbed back up and tottered on the swift moving log as it plunged and heaved up and down like a see-saw downriver.

"Pass me the lantern," Jules said.

Bitha shoved the lantern at him. "What are we going to do?"

"I was watching those three logs ahead of us." Jules pointed to rows of woodsy trunks sliding parallel to one another. Their own trunk had reached a gentler and wider part of Brooke Beginning and at least the see-saw movement had slowed down.

"Those logs don't seem to be affected by the current," Ralston said. "And they're really close to the water surface."

"They're floating toward the bank. If we get close enough we can hop down onto one."

Bitha squinted. "But why's the current not bearing them downriver like us?"

"Maybe they're caught in some cross current. We must hurry. We're almost close enough. At the count of three, we jump onto that bump on that first log."

Jules took something out of his cloak—the long ribbon that had secured Fiesty. He tied one end around his waist, the other around Bitha and told Ralston to hold onto the middle.

"It wouldn't do to separate again," he explained.

He edged down, clinging onto a branch trailing the water and cried, "Altogether, jump!" He and Ralston hit the bumpy surface of the log next to them, but Bitha missed and clung on to a protruding bumpy edge, legs trailing the water, until the boys heaved her up.

"It's a good thing you tied me," she told Jules. "But these logs don't even have a single twig jutting out of them."

"At the pace we're floating we'll soon reach the beach, so be ready to jump off." Jules began untying the ribbon from himself and Bitha.

"If the log turns downstream, we're goners."

Ralston tugged at Jules's cloak. "I know why—why there aren't any branches poking out."

"Rals, concentrate, will you? Handoverans are infamous for their mines, so let's be extra careful when we jump off, and the log may just turn and head downstream, too."

"But we're not on a log?"

"What?"

One end of the log raised itself out of the water and splashed against the surface of the river with a loud Whap! Whap!

"Hold tight!" Jules reached for Bitha just before she toppled as the log swayed from side to side. "We're so light it doesn't know we're on it."

The alligator they were on continued its course toward the sandy embankment where alligators lay sunning. When they reached shore, its companion lunged toward the reptile they were on and nipped their ride's snout. Jules and his sibling stayed paralyzed above the beast.

"It's not safe to get down," he said as he scoured the area. About ten alligators lay around in a daze. "We need to distract them."

"Don't look at me." Ralston spun his head about frantically.

"I have an idea. The good news is there're obviously no mines here with those alligators around. Guess Handoverans are scared of alligators, too."

Ralston said, "Saul mentioned booby traps, too."

"Stop it. I can't think."

It didn't take long for Jules to come up with his plan. He slid his pouch from his cloak and chose the precious stones with the most jagged edges. One after another he hurled the gems at them, aiming for their eyes. The afflicted alligators snapped at each other, serrated teeth lining their gaping jaws. They trashed their tails left and right, trying to find the perpetrator. Jules helped Bitha and Ralston slip down, and they stumbled to a nearby grove of brambles.

Bitha's panting became more pronounced. "Shouldn't we be more careful about those boobytraps?"

Jules said, "Reptiles have been sighted in these Rivers, but I never believed the reports."

"Maybe these are crocodiles?" Ralston said.

Jules shook his head. "Alligator heads are shorter and wider like shovels. A crocodile has a narrower jaw and a more V-shaped skull that tapers at the snout. These are alligators."

"I'm worried about the others," Bitha said. "Do you think they're okay?"

"We should find them," Jules said. "According to Saul's map, we're way off course."

"Let's not lose that map," Bitha said.

Ralston peered at the map in Jules's grasp. "I never knew Handover had alligators. I thought they had snakes?"

Jules looked at his brother. "Those, too."

29.
TENNESSON

HOLDEN ORDERED TIPPY and Tst Tst to hurry but they continued inching, and they kept falling behind.

"Just swing your leg forward like this," Holden said. He showed them how to take the strides.

"I want Jules," Tippy said.

"We can't wait on the beach," Holden said. "There's not enough cover."

Tst Tst reached for Tippy's arm and grasped it. "But we have the dragonfly lanterns. If we leave, how would Jules find us?"

"The lanterns may not shield us from bad Handoverans, or their soldiers. Come on."

Holden stopped suddenly, and Tst Tst tripped and bumped into him.

"You said to hurry," she said.

"Shh!" Holden pointed to what lay ahead of them.

From behind a log in the forest, they spied a clearing with a strange tent. It could pass as a house except it was made of canvas. The shuttered windows made it difficult to see if any occupants remained within. A fire pit with a used spit at the front of the structure confirmed that the house at least had one resident.

"From the size of the spit, I'd say not too may live here," Holden said, in his lowest tones. "Could still be an enemy position."

"How long do we wait here?" Tst Tst whispered. "Tippy has to go to the bathroom."

Tippy moved from one foot to the next.

"Why now?" Holden said.

But they didn't have to wait long.

"And what exactly are you hoping to see?" a hoarse voice croaked from behind them.

Holden gasped. Tippy and Tst Tst shrieked and squeezed their eyes shut.

"Didn't mean to spook you. But you are—ahem—on my grounds? Elfies, I presume? The usual greeting runs something like, 'Friend or foe?'"

The interrogator was a Handover Elf: a Handoveran. High forehead. Big nose. But he wasn't as stocky as Handoverans were supposed to be. Still, he was a whole head taller than Holden! His thick accent, too, wasn't what they were accustomed to.

"Our sincerest apologies," Tst Tst said. "We're friends, I hope."

"Trespassing is a crime with heavy penalties in Handover, especially for Elfies."

"We didn't mean to trespass," Holden said. "It's just that we're lost."

"So where was your destination?"

Holden locked eyes with Tst Tst.

"Right now, it's the bathroom," Tst Tst said.

"Makes two of us." The Handoveran smiled. He perked up and offered Holden his hand. "Tennesson is the name and tent making is my game!"

Holden hesitated, then shook his large, callused hand.

"Shall we hurry then?" He turned to Tst Tst and gestured at his tent.

Holden stepped forward, as if to stop Tst Tst but she'd already pulled Tippy toward the tent. Too late!

30.
CAMOUFLAGE

THE TENT CONSISTED of several compartments, like rooms in an apartment. Layouts, diagrams, and schematics lay scattered on the many tables in the relatively simple and dim interior that smelled of freshly baked cakes.

"Care to join me?" Tennesson said when they congregated in the kitchen.

"You have a strange home," Tippy said.

"Believe it or not," he announced flatly, "I designed it myself. Friends, and foes, come to me to have their tents designed, too. Although I must say I don't get too many Elfies frequenting these parts requesting my services. At least not since the edict. Come, I'll show you some of my most coveted prototypes."

They wanted to leave but didn't want to appear rude. So they followed. Down a dim corridor, in another cubicle, he showed them albums with pictures of tents, tabernacles, and canopies of various sizes.

Nothing was consistent with the Elfies' concept of a home. In one rendition a canvas home made especially for deception required the owner to dig a trench and use the covering to conceal the opening. Unsuspecting individuals treading above would never have guessed someone's hideout lay below. The finely woven tapestry covering the trench matched the textures and hues of the forest floor so precisely.

"Most of these homes look like they're for camouflage," Tst Tst said.

"In Handover you never know who the enemy is so it's best to stay hidden. That's what I tell my clients."

Another model, Holden's favorite, simulated a canopy of greenery, like the foliage of the forest. The user was to arrange the camouflaged invention overhead, securing the tapestry onto several boughs with strong twine. With a few of these woven rugs overlapping on top, the area under the tents remained dry even during the worst downpour.

Another pattern showed how a hollowed out upright tree trunk with an overhang affixed on top transformed the recess into a concealed hideout, indistinguishable except by the keenest eyes.

"My brother would love to see your drawings," Tst Tst said.

"And where might he be? This brother?"

"We don't know. Downriver, maybe."

"You're not the only foolish Elfie who'd tried to cross the River during a storm."

Holden leaned forward and stopped munching his cookie. "What do you mean?"

"There've been wrecks—Elfie boats, knickknacks, all come floating to our side of the beach. Makes good profit for some who sell to collectors. I come across all sorts of things living near the River."

"Those other wrecks had any survivors?"

Even Tippy and Tst Tst stopped munching.

"Hard to say. Never found anyone myself, but it's possible. Although with all the Scorpents around they'd better have some coverage. Too many Handoverans would love to sell an Elfie off for a few goodies."

Tst Tst heaved a deep sob.

"What's with her?"

Holden told Tennesson about Leroy and Bonnie's trip and that they might have lost their lives. "But we have hope. Some say they might have gone to visit a friend up north."

"Who's that? That friend?" Tennesson leaned in.

"Jules has the details, which is why we need to find *him*—among other reasons."

Tst Tst said, "Holden can't handle us."

"You children don't seem to realize how dangerous it is for you here, do you?"

"We can keep away from the Scorpents. We have this." Tst Tst brought up the lantern.

Tennesson raised one eyebrow. "And how about the snakes? There are even alligators in some parts of the River. And Elfie-eating insects?"

Holden scratched his chin and looked at the girls. "Maybe I can leave the girls with you and look for them myself."

"No need to be in a hurry," Tennesson said. "Give me news of the old country. There was a time I got news of it often."

"We need to get to Jules," Holden said.

"I don't live too far from this bridge you came on. If this Jules has any brains he'll make his way here—provided he hasn't—"

"Hasn't?"

"I have contacts. Maybe they have news about your friends' escapade." Tennesson stalked over to a closet where streams of ropes hung in different colors, widths and thicknesses. His fingers ran over the first few and settled on a thick, velvet, red cord. He pulled it.

Tst Tst and Tippy wandered about the room looking at old portraits faded with time.

"Who's this?" Tst Tst pointed to a lady dressed in white with a veil over her face. The lady in the picture had wide-set eyes so deep blue they pierced through the veil. Her light honey- colored hair was pulled back in a pony tail, with loose wisps cascading and fringing her face in soft tendrils.

"My wife, Luella. But she's gone." Tennesson stepped in front of the hanging portrait.

"I'm sorry," Holden said.

"Happened years back."

"What happened?"

"Gehzurolle rounded up Elfies living here—the edict I mentioned. He killed them all."

Holden and Tst Tst locked eyes. He was one of those who married an Elfie? Would that make him more trustworthy?

"In a few minutes," Tennesson said, "we'll see if anyone sighted any of your friends downstream. If we don't get a reply it could mean either good news or bad news."

"What's the good news?" Holden asked.

"They'd not been spotted by some eager for money types."

"And the bad news?" Tst Tst asked.

"They didn't make it."

31.
BOOK OF REMEMBRANCES

BEFORE HOLDEN COULD ask how they could avoid these Handoverans eager to sell Elfies for a bit of gain, a brassy clanging sounded in the room.

"Is that your doorbell?" Tst Tst said.

"My warning system—trespassers, like you were. They're not close by the sound of the bell. But, still, you'd better hide."

Tennesson glanced toward the front hallway, his forehead furrowed with worry lines.

"How can you tell someone's coming?" Holden asked as they rushed down the hallway with Tennesson.

"I've dug shallow trenches all over, and I covered them with my camouflaged rugs. Similar to the one that resembled the forest floor tapestry you saw in those sketches. I connected bells underneath the rugs. The different jingle for the different routes tells me which direction the visitors are approaching."

"So that's how you knew we were here?" Tst Tst said.

Tennesson nodded.

Another series of bells rang—this time tingling. "The visitors are arriving."

Tennesson whipped away a rug near the front entrance, and opened the trap door on the floor. The dug-out he pushed them into was small and cramped and smelled of stale onions.

Knock, knock, knock!

The raps sounded loud and jarring upon the doorpost. But that was all their straining ears heard from their hiding place.

Tst Tst groped about the wall like a blind person getting her bearings, and her hand came upon what seemed like a rope hanging down from the ceiling. She grabbed the rough hemp rope with both hands and tugged. Light spilled into the room. The lamp was a contraption whereby two liquids in separate jars, when mixed, one liquid spilling into the jar of the other when the rope was pulled, came alight.

"Shouldn't have done that," Holden whispered. "What if those visitors can see the light through the cracks?"

"There's a chest of drawers here." Tst Tst pulled Tippy toward her and brought her sister to the chest.

"Don't!" Holden said.

Too late. Tst Tst was already opening up the first drawer and peering in. And she gasped.

"What?" Holden strode over after a quick glance at the trap door they entered through.

"Book of Remembrances."

Bound volumes were stacked one atop the other in a neat manner in the drawer. Holden took one and flipped the pages quietly. A cross between an album and a diary, a Book of Remembrances also held scraps of letters, sketches, pressed flowers, and such articles like trinkets or tokens from a person's life. Numerous portraits of Tennesson and a lady Elfie—presumably his wife, Luella—filled the pages. Sometimes the pictures were of them in front of or inside the house, but the dwelling looked different from Tennesson's current home. Artwork lined one wall of the home in the pictures and neatly shelved books covered the other walls. It seemed that Tennesson had a different life when his wife was alive.

Tippy looked at the pictures closely, and pried one of them off. "Pretty."

When Holden took another book out and passed this to Tst Tst, a piece of paper slipped out and floated to the ground. It looked like an envelope. He quickly picked it up, but not before he saw the name on the top corner. "Saul Turpentine," it read.

He slid the envelope into his cloak and shut the drawers as the trap door creaked open.

32.
NOT ALONE

BITHA HUNG UPSIDE down swinging from side to side, narrowly missing the tree trunk. She'd stepped into a trap and the net had caught her up and had borne her, within seconds, to a high branch of the birch.

Below, Jules studied the height of the branch from which the net hung. The Handoveran booby trap looked rudimentary, but it still annoyed him. Why did it have to be so high up? "It's okay, don't struggle. Ralston's going to climb up and figure out the knots."

"Why me?" Ralston narrowed his eyes at Jules.

"You know I'm not the mechanical one."

Ralston sighed and set the dragonfly lantern next to Jules. Birch trees are not supposed to be that tall but this one towered over the rest of its relations nearby.

"Notice the spaces between the bark on the trunk? You can use them as footholds to climb. And don't shout when you're up there. Anyone could be listening in these parts."

Ralston glared at him.

"What are you going to do to get her out once you're up there?" Jules persisted.

"I'll figure something out—I'm the mechanical one, remember?" He stalked to the tree and grasped the woodsy bark. Like a lizard climbing a tree, slowly, he moved his hands and his feet up along the footholds on the trunk. Whoever set up the trap must have nicked the footholds for climbing. Ralston made his way up the trunk, higher and higher, never looking down. Jules thought it took him an eternity to get to the branch where the net was holding Bitha.

Two pairs of eyes, hidden between the golden and rusty fall leaves, watched Ralston as he edged his way toward Bitha in the net.

"It's too heavy," Ralston said. "I can't pull you up the branch."

"I have something in here, but I can't reach it. If I move the net tightens. Try and get to me or something and maybe you can get it."

"But the rope may not hold both our weight. We'll both fall."

Ralston stood on his tiptoes. "It's a fantastic view from here." He scanned the adjacent branches: a few were still full of green leaves but most of the other trees had turned to the burnt orange colors of fall, while still others had lost their greenery altogether. Something caught his eye. Strange. "There's a bridge of some sort up here."

"What?" Bitha shouted back.

"A web bridge."

"Are you going to help me?"

Ralston dipped his head lower, over the edge of the branch, toward the swinging net. "I think I can climb down the branch. Part way."

"Careful!"

"Not so loud. Jules said we must work quietly."

Head down, Ralston lowered himself along the curve of the branch toward the lead line that secured Bitha's net to the bough. He stopped when he got as far as he could go without toppling head first to the ground. With his free hand he examined the knot that secured the net to the branch.

If he could untie the knot he could free the net. Except that would mean Bitha would fall to her death. He tugged at the knot and, in the net, Bitha pendulummed.

"Stop! What are you doing?" she shouted.

Ralston stopped.

Bitha said, "I can reach it."

"What?"

"This!" Bitha brought out a familiar fabric bundling something within. "Jules passed it to me. It was in the pillowcase. Take it. Don't unwrap it, yet."

Ralston extended his arm and his fingertips touched the bundle. Something hard and sharp lay in it. "I can almost reach it."

Bitha strained her arm out even more.

"Got it." Ralston placed the bundle between his teeth and labored his way back up.

When he sat on the branch, he unraveled the wrap. The mirror shard Jules found in the mantel hiding place gleamed in his grasp. He read the message behind it—"ook within." What could that mean? But how could he cut the rope? Bitha could crash to her death. What did Jules expect him to do? He needed Jules up there. Maybe they could pull the lead rope up and haul Bitha up to the branch.

"I have to get Jules!" He shouted back down to Bitha. When he looked up he noticed a mist, like wisps of white vines that twined themselves between the branches and the leaves. It slithered toward him like a snake. When did the fog come in?

"Bitha!" But no answer came.

The mist felt denser now, like when he'd one day smashed into a cobweb and entangled himself in the soft, dense spider's snare. Perhaps the fog prevented Bitha from hearing him. He slipped the shard back into the wrap and bundled it hurriedly, slipping it into his cloak.

I hope I don't pierce myself with it. He reached out his arm trying to steady himself, and his fingers found a soft fuzz an arm's length away.

33.
VIPER

"RALSTON! BITHA!"

Jules had no choice but to shout. His breath labored as he thought of the climb to that awful height. A sort of heaviness fell over the forest and all around things seemed quieter. Less acute. As if the forest had fallen asleep.

He marched to the tree trunk and felt its scratchy surface. If he could just bring himself to get up there. It shouldn't be too hard. Especially since Ralston made it. Or had he?

All Jules could see were leaves, and the mist. He stared at the mist like ribbons twirling between branches and tree trunks. Was the mist there before? And what was that rotten smell, like soggy cucumbers, and that hissing sound?

Sss, like air seeping out of a balloon. Or a snake.

Ssss....

Jules swiveled around and came eyeball to eyeball with the yellow irises that thinned into slits. Unblinking, the elliptical cat-like glare wasn't the worse of it. The forked tongue flicked left to right nimbly. A pit between the nostrils and each eye on this beast's triangular head confirmed its identity: a viper.

When confronted with a venomous snake, the best form of defense would be, believe it or not, to run for your life. Jules knew that much. Yet, he couldn't move a muscle. He stood transformed into a pillar. The yellow irises entranced him.

His glazed eyes locked into the hypnotic draw of the serpent. He was unable to move. So this is how it'll end. Whose smart idea was it to come to Handover? And what had happened to Bitha and Ralston?

By now the mist had turned into a thick fog. Before Jules knew it, everything turned black, and he huddled into a ball.

34.
ABEL SEACREST, ESQUIRE

WHEN JULES CAME to, he looked around at the dim hole he was in. It smelled musty. Where was he? And Ralston? And Bitha? He tried to sit up and felt a cold pack on his forehead.

"Abel Seacrest, Esquire, at your service." The voice startled Jules.

Abel Seacrest? Could it be true that he was none other than *the* Abel Seacrest, the noted and renowned Fairy Elf legends spoke of?

Jules's mind swirled with things he'd heard. Uncountable stories abounded regarding Abel Seacrest. Aside from rumors that he was extremely old (which in itself was an achievement as far as he was concerned since no one lived past a hundred in Reign, what with the hazards of being so unacceptably small,) a famous lore linked the historical figure to the Ancient Books. Supposedly, Abel had learnt most of the Literature and could recite whole Passages from the Books off the bat. At least that was the rumor.

"Where am I?" Jules said.

"Not in a snake's pit, and you should be thankful for that."

That Abel Seacrest was believed to have the ability to fly. To fly? Jules craned his neck but the room was too dim. He couldn't see any wings sprouting from *this* Abel's back. Besides, he was undeniably hefty! And don't birds have hollow bones? Surely he'd need powerful wings to bear his weight.

"My sisters and brother. They're lost. I need to—"

"Everything in its own time," Abel said.

The tale of Abel implicated that he'd resorted to a forest life when the Kingdom of Reign became accursed. Some even blamed him for the losses their Kingdom suffered. But he couldn't be the old Abel Seacrest? That happened eons ago.

Jules clutched Abel's cloak as he walked by. "But did you see them—my brother and sisters? A boy and three Elfie girls?"

"Jules!" Bitha suddenly appeared at the open doorway. She carried a tray with brown bowls made of acorns and cups on saucers. "Abel said the candle will heal you. The snake bit you on the forehead."

Next to her, Ralston said, "Good thing he missed your eye!"

Jules felt the lump on his forehead, beneath the icepack, and felt nauseous.

Abel stepped toward him and held out a candle with three flames flickering on the tips of its wick. "Look at the flames, Jules."

Each of the three flames had a distinct color. One was blue, the middle blood red and, on the extreme right, the purest white, almost blinding. Intrigued and forgetting his queasiness, Jules leaned forward to study the strange flames and gasped.

"How'd you do that? How come I see my reflection in the red flame?" Jules asked, fascinated.

"What's important is how you feel now. Still ill? "

"I feel…fabulous."

"Precisely! Those who gaze into the flames will instantly feel 'fabulous'—as you put it."

"That's a valuable candle. It could cure sick people."

"If it was used properly."

"But how does it work, exactly?"

"It makes you, or rather your body, forget things. But enough of this. Promise not to breathe a word to anyone. I can't afford to share this." Abel tapped the candle with his finger and turned to face Ralston and Bitha with a grim look in his eyes.

All three nodded, but they continued to stare dazedly into the flickering flames as if something was drawing them to look.

"Are you the *genuine* Abel we study in history lessons?" Bitha said.

"It depends on what they teach in those *history* lessons these days," he said. "But what, pray tell, are you doing in *my* quarters?"

"First off, where are we in Handover, exactly?" Jules sat up and rummaged within his cloak.

Typical Elfie attire comprised of numerous pockets. Some boast as many as fifteen or twenty even thirty, pockets. These weren't the usual ones sewn in the breast of a jacket, or on the rear seats of pants. A secret pocket could be within another secret pocket. Pockets: in belts, in blankets, even in undergarments. But though Jules brought out pouches, and even items he'd forgotten he had and laid them side by side on the rough homespun bed sheet, he did not come across the map Saul had drawn.

"It's gone! The map's gone!"

35.
TO TRUST OR NOT TO TRUST

ABEL WALKED OVER and peered at Jules. "What are you looking for?"

Ralston and Bitha told him of their need to locate Holden, Tst Tst, and Tippy, but they never said anything more. And certainly not about the map.

"We need to get to a 'Mosche Falstaff,'" Jules said. Half of him regretted mentioning the name. Saul had said not to trust anyone in Handover.

"Ahh!" Abel rubbed his chin as if knowing some secret.

"You know him?"

"Of him."

"Look, if you can't help us, that's okay. We need to follow the curve of the river, and I'm sure we'll come across Holden and my little sisters. Holden's smart enough not to go gallivanting."

Jules swung his legs to the edge of the bed and stood up.

"Thank you for your hospitality. If you could point us the way to the Brooke?"

He walked to the doorway and noticed an opening where the sun shone through. The exit!

"Gather our things, Rals. And thanks." He gave Abel a small salute. It seemed appropriate somehow.

"Jules, wait!" Bitha said, hurrying toward him, as he stepped to the opening. She reached out and pulled him back in, just before he fell to his death. Abel's home was a hole high on a coniferous tree.

"Whoa!" Jules said, and he swayed.

Abel came over, and steadied him. "No need to zip about at lightning speed."

"How did I—we—get up here?" Jules looked from Ralston to Bitha to Abel.

Abel pointed to a branch out the entry opening where a bushy-tailed squirrel stood eating a nut of sorts. "That's Blaise, my pet. *And* your transport."

Jules stared at him wide eyed. "Is there *another* way down?" Could this Abel have flown up here?

"I am intimately acquainted with some of the local inhabitants. Care to meet one of my pals? One of them would be happy to assist."

"Was the snake your pal, too?"

Abel shuddered. "Your ignorance annoys me, boy. No Elfie befriends a snake, no matter how long they've lived in Handover."

"You don't understand, my mother's in danger!" Jules blurted out. "And now possibly my sisters, too. Not to mention my—my friends. We need to go."

Abel snatched the strange candle he'd placed on the table and brought it to Jules. The flames swirled before his eyes. Three colors twined into one. Jules wanted to turn his gaze away, but he couldn't. In a second, Jules spilled the story of their plight and their search for his grandparents. He went so far as to even tell Abel of his Keeper ancestry.

"So you see, if my mother didn't take her Book along, and she came here, she'd be dead meat. My Grandpa swore her in as Keeper before he left."

Abel grunted knowingly, the candle flickering still before Jules's face. Its light cast moving shadows all around them. "So your Grandpa knew."

"Knew what?"

Abel just nodded. "What spurred your Grandpa to leave?"

"It was all my fault." Jules trudged to a nearby chair made of twigs and fastened with twines of many colors. He slumped into it. Suddenly he felt tired and rested his head in his palms. "My grandpa argued with my mother one night. He didn't understand why she could have had five children when all Keepers only had one. I should never have spied on them."

"And your grandpa found out you spied?"

Jules shook his head. "I went to him and begged him to find out why. I thought maybe only one of us was a real Blaze, that the rest of us…were adopted. But which one? Me? After all, the Ancient Book never lies, right? It says a Keeper family is entitled to only one child—the heir to the Book."

Abel nodded again. "And you've read your Ancient Book?"

"Parts. Somewhat."

"Most of it?"

"Some. Okay, a bit."

Abel nodded, again. Jules felt intimidated by all his nodding.

"There was a time Keepers knew their Books," Abel said.

"But what good did that do us? We were still cursed. We still became small."

Centuries ago, before the curse, the Elfies of Reign stood tall and stately. But since the Keeper Falstaff lost the King's gift, and hence broke the oath that bound him and his fellow Elfies to the Majesty, the entire Elfie race was reduced to their puny size. For centuries Keepers have searched for the gift, but, for the most part, these efforts were futile since no one even remembered what the gift was. Their only consolation was that when the curse was activated Gehzurolle, his agents, the Scorpents and the Handoverans, were reduced, too. But still, the Elfies became the smallest of the lot. So much for being the King's favorite.

Abel held his arm. "But all need not remain lost. Destiny still lies in the hands of the Keepers. You want to be a Keeper, Jules?"

"I just want my family back, and for things the way they were before Gramps left."

"No grand scheme wafting through your head about how to restore us Fairy Elves to our former size?"

Jules stared at the ground. "There's something else."

Abel went to a chair and sat next to Jules at the rickety dining table as Jules explained.

"Grandpa went to Mosche. To find answers about our family. You know how the Books have to work together in synergy, and Gramps only had the one he inherited." Like a jigsaw puzzle each Book contained details and clues the others did not. To truly understand matters a Keeper would have to seek his fellow Keepers and together the five Books would unravel mysteries and explain the most worrisome of controversies.

"But why didn't your grandpa ask Saul? He's a Keeper? He'd have a Book?"

36.
PARTING WHISTLE

JULES COULDN'T STOP thinking about the Books and why his grandfather had sought Mosche when it would have made sense to simply inspect Saul's. He'd seen Saul bend over that Book. Together, Saul and Grandpa could have deciphered many codes the Books might have to solve this issue. Yet Grandpa opted to seek Mosche, who'd moved to Handover, instead.

Of course, to fully understand everything he'd need all five Books. Or at least four, since the fifth had disappeared centuries ago. What bigger secret was Grandpa hoping to uncover that required more than two Books? And to go to dangerous Handover?

"I am no Keeper, Jules Blaze. But I've had friends who were. Keepers are a complex breed, and Leroy must have had good reason to visit your Mosche Falstaff. "

When Abel finally gave them the use of his squirrel, Jules was relieved, yet sad to say good-bye to this odd, old man. Would he meet him again? Even Abel couldn't say.

"I've been in this old squirrel's nest, this drey, for so long. Maybe we'll bump into each other." But Abel didn't sound convincing.

Bitha tiptoed to hug Abel's broad shoulders. "You're *quite* acquainted with critters."

"It's a side effect of having lived in the woods for—ahem—some period, shall we say?" He brought out an intricate wooden whistle from his cloak. "And this helps, too."

"You made that?" Bitha peered at the whistle in his grasp.

It was carved out of hardwood with three holes on either end. An odd looking whistle!

"In my spare time." Abel handed it to her.

Bitha examined it closely and passed it to Ralston.

Ralston turned it this way and that in his hand. "Who gave you the design to follow?"

"Many designs exist, but this one calls on squirrels and small—by the world standard, of course—mammals of the land. Various designs for the various animals." He reached out and plucked the whistle out from Ralston's fingers. "Would you like one?"

Ralston glanced at Jules, who shook his head. "No. That's okay."

"So you've always lived in trees?" Bitha said.

"It's the best way to live—especially for befriending squirrels." He motioned for the squirrel to follow him, to a corner of the drey.

"Thanks again for helping, Blaise." Ralston reached into Blaise's soft fuzz and rubbed it hard. Blaise chirruped.

Abel said, "I have plenty of chums in the woods. If I see your Fiesty, I'd be sure to tell him to look for you. He might be able to hear one of my whistles. The sound reaches far."

Blaise pivoted on her hind legs away from Abel and Jules. Ralston and Bitha climbed on her back first.

"Peace go with you!" Abel said. He whistled, and Blaise upped and leaped from branch to branch, bearing the three higher and higher, to the apex of the tree.

Jules turned to Ralston. "Weren't we supposed to get *down* to tracc the River?"

37.
WEB BRIDGE

BLAISE RACED TO an overhang and, without warning, leapt across several boughs before bracing himself sure-footedly on a nearby offshoot.

Several acrobatics later, Blaise deposited them, to their alarm, on a commanding lone evergreen of the cypress family. A webbed landing where arachnids had woven a bridge connected one tree to its adjacent neighbor.

"That's the web-bridge I told you about." Ralston squeezed Jules's arm. "When I was trying to free Bitha."

"I think I'm going to be sick," Jules said. He turned to Blaise, but before he could wave good-bye to the squirrel who'd saved him from the snake, she leapt away. "So Abel travels on these web bridges?"

"Sometimes, but mostly he uses the animals," Bitha said. "I wish he'd come with us."

"I'm sure he has his reasons not to leave his comfortable *drey*," Jules said.

"There's no way we can identify the tree Abel's home is in." Bitha let out a long sigh as her eyes scanned the trees nearby.

Jules patted her arm. "I guess that's why he chose it for his home. It's hard for his enemies, too. I get the feeling Abel's not telling us all he knows."

Bitha nodded, face still glum.

"You'll feel better when we get to Tst Tst and Tippy," Jules said.

Through the leaves they saw the bits of blue that snaked north. Brooke Beginning.

"We'd best be going. I'm anxious about the others and Mom."

"And Grandpa," Ralston said.

"I wonder," Bitha said in a small voice, "if he made it to Mosche's with Grandma. And we haven't even heard from Dad for months. I feel so worried about him. What if something bad happened to him?"

38.
NO ACCIDENT

"I SEE YOU'VE made yourselves comfortable?" Tennesson raised his eyebrows at Holden and Tst Tst as they strode toward him at the bottom of the dim staircase. They managed to close the drawers just in time.

"So are your guests still here? Who were they?" Holden said, hands in pockets.

"They're not Scorpents if that's what concerns you. But they have bad news. Terrifying news, actually."

"What?" Tst Tst leaned closer toward Holden, holding Tippy's hand.

"I can't explain it, too. And we'd never heard of such a thing—except maybe decades ago, before my time. My grandpa may have told me something similar."

"Well, what is it?" Tst Tst sounded impatient.

Tennesson rubbed his chin. "Locusts. The guests were my informers—traders who roam the land buying and selling so they catch up with plenty of news. And even prophesies."

"Prophesies?"

"We have tellers in the city Heritage who can forewarn you with omens of the future." He shot Tst Tst an impatient glare. "About the locusts, sentries on guard on some of the highest treetops saw a swarm—maybe an acre or more—of a black cloud floating this way. They *think* it was locusts. So far the insects haven't settled anywhere, which could mean bad news for us."

"Why?" Tst Tst asked.

"Because it means they'd have to stop soon, and it could very well mean they'd pay their respects here where we're at and ravage our vegetation, leaving patches, if not the whole forest, barren."

Tst Tst and Tippy gasped. Even Holden's eyes popped wide open.

"Of course they may not stop here. They could be on their way to Reign."

Tst Tst drew in a loud breath.

"Nothing to worry about. We'll just stay indoors and keep our shutters and doors closed. You can help me stuff rags in the door gaps." Tennesson turned and went up the stairs.

Once back in the living room they hurriedly tore strips to stuff under doors and cracks in window flaps.

"Can they eat up your house?" Tst Tst said.

"The coating on the house would make them sick if they tried, and we'd really be in trouble if we're outside, especially if we were on one of those web bridges."

"What do you mean?"

"Web bridges? They're everywhere up on the branches. They were spun by the spiders and have been there for as long as I remember. Useful, especially useful, when we want to avoid death pits, mines, and traps. Most Handoverans don't know about their existence, and those of us who do like it that way."

"So that's how you get to town?"

"You mean to Heritage? I never go there. But I use the web bridges for other places. I was going to recommend you to get up there if you want to travel to places here in Handover, but after this, who knows if the locusts might destroy a lot of the bridges when they fly through."

Tst Tst wrung her hands. "I'm worried for Jules and Ralston and Bitha." She tugged at Holden's cloak as they busied themselves stuffing rags under a wide opening in a particular shutter.

"They'll know to hide." Holden said.

"But what if they're up on the bridge?"

"Jules will never get up there. He's scared of heights."

"Acrophobic," Tst Tst muttered.

"What?"

"Acrophobic—scared of heights. Mom said he got that way when a family friend dropped him when he was a kid—a baby, I think."

"Who did that?"

Tst Tst shrugged. "Grandpa said it was an accident. But Jules never recovered. I'm still worried for them. How'd they hide if the locusts suddenly appear?"

"Maybe it's providential he's afraid of heights." Holden stole a glance at Tennesson and whispered to Tst Tst, "Do you remember if we mentioned Saul to Tennesson?"

Tst Tst stopped her work and shook her head. "Why?"

"Nothing," Holden said. "We have to leave."

"But not till *after* the locusts."

"How do we know that's even true? What if he just wants to trap us?"

"Why'd you think that?"

Holden slipped the envelope out of his pocket and shoved it toward Tst Tst. She read the name on it: Saul Turpentine, at Lower East Riverbank, Kingdom of Reign.

"That's our Saul!" Tst Tst said, almost too loudly.

"What should we do?"

"Let's test him," she whispered back.

"Don't do anything drastic," Holden said.

"How are things going?" Tennesson's voice boomed.

Tst Tst swiveled around and slipped the envelope into her cloak pocket.

"Mr. Saul? I mean, Tennesson? Could Tippy take a short nap?" Holden asked.

Tennesson stepped toward him and looked taller. "What did you call me?"

39.
WRONG DECISIONS

"HAVE YOU FIGURED how we're going to get down from here?" Jules looked down the flimsy railing of silky threads that he'd clutched several times as the bridge swayed when they walked a bit too fast.

Ralston scratched his forehead. "Same way I got up, I guess."

None of them had remembered to ask Abel for a suitable way to get down.

"We don't even have Saul's map," Ralston said. "How will we find our way around Handover?"

"Abel's map's not too hot, but maybe once we get to that town Heritage we can find a better map," Jules said.

Bitha shielded her eyes from the gleaming sun. "What's that black mass floating this way? Sure doesn't look like a cloud. It's shimmering."

Ralston went to her, unslung the pillowcase from his shoulder and rummaged within it. "I know I brought that spyglass. You didn't lose it, right?"

Bitha glared at him.

"Here!" Ralston focused the spyglass over one eye. He gasped. "It is glittering."

Jules snatched the spyglass from him and studied the cloud. "I don't like the looks of it."

The last he'd seen things in the sky it'd meant several things: first strange flashes, then ravens, then lightning bearing clouds. And they all spelled trouble. "Better hurry," Jules said.

They trudged on the web bridges for at least three hours, choosing always the fork that led them closest to the Brooke. They figured they must be close to the beach they'd last seen Holden and the girls. Assuming this was the same river they'd almost drowned in. Once they even came across an intricate webbing attached to a rope which seemed to lead to the ground.

"That must be like another one of those booby traps that snagged Bitha," Ralston said, examining it closely.

"Try to unravel the webbing. It could come in handy. Maybe we could snag a Handoveran with one of their own traps." Jules scoffed.

The sun had reached its apex, and the air weighed heavy and humid. Even the lemony scent of the conifer didn't help revive them from their sluggish mood.

"It's not that difficult to climb down," Ralston said.

After another half hour of trudging Ralston tugged a fraying spider line on the flimsy railing.

Bitha said, "Do you mind not unraveling the bridge? Do you want us to—"

Jules gasped.

"What?" Ralston said.

Jules clapped him on his back. "Rals, you're a genius!"

"What?" Ralston said.

"Pass me that mirror shard." Jules went over to the pillowcase still slung on Bitha and rummaged through it.

"You carry it." Bitha handed the case to Ralston. "I'll take the lantern."

Shard in hand, Jules sawed a line from the railing with the sharp edge and unfurled the cut end from its main line. Bitha and Ralston stared at him as if he'd lost it.

"I'll start another one this side." He pointed to the railing on the opposite end. "Bitha, you unravel this as I've done. Got it?"

Bitha still looked confused, but she nodded.

Ralston followed Jules to the other side. "You're making something?"

Jules explained that the web thread, though fine and silky, was tough. Tough enough to hold their weight, he ventured. "If we can twine a few strands together and make a rope long enough we can secure it up here and tie the other end as a harness. Then we can sort of rappel down the tree trunk. If we lose a footing we won't crash to the ground."

"That's impressive," Ralston said.

"Do you," Bitha said in a small voice, "hear that?"

A droning was now added to the swishing of the leaves swaying in the wind. It was barely perceptible, but if Jules strained his ears he could hear the whirring buzz. He took the spyglass to his eye again. "Oh, no! Insects! Their wings. Just cut off the length you've unraveled and let's seek shelter—maybe in that bunch of thick leaves over yonder." He pointed ahead, to where the bough met the main trunk.

Ralston's eyes grew round. "We mustn't be in their way. They could devour us."

"Follow me," Jules said, but he didn't know if this was a good idea. Maybe their best bet was to use the length of spider twine and see how far down it got them. At their height, the insects would fly smack into them. If only they'd never been reduced to this helpless size. If only Falstaff had not lost that gift. If only.

When they reached the section abundant with leaves, they parted the greenery in search of a suitable hiding spot. A hole in the trunk, or an unusually huge knot in the branch they could snuggle into would help. But even after running here and there and poking about behind this and that clump of leaves, they found nothing. The droning had heightened by now and drowned out the swishing of the swaying canopy.

40.
LOCUSTS

WHERE TO HIDE? Jules scanned the canopy above. Suddenly, a large furry animal bounded from behind them and landed almost on top of Jules.

"Blaise!" Bitha said.

"Wait!" Jules stayed her with outstretched arm. "We can't be sure he's Blaise. He could be a wild squirrel."

"It's Blaise!" Ralston said. "I drew a picture of him while we waited for you to come around. I recognize his white markings under his chin." He rushed toward the squirrel and buried his hand in its fur, rubbing its chest, and the squirrel chirped. "See?" Ralston said.

A whizzing din shook the trees around them and the beating of millions of wings sent chills up their spines. Several trees away the locusts blanketed the sky and the entire forest dimmed considerably.

"I hope," Jules started to say, but then Blaise nudged Ralston, lifted him into the air and swerved his bushy tail, catching Ralston before he fell off the branch.

"Whoa!" Ralston said, from his perch on Blaise.

"C'mon!" Jules tugged at Bitha's arm and gave her a leg up onto Blaise. "I hope he knows where to go."

Before they even had a good hold of Blaise's fur, the squirrel upped and leaped from branch to branch, away from the throng of locusts which could not have been more than several trees behind them. With one lurch, Blaise lunged into a hollow of a trunk, dark and musty with the smell of stale nuts.

"Quick, plug up the opening with those acorns." Jules pointed at a stack of stale smelling acorns by the opening. With the lantern they could see that this opening was once a drey. Probably an abandoned one. Bitha and Ralston helped Jules stack up the acorns but Blaise dug at his neck with his front paw and a scroll dropped from his neck. Ralston picked it up but before he even looked up, Blaise squeezed out the half-covered opening and leapt out onto the branch directly outside. An onslaught of locusts dashed into him.

"Oh, no!" Ralston cried.

The squirrel yelped and made a pitiful cry. By now they had almost closed up the opening entirely.

"We have to pull him back in," Bitha said.

Between acorn slits they saw Blaise fighting off the locusts, as hundred dashed against the branches.

"Please, Jules!" she pleaded.

Jules reached his hand up as though he was going to take down an acorn, but hesitated. He bit down into his lower lip and pulled Bitha away.

"What are you doing? You can't…." She sobbed loudly.

But Jules and Ralston blocked the stacked acorns from falling with their backs. The clamor of the locusts' vibrating wings resounded in the trunk, and the Elfies stopped their ears as best they could with the heels of their palms. Jules thought he heard a faint scream coming from outside, and pressed down on his ears more.

The buzzing of wings outside droned louder. A locust feeler poked through a crack in the opening. Jules sliced it off with the shard.

"Blaise brought back Saul's map." Ralston handed Jules the scroll he'd picked up by Blaise's feet. "Do you think Blaise…?" Ralston gulped and wiped his eyes.

"Abel must have found the map and got Blaise to track us." Jules shoved the map back into his cloak. "I wish he hadn't done that." He looked up and saw Bitha's accusing eyes. "I'm sorry, Bitha."

She avoided his gaze. "Aren't you going to look at the map?" She said between sobs.

"Later. I feel so bad Blaise had to suffer on account of us."

"You think he survived?" Bitha asked in a small voice.

Jules kept away the horrible visions of Blaise being attacked by the locusts. Suffering.

It was so dark outside they couldn't even make out Blaise's outline, or even determine if he was still there. But the whirring had ebbed, and the tree had stopped vibrating.

"Should we go out?" Ralston said, peeking between slits in the acorn stack.

"I can't see Blaise." Jules removed a few of the acorns and poked his head and shoulders slowly out of their hiding.

The plague of locusts that had covered the land like a massive blanket had moved on. Jules couldn't guess where they planned to land. He hoped it wasn't Reign. Locusts were infamous for obliterating whole plains and fields where they landed. Their powerful jaws usually ate everything green in their paths. Thankfully, these were only rumors passed down through the years, and no Elfie could vouch the insects ever terrorized Reign.

"Do you see Blaise?" Bitha sounded hopeful.

"Just shreds of leaves. I don't know if it's safe to even go out yet."

Jules plugged the hole back with the acorns, and scanned the drey. Lantern in hand, he walked to each corner of the den. "I can see why Abel would want to stay in something like this. Feels snug. Maybe we should go back to him and see if Blaise is fine."

"We don't even know which tree Abel's in," Bitha said, wiping her eyes.

"You're right. We have to go find Tst Tst and the others. I hope Tippy's listening to Holden." He worried that the locusts might hurt them. Jules snatched up the pillowcase and handed it to Ralston after taking out the Handoveran trap webbing. He found the spider twine in his pocket. He unwound it carefully. "It's time to test this." He tugged at the twine with both hands as hard as he could.

41.
HARNESS

ONCE THEY'D CLEARED the acorns out of the opening, they stepped out onto the branch. The leaves were still intact. With ties they brought along, they secured the webbing to a twine and made a harness. Ralston volunteered to rappel down first. He peered over the web railing.

"What happens if we don't find them? Tst Tst and the rest. "

Jules shrugged. "We can't even get back to Reign without that log bridge. And I don't know what'll happen. We're supposed to find Mom, and Mrs. L and Grandpa and Grandma. And even Miranda. But instead we're losing people."

Bitha sobbed. "I hope Mom brought her Book."

Ralston felt the harness secured to his waist, then tugged at the twine and edged over the branch. "What should I do if I see a snake?"

"Run," Jules said, and let the twine go a bit at a time.

Jules had instructed that, once on the forest floor, Ralston would have to find twenty large stones and fit these into the webbing until it looked like a giant net filled with rocks. Ralston would use this as his anchor for the rappel system Jules and Bitha would come down on. He'd made a rope and pulley system before in their backyard. But this one would have to be strong enough to bear Jules's and Bitha's weight together. The brothers had worked out that twenty stones would suffice to counterbalance Bitha's and Jules's combined weight. If not, Jules and Bitha ran the risk of rappelling too fast, and crashing to their death.

Jules wondered what was taking Ralston so long but he learned not to shout.

Finally, Jules felt someone tug the line from below—the signal for Jules to start his way down using the upper end of the twine. Jules tied the mid-section of the rope twine around both his and Bitha's waists and slung the free end down toward Ralston who would have to help add weight to their side in case the stones were too heavy.

They eased themselves round the side of the branch opposite the line bearing the stones.

"Ready, Bitha?"

Bitha nodded.

He squeezed her hand. "Don't worry. If we fall, we fall together."

42.
BOXED

JULES COULDN'T BELIEVE it when Bitha and he finally landed safely on the ground. Ralston could be relied on for some things. Even though it was late, he, Ralston, and Bitha continued trudging across grown brambles and tumbled logs. The rush of the River guided them toward the water. Despite several cuts and bruises, they made good time. Even their rappel down the tree went without incident.

"Look out for suspicious logs." Jules grinned at Bitha. He bared and snapped his teeth as he pretended to be an angry alligator.

She rolled her eyes at him. "How can you joke at a time like this?"

"If I don't, I'd go insane."

Ralston said, "Hope the locusts didn't get Tst Tst and the others."

"By the dense greenery on these conifers it looks like the locusts had a different destination. But where? I don't have a good feeling about it," Jules said.

Locusts never threatened Reign before but then neither had Scorpents, or those strange robberies. Odd things happen when Keepers invite Scorpents to Reign.

Ralston nodded. "Did you find out about the flash that night?"

"No. Nothing makes sense. We have to find a way to look for Mosche Falstaff. I get the feeling he'll have some answers. At least his Book should help, provided he will help, of course."

"Shh!" Bitha said. "What's that?"

Below the growing *whoosh whoosh* of the River tiny tinkling sounded, faint but still audible. An owl flapped overhead and Ralston stepped back and stumbled on Bitha's foot.

"Sorry. Whoa!"

"Rals!" Jules said, "Where are you?" Even with the dragonfly lantern, the dim lighting made it hard to see.

Ralston had disappeared.

"Help!" this time it was Bitha. When she disappeared, the forest plunged into darkness because she took her lantern with her.

"Bitha? Where are you?" Jules let his eyes adjust but stumbled forward. "Help!" It sounded muffled.

"Rals?" Jules was afraid to take another step forward. It was late and the forest had suddenly blackened when Bitha disappeared with the lantern.

"Here, here." Ralston sounded winded.

"Here? Where is here?" Jules could barely contain his frustration.

"Below," Bitha said. "If we can shine to the top we can see how to get out. Be caref—"

Jules took a step forward and slipped. "Ouch!" The ground felt as if it had caved in under his weight.

"Whoa!" Something brushed his arm.

"It's me," Bitha was next to him. Her voice sounded hollow. "I think I broke the lantern."

Great! Where were they? Jules groped about. "You okay?"

Amidst the gushing and whooshing of the tumbling river water in the background a soft rustling arose, as if runners had slid on the grass. Then even the rush of water quieted. Jules groped about as if blind, and his palms hit something hard. But it wasn't packed earth as he'd imagined since it felt like he'd fallen into a hole. The texture, rough to his fingers, had the feel of the warp and weft of a weave, as if it was a thick blanket or a rug.

"Jules?"

It was Bitha. The dragonfly lantern turned on dimmer than before. But when Jules tilted his head up he saw only a woven sheet that had sealed them in. Even the trees and the sky had disappeared.

"We're in some sort of closed box." Jules took Bitha's lantern and shone the dim rays at the ceiling of their trap.

"Let's see what we have before our lantern goes off, again," Ralston said. The light flickered on and off.

They peered into the pillowcase sack, and Jules took the shard out. He read the message again : "—ook within." What could that mean?

"Something's happening!" Bitha said. "Why is the box moving?"

They held their breaths and waited.

"Jules? Ralston?" An unfamiliar voice whispered from above.

Jules cupped his hand over Ralston's mouth.

"It's okay," the voice continued. "Holden and the girls are at my place. I'm Tennesson, a friend, not a foe."

Bitha fell and sat on the lantern—crushing it, and now the box was pitch black.

Tennesson said, "Don't waste time. I'm risking my neck out here at night." Something was thrown into the box now and with its top slightly ajar, a Handover face peered in, his lantern lighting the box, which wasn't a box at all but a ditch with wall to wall carpet floor and tapestry rugs hung on four sides, with the top, also a rug, that slid to the side.

"Is this your trap?" Jules accused.

"*Not* a trap—my hide-out. One of many. Are we going or do you wish to discuss the uses of this contraption and wait for Gehzurolle's forces to catch us? Because I *will* be implicated in aiding and abetting the enemies of Handover. *And* the Master of our Land."

"How do we know you haven't trapped the others, as well?"

"Your sister—Tst Tst—warned me you'll put up resistance. She said to tell you the code—Something you all came up with. 'XYZ'. Satisfied?"

Jules hesitated. Saul had said to beware of all Handoverans. Deception ran in their veins. Yet who but Tst Tst would say something like that?

Tennesson said, quite fiercely, "If you'd rather I left you for the Master of Evil himself, be my guests. My spies tell me he's out roaming tonight." Tennesson made as if he was leaving.

"Wait!" Jules ran to the rope—which was what Tennesson had dropped earlier—and tugged at it. "Quick, Bitha!"

Once out of the carpeted hide-out, Tennesson kept hurrying them on and looking up at the branches. A cold wind had stolen into the night, and Bitha wrapped her cloak about her shoulders tightly and stumbled a few times. No pleasantries along the way, Tennesson advised. No time. And too much noise for the night.

But before they arrived at his tent home, the leaves above rustled, and Tennesson beckoned to hide under a rock. "Shh!" he motioned with forefinger to lips.

Shadows moved before them. The hair on Jules's neck rose, and he bit down into his lips even as he placed a step toward the figures. The crunch-crunch his feet made sounded abrasive. His mind clouded with images of Scorpents he'd heard of. Twisted faces, hardened with hate and eyes in pitted sockets like shallow graves.

What was Tennesson taking them to? Was the Handoveran aware the meeting ahead was going to happen? Was this a trap after all? Who can I trust?

43.
BETA

A DENSE ACACIA bush was before the rock, and Jules willed himself to step into the bush for a peek. He might find out something that could help him with their search—about his mother, or Mosche. Tennesson tugged at his sleeve but Jules continued to crawl toward the tiny opening in the dense bush, as voices became audible.

Within the bramble, he stared at a glimmer a stone's throw away. In front of a Noble fir, a creature stood erect. They could not perceive the speaker's face, but a luminous radiance emanated from his body. (This iridescent gleam enabled Jules to survey the meeting taking place in the inky forest.) The individual wore a black mantle. His long cloak flowed like liquid fabric. It absorbed any light from the stars above that dared to get near it, yet it didn't swallow the gleam that shone forth from the individual's body.

Jules slowly shifted his gaze to Ralston behind him and put his forefinger to his lips as Ralston sidled next to him. Ralston had his hand covering his mouth and Jules noticed his brother shiver.

The breeze changed course, rustled the leaves, and brought with it the conversation before them. The cloaked individual was addressing someone they couldn't yet see. The voice from the glowering figure sounded smooth like silk, with a tinge of melody. But it was the contents of the dialogue which wafted to the hidden boys that froze them.

"No one must know." The voice was smooth as honey, sweet to the point of nausea. Like the faint smell about them.

"Yesss, Masterrr," a croaky tone answered. "And I almost have the gift for you. You will be most pleased."

"—*sure*, Whisperer?" the smooth voice continued. "—red crystal—fell—King Star—where is it?"

"Beta will get it."

"I need proof the Keeper has fallen—"

"Quite S-Sire. The Hanfiesss charged with the job-b-b—the last we heard they accomplished asss we hoped. Everything's planned." Wind wove through the leaves, and the broken bits of twigs and dirt swirled before the acacia plant.

Jules held his breath. Was Beta going to steal for this Whisperer? Who was Beta? A red crystal that fell? And a Keeper who'd fallen? Dead? Bile crept up his throat, and he swallowed several times. Surely the Keeper couldn't mean his own Grandpa? Or his mother? What if it was Mosche? And the King Star was related to this?

The snippets of exchange continued in intermittent spurts. If only the wind didn't blow the words away.

"I am not particularly fond of your informant. That is your business. Progress with the next task. Are the soldiers back?"

"Yes, S-Sire. They took-k—"

"When will Beta complete the project?"

"That Book'sss—raiding party already waiting there. Made neccs ssary arrangements."

"I don't deal with Elfies—"

"But Beta is—no ordinary—"

"Really—where is my red—?"

"Beta has located the carrier—"

"—once you're done—get rid of B–," came the icy reply. But now another individual in a charcoal cloak swooped in. The shadow dived in without a sound. It landed but a few paces in front of the velvety voiced individual. Jules and Ralston jerked back.

"I apologize for my delay and interruption, my honorable Master," the intruder heaved out in a great huff. His voice contrasted with the croaky whisper. It sounded almost like the 'whoosh' of the wind. "But I have news of significant interest."

"Yes, Rage? We've been contemplating your quest, or rather its lack." The silky voice held not the slightest hint of anger, yet a foreboding tone exuded in his delivery.

Whisperer mocked: "*Finally* you're here? Late as us-suallll? How difficult—to capture—unsuspecting kii—?" Once again the wind shifted its direction. "Your contact deserves-ss—"

The boys couldn't see the individuals speaking with this prominent figure but they wanted to get away. The words "intention," "weather," "storm," "swarm," drifted to them. Was this the swarm of locusts? Or was it "swam?"

Jules couldn't identify this individual but *who* were they planning to capture? *"Kii—"as in Keepers? Or "Kii—" as in kids?* The questions swirled in his mind. And how to extricate themselves from this delicate situation? It was a mystery no twig snapped under their feet, or rustling of leaves exposed them so far.

He scoured his brain, wondering what to do. What if these conspirators discovered them? They couldn't even be sure the lantern still worked, or that Tennesson would not sell them off. And who was Beta? An Elfie Gehzurolle eventually wants to rid? Was B, Bitha? Or Beta? He cast a look behind him at his sister behind the rock, her cloak barely visible.

44.
LAND OF THE DEAD

OF ALL THE problems surrounding them, the fallen Keeper worried Jules most. Who was this? Five Keeper families supposedly survived the curse—his own through Grandpa Leroy, Saul Turpentine, and possibly Mosche Falstaff. Who were the other two?

The wind altered its course even more, and the sentences drifted away, sounding muted and unclear. Jules straightened himself so he could hear better. His uncomfortable stance left his back as stiff as a board. As he scrunched his shoulder blades together, his back cracked. He shuddered and stood still, not daring to breathe.

"The smell of the Elfies is overpowering here," the tall figure said.

"The ones-ss on the bridge should be dead," Whisperer said. "And my spies located the others. They are not far away." Whisperer stopped and whirled on the spot and moved closer to the acacia bush. "You only smell the dead, S-sire. From weeks back. The Handoverans performed an excellent job-bb. I have a lessss offensive meeting place…."

Again the wind blew away the rest of their words.

The company of three lifted their black cloaks above their heads and vanished.

Jules and Ralston turned, and their eyes locked.

Later as they continued trudging toward Tennesson's home, or so Jules hoped, Jules grasped Ralston's arm and asked in a hoarse, panting voice, "What do you think? Who is Beta?"

"Did you smell something there, too? That pungent smell—almost sweet?"

"If I have to put a word to it, I'd say it smelt of 'hate.'" Jules didn't know what he meant exactly, but the word "hate" popped into his mind. "I thought I smelled it before."

"At our home, when we first walked in," Ralston said.

They'd ask Tennesson what he thought of this meeting but strangely he'd only heard murmurs and had neither seen the figures, nor could he confirm their identity but he was afraid. Was he blind? The murmurings sounded like the rumblings of thunder, he'd said.

Should we believe him? Jules discussed with Ralston and Bitha as they lagged behind Tennesson.

Bitha said, "I hope Tennesson's house is safe for Tst Tst and the others." And she cast a furtive glance at Tennesson trudging ahead.

"That Whisperer seemed to think we, or some other Elfies, are not far from here," Jules said.

They found Holden and the girls safe, albeit upset. Tennesson had restrained them with rope and bound them to their chairs.

"Afraid they'd sneak off again," Tennesson added amiably as he untied them.

Jules determined it best they rested for the night and set off before dawn. Tennesson had never heard of Mosche, but when Jules mentioned the waterfall Mosche was rumored to have hidden himself through the ages he advised them to visit a merchant of antiques he'd dealt with.

"I can draw the map to get there, but it's too dangerous for you to go to Heritage now. My informants said Gehzurolle has left Euruliaf and was roaming the streets."

Jules thought of the cloaked figure. "We have to find Mosche, no matter what. My mother's and grandparents' lives depend on it."

Tennesson said quietly, "The dealer's name is Starkies, and he might have answers for you. But be careful. Like I said, I don't know where Starkies stands. He could be a friend." Tennesson lifted one eyebrow and added slowly, "Or a foe."

"It's a risk I'll have to take."

"If you have something he's interested in, he might trade that for information."

Jules thought of Tippy's sardius and wondered if this was the red crystal referred to. He'd checked his pouch and had not found it. He hoped Tippy still had it on her. But other matters pressed for his time. Who did Whisperer say was not far from there?

"Is this the fastest way?" Jules pointed to the route on the map.

"The fastest way is to cut through the cemetery—Land of the Dead." Tennesson said. "Are you sure you want to take that route?"

Holden and Ralston stared at Jules but he looked away.

"We don't have a choice," Jules said. "It'll be daytime." He comforted them and watched Tst Tst's and Tippy's faces.

Their eyes were wide discs.

Jules's heart sank thinking about what he'd have to do. "Could the girls stay with you, Tennesson? It's only till we find Mosche. Maybe you can hide them somewhere safe, and I'll pick them up on our return."

"Do you think Handover is a walk in the park, boy?" Tennesson threw up his hands. "I'm sorry, but the penalties are too extreme for me. I've already risked enough, you realize?"

Jules stared glumly at nothing in particular. If something happened to his sisters in the Land of the Dead what would he do? But what choice did he have? His mind strayed to the red crystal, and he wondered which Keeper died. He needed to check with Tippy to be sure she still kept the red stone but Tennesson afforded them no privacy.

"Rest now, for the walk would take you the entire day, and you don't want to stay outside when darkness covers Handover, even with your lanterns." Tennesson jerked his chin at the dragonfly lanterns set side by side on the dining table.

Jules hoped the lanterns still worked.

45.
HOLDEN'S SECRET

BEFORE THE SUN awoke the morning glories in the land, Jules and his company plodded toward Heritage dressed in Handover merchant attire, courtesy of Tennesson.

They passed Woodsbury, the last subdivision before the cemetery that bordered the copse before Heritage, the capital of Handover. Everyone looked uneasy. Shadows loomed large and ominous in this part, and every now and then wisps of thin strands seemed to touch their arms and faces.

"It's just forgotten webs. Nobody visits these parts," Jules said to them.

Not a sound could be heard, as if even the woodland animals avoided the burial area. A broken-down signboard with faded words read, "Let the Dead bury the Dead."

Jules pointed at the signboard. "I heard of that saying before."

"Me too!" Holden said.

"Wait up," Jules said. "Who told you?"

But Holden sped up, swinging the lantern he was carrying.

"How'd you know about that saying—bury the dead? That's not common knowledge."

"Don't know." Holden shrugged and hurried ahead.

"Why are you avoiding me? Only Keepers heard of the saying?"

"Is that a question?"

"Why so secretive?"

"Because I don't know who we can trust anymore."

"What'd you mean?"

"You said that dark figure mentioned Beta is helping this Whisperer?"

"So?"

Holden continued trudging, steps so fast he stumbled over the overgrown roots and twigs. He mumbled something under his breath.

"What?" Jules hollered at him, and immediately regretted his volume. What if there were Scorpents nearby?

"I said, 'I know who Beta is.'"

Ralston and the girls quickened their steps toward Holden.

"Explain." Jules grabbed Holden's arm.

"I have secrets, too."

Jules narrowed his eyes at Holden. Was Holden Beta? When they were little they'd been close friends, but as Holden became more reserved they'd drifted apart, and Jules always felt Holden kept to himself. Then when they turned fifteen and both showed much interest for Miranda, their friendship dipped below the freezing point. Especially since Miranda preferred visiting Holden to Jules.

"Is it safe to spill secrets here?" Holden asked.

Jules shrugged. "It's your choice."

"Let's keep walking." Holden looked about the branches. "I'm sorry we're not friends. Ever since I turned twelve my mom told me something, and it became hard for me to talk to you lest I accidentally broke my promise to my mom."

"And you want to break the promise now?"

"I don't even know if my mom is alive. Or my dad."

"We're in the same boat there." Jules looked to the ground.

Holden's shoulders drooped. "But you have your siblings, and I have no one. Except maybe Miranda. She knows my secret, you know."

"I'm not surprised. She likes you."

"I liked her, too. Until ..."

"Until?" Tst Tst chimed in.

Holden drew a deep breath. "She told them about my mother."

"Told who what?" Tst Tst said.

Holden shook his head at her and smirked. "Told whoever took my mother that she's a Keeper."

"Keeper?" Jules reached out and stopped Holden from walking. "Your mother's a Keeper?"

Holden nodded.

"So you're a Keeper family, too. I can't believe there're three Keepers in the same region of Reign."

"A long time ago all the Keepers came from one family. But they separated. So my great grandfather followed the directions in our Book and built the house I live in now. The Book must have wanted us Keeper families to live close together."

"Are there directions in your Book?"

"Our Ancient Book specializes in Maps and Symbols. It's always helped us find Paths, but sometimes the codes and symbols are not explained. I think Beta stole our Book to find the way around Handover. Which means my mother is wandering around without her Book, or the enemy's already got rid of her."

"So who's Beta?" Jules felt sad. Fear of Gehzurolle had kept each Keeper family to themselves. Maybe if they'd known Jessie Lacework was a Keeper Grandpa could have gone to her for help.

"Miranda's Beta," Holden said flatly. "I just put it together when you mentioned the name Beta. She always joked that I was Alpha and she was Beta. She must have never guessed I'd get to hear about it. It doesn't matter now, anyway. She sold my mother. For what?" He threw his hands in the air.

"Remember, Saul said Miranda's looking for her mother?" Jules said. "She's desperate. Anything to get her mother back. I think she sold my mom, too."

Ralston tugged at his arm. "Why'd you think that?"

"It's strange she knew we were going to have potato soup for supper," Jules said. "As if she'd already been to our place. Then that pot with the word Lacework written on the bottom?"

"What about it?" Ralston said.

"That was not there before we left. Mom would never have cooked *another* pot if she'd already had one from Mrs. L. Miranda'd brought it to our place—maybe as an excuse to see Mom. That's why I thought it was a message. I thought Mom wrote it and put the soup in for me to find. But maybe Miranda did it. She set us up."

"You mean she wanted us dead?" Ralston's eyes widened. "*She* tried to get us to the Laceworks' knowing we'd get blown up by that lightning?" He sounded incredulous.

"I can't believe it, either," Holden said. "We *were* having potato soup when she came. She said it smelled so good she was sure Mrs. Blaze would like some." Holden paused and rubbed his eyes. "I'm kinda glad we might never see her again. One more thing…."

"What?" Jules eyed Holden suspiciously. What else could he have to tell?

"About my muttering you asked about?"

"When you were crossing the Brooke?" Who'd have thought Jules would learn so much about his neighbor of sixteen years in Handover, right after they walked through the Land of the Dead, too!

Holden's eyes flitted about. "I was afraid, but I didn't want you to think I was a coward."

"Confession time: I was cowardly, too."

"I was repeating, 'Perfect love casts out all fear.' Mom taught me from the Ancient Book."

Jules barked a short laugh. "High five! I was saying that very verse, too!"

46.
HERITAGE

JULES STOOD AND cast his gaze about the leaves above. The wind whistled through the boughs, and suddenly he shivered. "If Whisperer gets to Miranda before we warn her, we'll probably never see her again."

Ralston turned his head and looked over his shoulder. "You mean if Whisperer takes her out?"

Holden and Jules locked eyes.

"We can't let him get her," Ralston said. "We'd better look for her. She's our friend."

They were so engrossed with the conversation that they had not kept alert. From between the tall blades of grass, Handover soldiers approached. Their trudging march grew louder and more determined with each step.

"Quick, the lamps." Jules postured himself before Tst Tst and Tippy and jerked the light into their faces to expose them even more. Ralston reached out for Bitha as Holden cuddled them both.

They were uncertain as to the extent of the lamps' ability to shield them from the Lord of Shadows, or the Scorpents, or even the Handover enemies. They tried them on Tennesson, and he'd still seen them. Hardly daring to breathe, they waited for the soldiers. But the sentries trudged on, as though the Elfies were invisible.

"We better hurry," Jules urged after the soldiers' footsteps faded into the darkness.

At the outskirts of Heritage, the Town Square came into view. From a knoll before the Town Arch, the official entry point into the Handover Capital, they detected the avenues crisscrossing the urban sprawl. Each dwelling and edifice in that sophisticated province sat atop rocks or sawn off tree stumps, meticulously ordered into neat rows. Elaborately trimmed shrubs and bushes bordered the promenades.

Even in the twilight, the weary travelers spied the profusion of hues thanks to vibrant street lights and the bejeweled lamps that hung at regular intervals from brightly tinted poles. Plants lodged in walnut shells boasted of blooming flowers in a spectrum of colors. The flowered shells hung from lamp poles in front of every structure and perfumed the night air. The ground was paved with colorful pebbles whose rough edges had been smoothed out and colors muted by the constant tread of traders and residents of that country.

"Hey! Look at those trees." Jules pointed to the shrubs.

A grove of unfamiliar-looking trees with branches laden with deep red fruits stood in the middle of the Square. Everything looked uncommon, but what stunned them most was the fruits.

"Where have I seen them?" Jules said.

After two more wrong turns, they stood before a cluster of multi-hued tents above a cluster of fallen logs.

"Looks like Tennesson's sketches," Holden said.

The uppermost pavilion, which formed the front portico, was constructed out of a vertical striped canvas of blue, white, and yellow with multi-colored ribbon streamers flowing from the top. Each of the canopies held a flourish of gold trimmings.

Jules paused, took a deep breath and knocked on the doorpost.

"Who's there disturbing my peace at this ridiculous hour!" a gruff voice said.

47.
FRIEND OR FOE

TENNESSON HAD TRAINED them on what to say. In two minutes, a tall Handoveran with a wide forehead and thick, dark eyebrows flung the entrance flap open. He could have been handsome in his younger days, but his gaunt cheeks told a story of trials, and the corners of his mouth drooped down giving his face a sad look.

"So Tennesson sent you? He speaks of me after all?" Starkies surveyed the streets beyond with darting eyes. "Come in, quick."

The visitors stumbled into the abode. All sorts of knickknacks, and ancient artifacts spilled from bookcases and cramped table tops. It was apparent Starkies wasn't one for orderly housekeeping. And it looked like his residence and store shared the same address.

"Follow me, quick. You shouldn't be here. It's dangerous for you. And now, for me, too," the graying Handoveran spoke between gritted teeth. He gestured for them to descend a flight of narrow spiral stairs concealed behind a sizeable painting of a country cottage with a woman Elfie by its front door. The face and figure looked faded with time.

Starkies gestured for them to sit on the stools in the underground room which held chests of drawers and some stools around a square dining table. "So what brings you here?"

Jules unfolded the story leaving out parts he felt should be kept secret. "So have you heard of a Mosche Falstaff who lives by the waterfall?" he finally asked.

Starkies rubbed his chin. "I have heard of all sorts of things, and I *may* have heard of him." He cast a glance at the dragonfly lanterns. "But everything comes with a price. What do you have in exchange? I've already risked much having you here. Handoverans do not like to do business with anyone partial to Elfies, and I have a reputation to upkeep."

Jules groped for his pouch in his cloak, hefted the velvety sack in one hand and laid it on the table. But Starkies reached out and snatched a dragonfly lantern Bitha was holding. "This will do nicely, thank you."

"I'm sorry, but the lanterns aren't for trade."

"And why not? I thought this Mosche was pertinent to your search—was it your grandpa you said whose life depended on your quest? Surely your grandpa means more than a couple of lanterns." He now held the other lantern he'd snatched from Tst Tst in his other hand, and his eyes drank in the cut glass pieces of the lantern held together by lacy ironwork as though inspecting for breakages.

Jules kept his voice calm though his heart threatened to explode. "I have rare gems in the pouch. You can't find these in Handover." What if Starkies stole their lanterns and sold them to the soldiers, or worse, the Scorpents? But as he spilled the glittery contents of the pouch, and spread them on the table top, Starkies set the lanterns back on the floor, by his feet, and leaned toward the gems. They glittered as they caught the light of the dim candles on the wall sconces.

"Impressive," Starkies breathed out. "I have heard of one looking for red crystals. Not only red, but sometimes blue, or purple. But red is the color of the month it seems. A hefty prize is promised to the bounty hunter who locates it."

"What," Jules began slowly, "exactly is this red crystal?" He was so occupied with getting to Heritage and surviving that he never had the chance to see if Tippy still had the sardius with her. Surely, Tippy's stone couldn't have been the red crystal? And why all the fuss about a stone? Wasn't Saul even mesmerized by it? Did it have hypnotic powers?

"Some traders from up north near Gehzurolle's city of Euruliaf dropped by, poking around my displays and asking for it. They said it was last seen in Reign. Rumor has it that Gehzurolle collects crystals when they rain from the sky, from the giant star, and they don't come very often, usually one at a time, and at most, once every twenty years or so. A rarity."

Jules covered his gems with his spread fingers. "What do you mean?"

"Apparently this phenomenon occurs when an important Elfie, from a rare Elfie group, dies. Gehzurolle rejoices when his spies tell him of its arrival, and if it makes the master happy, he makes life easier for us in Handover. Anything for peace. I'm sure you agree."

Jules wasn't sure he agreed, but he swallowed a lump thick in his throat. "Any idea who this rare Elfie was who died?"

"One important Elfie. One of many. I don't care for details. What's it to me? I hear of Elfie deaths often, especially those who come to our land. Better, I even inherit their relics on rare occasions." Starkies stared at their faces and smiled. "One cannot complain."

"Their relics?"

"Sure. When an Elfie dies here with no heirs, nothing, the roamers come across their goods and sell these to me for a few bucks. They win, I win. Everybody's happy."

"Except the dead."

"Once dead, always dead."

But this was not what Jules had heard. Dead Elfies just changed realms, Grandpa had said. And they left a token behind to show they were still alive. Was that what that red crystal was? It was explained in the Book somewhere, but Jules had never read it for himself. A token left behind by an important Elfie? A Keeper? Which one? But Jules had a mission now: locate Mosche and see what he had to say about his grandparents and his mother. And Mrs. L, too.

"I might be able to get this red crystal," Jules said. "Imagine the favors Gehzurolle would grant you if you passed it to him."

"Really?" Starkies leaned into Jules's face, and Jules stepped back.

"Where's the waterfall? Tell me. I will hand you the red crystal when I get back. I promise." Jules locked eyes with Tippy for a second and knew what she was thinking. But he wasn't betraying her. What's a crystal worth compared to his mother's and grandparents' lives? But Tippy's eyes spoke of hurt.

"You don't have it on you?"

"No." It wasn't a lie.

"Done!" Starkies's boom jolted Jules. "But you will leave me your siblings as collateral, so I'm assured of your return?"

"My siblings are not part of the bargain. I'll give you *all* the gems in my pouch. And my word—the red crystal is yours when I return."

Starkies turned around and walked to a chest, a feather duster now in hand. With his back to Jules, he said, "No deal. They stay with me. I've been fooled too many times, especially by Elfies. So much for *their* word."

Ralston reached out and touched Jules's arm. "It's okay. I'll take care of the girls here. I won't let anything happen to them. It might be safer here, too, if he hides us."

But could Jules risk it? Scorpents had taken over the command of the Handover Army. Several prominent Handover generals of the various regiments who objected to Scorpents in the past had conveniently disappeared, and Scorpents have ransacked habitation in Heritage and other neighboring Handover Cities, too. Tennesson had warned them. What if the Scorpents searched Starkies's place and found them?

Jules turned to Starkies. "Promise me you'll keep them well hidden? Somewhere Scorpents can't smell them out."

Starkies nodded. "Naturally. I wouldn't want to be accused of harboring Elfies. Think of my reputation. " He swept Jules's hands away from the gems and meticulously picked and dropped each gem, one by one, into the velvety pouch. *Click, click, click.* The gems hit each other as he dropped them into the pouch.

There goes the last of my connection with Grandpa, Jules mused. His shoulders sagged.

"No one can find them if I hide them in this secret cell," Starkies said. "I'll provide sustenance. I live alone, so at least they won't be bothered." He drew out a paper from a drawer and sketched on it. "This map will get you to the Slippery Slope, which runs close to Roaring Waterfall. I heard an old Elfie family lived in that vicinity for decades. Maybe even centuries. Scorpents have been searching for their abode for just as long, my grandpa told me."

Jules studied the rudimentary map. "But where exactly is the home?"

"Near the waterfall. Somewhere. If it was easy to locate, the Scorpents would have accessed it. And speaking of Scorpents, you'll have to travel through Slippery Slope."

"Why'd they call it Slippery Slope?" Ralston asked.

"The grade there is so steep anyone on it will have a hard time staying up. But the Scorpents roam the area much, and they seem perfectly able to handle it, so it can't be that bad."

48.
LEGEND

THAT NIGHT AS they slept in Starkies's cellar, Jules tossed and turned until a faint song awoke him. It wafted in from somewhere in the corner of the cellar, but Jules couldn't be sure. The singer's voice sounded feminine, but before he could dwell on it further, sleep enveloped her warm embrace upon him again and, finally, overcome by fatigue, Jules dozed off. Or so he thought.

Legends of old boasted of tales regarding dreams. Some said it was the subconscious mind acting out what one couldn't make sense of when awake. Others said dreams contained myriads of confused thoughts rearranging themselves when the mind had no other distractions. The Ancient Books said in the not too distant future a generation of Fairy Elves would see visions and dream dreams. But some also warned it wasn't always possible to awake from such a state.

Jules sat up when he heard the barely perceptible singing again. How can anyone get any sleep like this? At first he thought it was his mother. She'd come to get his assistance which was her custom, especially when he was napping. It was a feminine pitch like hers. But this was impossible since he was in Starkies's cellar that smelled of mold and old furniture. His snoozing companions didn't appear aware of any music. He strained his ears to hear the words but the lyrics eluded him.

Where was it coming from?

Stealthily, he tiptoed out of the cellar, fumbling up the staircase. There was barely light to see beyond his stride. Only one candle remained burning on the wall sconce. Up and up, round and round the steps spiraled. He didn't recall the cellar being so abysmal. He even forgot about the lantern.

Finally, he popped up at the top of the staircase. Once in the living room, he saw the tapestry hanging that acted as the front door flap of Starkies's home. The song was coming from outside.

Would he dare venture into the wilderness of Handover? Where was the tune taking him to?

As the draw of the vocalist grew stronger, Jules lifted the tapestry flap and breathed the fresh air. The day just broke, and mist rose from the dewy grass. From his roost on Starkies's porch he perceived a silvery blue glistening between the pine trees in the distance. He shook his head vigorously to clear his mind. Maybe he should go back in? But the melody beckoned to him, again. And this time, he obeyed its call.

He skipped down the steps and ran away from the front door and into the vast span called the Wildering Woods. The enchantment drew him on. It wasn't getting any louder, but the words became more audible. Something else besides the voice accompanied the singing. A harp.

By now he was standing at the edge of the River, sprays hitting his cloak. Only minutes ago the River seemed deep in the woods. Odd. He was also no longer afraid of Brooke Beginning and all the tales affiliated with it, or even of Handover.

Is this Brooke Beginning? If I reach my hand out toward the water, will I fall in, or drown? After all, everyone knows Elfies cannot swim.

But his acute thirst needed quenching. He must steal a drink. Even if it's just one gulp.

49.
ARNETT

THE WATER BABBLING in the river seemed crystal clear and inviting. Jules treaded to the brink of the ledge that separated the dry ground from the swiftly flowing waters beneath. *Would he really lose his memory if he took a gulp of the water?*

As he cupped his hands together and knelt to take his sip, he scanned his surroundings just in case. Then he realized where the tune was coming from. When his gaze wandered to the spot a gasp escaped his lips.

How could that be?

Inside the surging current stood a lady staring at him. She held a harp in her left hand. She was submerged in the waters but Jules could clearly see her gazing up as if he was looking in a mirror, except the reflection wasn't his own. She didn't look the least bit wet.

Framing her pale face, her hair, red like tongues of fire, flowed freely as though caught in a breeze. Jules leaned forward and reached out for the lady's outstretched arm, her fingers slender and open toward him. Subsequently, her pale, pristine hand broke out of the water, and without hesitation, Jules stooped over more and grasped it. The beautiful nymph tightened her grip and dragged Jules toward her. The water splashed onto him and swallowed him whole.

"Arnett? It's Arnett isn't it?" Jules whispered, overwhelmed by her beauty and the splendor of her presence.

"Welcome, Jules. I have been considering you," she said in a soft voice.

Some legends of Arnett insinuated she was nothing but a figment of one's imagination. Others swore they'd seen her. Nothing specific, but the accounts had corroborated. Jules always listened to these stories with awe. Sometimes he speculated that Arnett must just be a ghost, since some could see her, while others couldn't.

"Where am I?"

"You are in a secret cavern under the river, Jules."

"Brooke Beginning?"

"Many Elfies lie buried there, their wealth hidden in drawers."

Hidden in drawers? Jules opened his mouth to say something, but she cut in.

"I see you are thirsty and hungry. It has been hours since you partook of your last meal. Come!" She turned and floated away, as though she had no need for feet, even though her white satiny shoes peeked from under her robe.

Jules tilted his chin up to look beyond her. He followed closely, careful not to tread on her trailing gossamer gown. A glow radiated from her body, and he felt drawn to her light. He spotted a table prepared with glass goblets filled to the brim with scarlet juice and numerous silver trays laden with fruits and delicacies he didn't recognize. The food looked delectable and smelled sweet and savory; of honey, lemon cakes, cinnamon apples and delicious mince pies. Deep purple fruit bursting with juice, ruby red pommes he wouldn't mind sinking his teeth into, freshly baked goods dripping with what must have been creamy butter he'd gladly devour lay on the dazzling white tablecloth.

Arnett moved aside and Jules found himself before the fare. Instinctively, he picked up a golden chalice. He handled it gingerly between finger and thumb and studied its ruby red content, swirling it around inside. When he placed the surprisingly warm golden goblet to his lips the juice was tepid. Still he gulped the sweet extract to the last drop.

"Jules, it would please me if you would take a bite of the cake I have for you."

On a silver plate lay a slice of chocolate cake frosted with dark pink crystalline sugar.

"Treat yourself." She prompted him with tender tones.

He took the slice and shoved the moist cake into his mouth, savoring the chocolate and raspberry taste that swirled on his tongue. Staring at her, he asked, "Why did you bring me here? What is it that you require me to do?"

"There is nothing you can do for me that I cannot perform for myself. I am here to help you overcome."

"Overcome?"

"You don't understand now, but later you will."

"Oh?" It suddenly dawned on him that he must be inside the Brooke. *Did I drown? Like Grandpa?* He shivered.

Arnett asked gently. "Tell me what is troubling you, Jules, son of Jon Blaze?"

"My grandparents and mother are missing. I hope to find them. My mother's Book, too. And my father. Can you help?"

"Is that all?"

"We need to get to Mosche Falstaff's hide-out near Roaring Falls, and persuade him to return to Reign. And there, Miranda…." His words trailed.

"Shh! Keep your heart at rest." Arnett leaned over and stretched out her unnaturally pale fingers to grab his hand.

She cast a gaze at the spread. "Have you dined to your heart's content? Is that all you desire to partake of my table?"

Jules merely shook his head slowly. He couldn't keep his eyes off her face.

"It is time for you to preview." Her tone remained melodious although urgent. "It is a lighted path of things to come. Focus on the light in the darkness, and swim toward the light. I will help you overcome. Behold the image in the mirror! Some things you need to forget. Some things you need to remember. Your Kingdom needs you."

Jules was certain he didn't understand Arnett's instructions, but he followed her gaze. Before him a gilded mirror was suspended in midair. A mirror? He peered into the shimmering reflection. In the background Arnett was strumming her harp and singing the song that had attracted him from the start. Now, he heard the words.

"There was a fire stark and bright,
That cast out shadows in the night,

That roared and danced, sparks alighted;
It soared and pranced, the demons chided.

The fire so wondrously flared,
Its heat with all nature shared.

Where did it come from? No one knew,
But one certain thing for sure is true.

That fire came from something small,
Then slowly grew, consuming all.

At times it faltered, almost failing,
But then returned with flames unwavering.

Until it grew so vast and strong,
That nothing challenged it for long.

You have been made just like that flame,
No matter beaten, broken, shamed.

Overcome you will as your flames soar,
Until you too can flare and roar.

And be a fire shining out,
Devoured not, no fear, no doubt.

50.
NOTE

WHEN JULES AWOKE abruptly, he sat up and found himself back in the cellar. He rubbed the sleep out of his face and surveyed the room.

Why was his hair soaked? And why was he feeling full? And stuffed?

He wasn't sure who or what he'd encountered. Perhaps his worry about locating this waterfall had seeped into his dream. But something kindled in his spirit. He wished he could recall what it was Arnett had showed him in the dream. The image lingered in a small corner of his mind, but tried as he might he couldn't bring up the image.

"Jules!" The harsh whisper startled him. It was Tst Tst.

"What is it?"

"Look what I found."

Jules got up and tiptoed to his sister who stood with her back to him, both her arms in a deep drawer moving left to right, her hands obviously groping. Even in the dimness he could make out the outline of the item she eventually pulled out. It looked bent and one winged portion was missing, but Jules didn't doubt what it was.

A dragonfly lantern. Crafted by an artisan rumored to live in the eastern hills of Handover called Extreme. The full powers locked within these lamps were hardly understood, and though each bore similarities to its sisters, the craftsman made each unique.

Jules wasn't even sure the craftsman still lived, or that anyone else in the Kingdom owned one. But he was sure of one thing, this tattered lantern was their grandpa's. The very one the old man had taken with him on his fateful trip.

Jules fingered the broken frame of the lantern lightly.

Tst Tst stared at him. "How come it's here?"

"Starkies isn't telling us everything." Jules groped deeper into the drawer and searched for something—what exactly, he knew not. But as he was about to give up a latch at the drawer's rear end caught his groping finger. He tugged it. The entire back came loose. He peered into the drawer, but it was dark. "Bring our lantern."

A piece of white poked out from a slot in the rear, like a secret pocket meant to hide letters, or notes. He yanked it out and a tiny corner caught the edge and tore, but for the most part, the paper was intact. He unfolded the paper. It was water stained and crinkled, and when he read it, he gasped.

"What?" Tst Tst pulled his arm.

"Wait!" It was a short note in a vaguely familiar handwriting, but he couldn't pinpoint where he might have seen the writing. It was addressed to Leroy Priestley, although it only began with LP. He read it to Tst Tst.

"LP, your father and mine knew one another way back. I write to urge you to visit me. I know Handover is an unlikely place to visit, but as a fellow Keeper I entreat you to come. I have news that relates to your family. All may not be lost if I am correct in the reading of my Book. I live in the waterfall. I cannot risk detailing my precise location, but if you go to your

Book, my precise location is stipulated. It's best you visit me when darkness reigns.

MF"

So that was why Grandpa left in a hurry. And he asked Mother for the Book that night. Could Grandpa have brought the Book with him? But alas, Jules didn't possess the Book and MF's location must remain a mystery to him. He must assume MF to mean Mosche Falstaff.

Someone had given this letter to Starkies, possibly at the same time the trader obtained the lantern. What could that mean for Grandpa Leroy? Did they steal it from him? Surely he still stood a chance to survive Handover if his Book was with him. But did Grandpa bring his Book?

Jules folded the letter back upon its creases and pocketed it.

Tst Tst tugged at his sleeve. "Jules, I'm scared for Grandpa and Grandma."

"I'm scared, too. That's why I must find Mosche." He replaced the broken lantern back and gave Tst Tst a quick hug. He missed hearing her big words. "Maybe they're with him." But Jules knew he didn't sound convincing.

51.
PIT FALLS

"BEWARE OF THE pits!" Starkies had warned them before Jules and Holden slipped out in the cover of the mists early that morning, even before dawn.

"What pit was Starkies whispering about?" Jules turned to Holden.

Holden shrugged and adjusted the lantern in the crook of his arm. They never asked Starkies about Leroy's broken lantern. Jules insisted on it. There was no point in antagonizing the trader, and besides, if they angered him, he might even call in the soldiers on them. Best to feign ignorance, at least for the moment. And Jules kept the letter to himself, making Tst Tst promise not to say anything. It only confirmed what he already knew—that Mosche lived "in" the waterfall. He'd have chosen a different preposition—maybe "at" the waterfall, or "by" the waterfall. But he'd have to scout the area to see how anyone could live "in" a waterfall.

Jules said, "What pit?"

"You have to wake up from this stupor," Holden said. "Starkies warned us about these dangerous pits."

"There's a pit that goes into the center of our world's core. Molten rocks and all sorts of unpleasant stuff there. That sort of pit?"

Holden turned to him. "No, this is a more ghastly kind. I've heard of them. People say Gehzurolle throws his own servants in these pits. My mom showed me the map of Handover once with pits everywhere."

"Did the servants commit crimes? Break his laws?"

"She never said. But I sure wish we had her Book."

The wind rustled the leaves above, and a morning lark sang a lonesome tune. "We-ware—we-ware…," it seemed to say.

"Your mom read you anything else about pits?"

Holden nodded as he continued trudging. They hadn't even left Heritage yet, but still he looked furtively at the homes on tree logs before them. Fingers of mists wound their way in and out of the tree stumps, hiding some homes almost entirely.

"Once she read about someone being brought up out of a horrible pit," Holden said. "But I don't remember much."

"I don't remember much of our Book, either. We better watch our steps." They halted beside a clump of dense bushes and Jules straightened the map Starkies had drawn. It was rudimentary—mere lines and crosses to signify landmarks. "It says to head north once we get to the City Square."

"You think those web bridges are up there?" Holden jerked his head at the boughs overhead. "We could see if there's a way up there. At least bypass soldiers or pits."

"Let's just get to the Square first."

But even as they turned one corner then another, the rows of Handover homes upon the logs began to look too similar, all the same, until they realized they had circled the same street thrice and were lost.

"This fog doesn't help," Holden said.

"We must remain quiet," Jules whispered into Holden' ear. "It's almost daylight."

"Let's just talk with hand signals."

"If you wish."

"Maybe we should climb up and scout the area from above."

"Let's re-start from there," Jules pointed to a corner between two avenues lined with trees of ruby red fruits. "Those fruits look familiar. Maybe they'll take us to the City Square."

For a moment they stood with their backs against a redwood, fumbling. Even though a breeze wafted in a steady stream from a lake nearby, the boys sweated profusely. Beads of perspiration pooled above their foreheads and on their temples before dripping down their faces and into their eyes, blurring their vision.

With hearts pounding, they scanned the map. A few stray fireflies afforded them some light in that darkest hour before dawn. Jules reached out and swiftly nabbed an ill-fated fly. He lodged it in one of his many pockets. He'd decide its fate later.

"We can't wait here, studying this forever." Jules waved the map about. "By the time we find Mosche, everyone could be dead."

"Since you're so smart, you decide." Holden shot him a glare.

"Let's just go, okay?"

They hid behind some brambles at the edge of the City Square. Several groupings of Handoverans huddled together deep in discussion. Some warmed their hands in nearby fire pits, in the dusky air.

"That group over there seems riled up." Jules gestured for Holden to follow. "Let's get closer so we can hear."

They dodged in and out of branches, their steps making loud scrunches as they crushed the dry leaves under their boots for Starkies said their sandals would never survive Slippery Slide. They avoided the streets where possible till they came to a grove with short trees arranged in a square. The City Square, Jules thought with relief.

"In here." Jules shoved Holden into the underbrush.

"What type of plant is this?"

Jules shot him a glare."There's no time for botany lessons." He slipped in after Holden.

"Did you see the Scorpent soldiers here earlier?" A larger than normal Handoveran walked toward their direction and asked of his companion. His voice low and rough.

"They found an Elfie, eh?"

"There's a reward for their capture."

Even in the early hours the City Center thronged with Handoverans. People quarreled in loud voices. Some gestured wildly with their hands. What was up? Several larger shapes, Scorpent shapes, scattered here and there in a far side. They seemed to be moving away which was just as well.

Jules and Holden edged closer. If they turned the lantern on, the Scorpents wouldn't see them, but then the Handoverans might. Better just keep them turned off and hide in the shade, Jules advised as he pulled Holden under the mass of ragweed.

"...the Scorpents think it best for us if Elfies didn't exist."

"As long as Gehzurolle's happy we can abide in peace—"

"And harmony."

Holden nudged Jules and Jules put a finger to his lips.

Another with a thick accent said, "It's a pity the spy was caught. Now Gehzurolle will surely not get the Books he was after."

"If you want to please the Master, best keep an eye out for Elfies. They've gotten braver, and must be eradicated. They have no business in our Land."

It was then that the worst possible thing happened. Holden sneezed. Continuously.

52.
TAKEN

"ACHOOH! ACHOOH!"

THE Handoverans gaped at each other, faces bewildered, but the largest one must have had an exceptional knack for tracking sounds, for despite the mist, he rushed toward the ragweed and parted the branches and leaves.

"Quick!" Jules reached for the lantern and turned it on. Too late. A pair of large hands, like overstuffed pillows with claws, grabbed Holden.

"Well, what do we have here?" The Handoveran's voice boomed. "I smell Elfie meat. You're the cause for our troubles, eh?"

"Look, we don't mean any harm." Holden wiped his nose with his sleeves.

Very soon a horde of onlookers surrounded them, questioning glares upon their faces. The multitude peered upon the cowering boys, their intimidating scowls deepening with each minute.

"We're friends!" Holden pleaded timidly. "Truly! We don't mean any harm."

Jules's stomach turned and his heart pounded so loudly in his ears he feared his eardrums might burst, but he didn't say a word. Holden must have not realized Jules remained undetected.

But even as Holden tried to placate the Handoverans, they weren't interested in clarifications. They didn't want justification. They didn't want a solution. The anger within them festered and turned to hatred. They lashed out with words, and a few even smacked him on the head. Their anger was like the fury in a tornado, destroying any order that stood in its way.

But still Jules didn't say a word. The light prevailed. Before being dragged away Holden had stood a few feet from him and was not in the light of the lantern Jules held in his hand. When the large hands dragged Holden, his lantern was thrust toward Jules and now lay by Jules's feet. Jules wondered what he should do. Will they see him if he moved?

"I *know*!" another heavy accented Handoveran voice boomed out. "We can give him up to the Scorpents and claim a prize."

Low rumbles of sinister laughter and hails of affirmations bellowed forth.

"I humbly seek your pardon. Epic Elfie apology." Holden backed away, but a hand shoved his back, hurtling him forward from the rear. "Jules? Jules?" he cried.

"Who is this Rules? Jules? Who's he seeking?" a taunting voice sounded. Several of the Handoverans looked about and even parted the ragweed further.

But burly arms scooped Holden up by the scruff of his neck like a kitten and everyone's attention re-focused on Holden.

In a quiet voice, someone said, "I think it's a stroke of genius to orchestrate a claim. The Scorpents might buy our treasure. He's fodder for our Master."

The strong Handoveran lifted Holden and maneuvered his steps away from the City Square, out a pair of large iron gates that held heads of crickets topping the pillars on each side. Toward the direction of the forest the burly Handoveran and his followers, an assembly of Handover natives, some attired smartly with official badges, pressed on making a raucous, with jabbering and ranting.

53.
DOWN TRODDEN

NOW, WITH TWO lighted lanterns in one hand, Jules followed the procession a stone's throw away. The Handoverans' lengthy strides made it difficult for him to keep up, but he tried anyway.

They kept a swift pace and Jules lagged further and further behind until the congregation became a small mass in the distance, and he hardly heard their loud scolding. Birds chirped and swooped about, but the voices of the Handoverans ceased. Would he even find his way back to Starkies's at this rate? Would he lose Holden?

The mist had lifted, but here in the forest it was dark. Just when he felt certain he'd lost them, between the swaying grasses and twigs, he saw the quivering flames from their torches further ahead. They were under a massive oak with widespread branches. A ruckus followed as Handoverans shouted here and there and Jules realized the reason as he came close enough to see.

Scorpents! These looked massive, larger than the ones at the City Square, Jules was sure. Shoulders bulked and hulking over too-small waists, and they wore gray metal vests that gleamed even in the dim morning sun. Their voices sounded like wheezing: hot breath forced through a narrow larynx came out in dark puffs around the nostrils.

More vivid descriptions of Scorpents swam around in Jules's mind. The Ancient Books explained that no blood coursed through these savages' veins, and a scrutiny of the Scorpents' vulgar faces revealed eyes hooded beneath scales of hatred. Rumors claimed that Gehzurolle, their master, had sliced off their ears. Jules didn't know exactly why. Jules stepped closer to the wheezing, curious to see the truth for himself. Surely the lanterns would protect him; they had so far.

But as Jules took another step away from the shadow of the tall stalks of grass and into the clearing, the wind brought something to his ears.

"—the girl is already there." The wheezy voice rasped out. The Scorpent voice.

Somehow Jules knew they meant Miranda. Beta! But where was she? And how was he to help Holden? Could he squeeze through and get to Holden, bathe him in the light of the lanterns, both of which blazed bright in his grasp, and made Jules invisible?

It happened so fast, Jules didn't know what hit him. Next thing, feet trampled over him—heavy feet in heavy boots and thick-soled shoes. Some even had spikes. Jules rolled on the ground to avoid the trampling, but someone's metal toed boots crushed his forehead. It felt like his temple was caving in, and then everything went black.

54.
BY HOOKS OR BY CROOK

"HOLDEN?" JULES RUBBED a sore spot on his temple and felt a scab above his brow.

"Sleeping Beauty is up?" The voice sounded rough, but held not the accent of the Handoverans who shouted and captured Holden. Nor did it sound raspy like a Scorpent voice.

"Who are you?" Jules peered at the dim setting from his bed. Vague shapes in shadows resembled furniture, maybe a desk, and some chairs. The speaker stood over him with the dragonfly lantern in his hand. With the glare from the lantern Jules couldn't make out details of the individual. Just that he was slender and towered over him.

"Did you save Holden?"

"By Holden you mean that foolish Elfie boy they caught?"

Jules sat up and groaned. The room spun like the eye of a tornado. "My friend."

"*They* have him—the Scorpents. I don't normally make it my business to check out their prisoners, but I have to say, I couldn't believe they found another Elfie. Two in a day in Heritage is quite an achievement for them."

An assortment of shapes that looked like hooks of various sizes hung from the walls about the room.

"Did you see who the other Elfie was?"

"A lad with long untidy hair. Slender and a real squealer."

"A lad?"

"Looked like it. But what are these lanterns you have? They're unique."

"My Grandpa gave them to me, to us, my family." Jules reached out and snatched the one at the foot of the bed by his ankle. They looked somewhat mangled. He turned one on and off. Then the other.

"Is it broken?"

Jules shrugged. "Can you see me?"

"Do I look blind?" The older man leaned over and stared at Jules's face.

"I'm Jules." He reached his hand toward the stranger.

"Rude of me, but with all the excitement—I am Hooks, the fisherman." His face was round and his thick lips reminded Jules of a fish's but still there was something kind about him. Hooks gestured at the hooks on display on the walls. "Like my décor?"

Jules drew a deep breath and told Hooks he needed to get Holden back for his search of the waterfall.

"I don't know if it's possible or wise to look for Holden. You'd better cut your losses, and go on your own. Know what I mean?"

"I can't just leave him."

"Might not have a choice. From what I'd heard, they threw him in the pit."

"Pit?" His words sounded stupid to his own ears. Was Holden gone? Dead, maybe, like Mrs. Lacework? A Keeper family annihilated in a week? How many annihilated in a week? His own, too, maybe? His grandparents? His mother? Don't panic.

Hooks snapped his fingers in front of Jules's face. "The death pits. Most of them are scattered on the way to Blood Ridge. The closest is a day's run from here."

"Blood Ridge?"

"You an ignoramus? Blood Ridge is Gehzurolle's Headquarters in Euruliaf. Do you often travel without a map?"

55.
BLOOD RIDGE

JULES DUG INTO his different pockets and came upon the map Saul drew and Abel miraculously found. It seemed like a lifetime ago. He must have lost the rudimentary one Starkies drew. He remembered he waved it about. Maybe Holden had it when the Handoverans snatched him. And he'd thought they were in a bind then.

As Jules straightened the creases to show Hooks the map, a scrawl on one side of the map caught his eye. A note from Abel? He felt like kicking himself for not checking the map earlier when the squirrel brought it to him. In the dim light, he strained and read the short message.

"Behind the waterfall." Abel wrote and drew an arrow to a spot on the map. Under this first message, Abel continued, "If this Falstaff is of old, his Book holds your answers."

How would Abel know?

And below that message, in even smaller print, so small Jules had to squint and slant the paper to the light, was written: "I placed a whistle in your cloak in case you needed a critter."

Jules fumbled about in his pockets, patting each part of his cloak until he found a whistle in his inside pocket. Except he'd never have thought that was what the curious wooden object with multiple holes was. He brought it to his lips, but then stopped. What strange critter might come if he blew now?

"What is that?" Hooks took a step closer, his eyes large.

"A gift from a friend." He handed the map to Hooks. "Maybe you can tell me where we are on this map and how I can find Holden."

Hooks crinkled his nose while studying the map. "Slippery Slide is the *long* route to the waterfall. Did your map maker tell you that?"

Jules shook his head.

Hooks cleared his throat. "But this is the good news. If you can call it good. It will get you to some of the pits because it's the *only* way to Blood Ridge. But still I'd avoid it if I were you."

"I don't have a choice." Reign only had four Keepers Jules knew about—his family, Saul's family, the Laceworks, and possibly Mosche Falstaff. And the way Keeper families were disappearing, how many would be left by the time his journey ended?

Maybe his family was already doomed, like Reign would be, once all the Keepers were annihilated.

"Most Handoverans," Hooks said, "are afraid of Blood Ridge. They'd avoid any path that could lead there like the plague, which is why the Scorpents dig their pits there—fewer prying eyes."

"Can I be sure I'll find Holden there?"

"Nothing is for sure, mi-lad."

"It's a risk I'm willing to take."

"All approaches to Blood Ridge are fraught with peril," Hooks said. "Merchants have some horrific tales regarding that trail. And I must warn you, I've heard if you encounter a Scorpent encampment, you'll find your pit for sure."

"Hooks!" A shrill voice came from somewhere beyond the doorway of the bedroom.

Hooks gave a start and swiveled around. "Coming, Dear!" To Jules he whispered, "It's the wife. She doesn't know you're here, so be quiet, and turn that light on or something. Quick." He winked and smiled.

A swollen figure appeared in the doorway. "Who were you chattering to? Not to yourself I hope."

"As a matter of fact, I was quarreling with myself."

"And I'll be quarreling with you if you don't catch me the fish you said you'd come home with."

"I caught a fish, but not the sort you'd like. And by now, you know, they don't bite so late in the evening, Dear."

Jules could not tell that he'd lain unconscious for the better part of the day. How late was it, and where was Holden by now? He lay quietly by the bed, both lanterns on his lap. Hooks could still see him but the other Handoveran could not. Why? Jules could not fathom, but clearly, the lanterns clouded Mrs. Hook's vision. Was Hooks a Hanfie? Was that what separated Hooks from other Handoverans? He was rather short for a Handoveran.

Jules planned to leave the instant he had the chance. Slippery Slide or not, he must find the pit, even if it was one of many. He couldn't leave Holden to die. Somewhere in the recesses of his mind he recalled Grandpa Leroy's warning: At least five Keepers must remain or their Kingdom of Reign would be cursed forever. If Holden was the remaining heir to the Lacework Book, Jules meant to save him, unless it was too late. But Mrs. Hooks still stood, arms crossed rigidly over her ample chest, guarding his bedroom door.

Hooks gathered things from about the room—fishing rods, tackle boxes, and two or three sizes of giant hooks he carefully wrapped in thick blankets and placed in his sack. With his wife still eyeing him from the doorway, he said, "If I went to the lake, I could possibly get quite close to the pit. At least, one of them."

"Are you threatening me, Hooks?" his wife said in a shrill voice, obviously confused by Hooks's words. "If you fall into a pit it's your fault. But don't think you can escape me. I'd find you for sure if you don't get me that fish. By hook or by crook." She gave a snotty cackle and stormed out the door, obviously thrilled by her own joke.

Jules almost chuckled, but he felt sorry for Hooks who seemed helpful, and helpless.

As quick as June bugs, Jules scurried and gathered his things by his feet. "If you point me to a pit, I'll help you catch your fish."

Hooks practically shoved him out the door. He was afraid of his wife's detecting Jules.

"You cannot imagine who she'll take you to, and I won't be able to help one bit. You know the price we pay for helping Elfies?"

56.
SLIPPERY SLIDE

BUT HOOKS WAS good to his promise. His house, a ramshackle tent-like structure atop a lightning struck stub of a trunk, sat by the edge of the City Square, a stone's throw from the forest called Wildering Wild. Hooks led him to it and up to the top of a steep incline.

Hours later when they arrived at the top of Slippery Slide, Jules's heart sank lower. Before them lay a steep slant with the gravel and loose earth—the sandy expanse they had to conquer. The decline was worse than he'd imagined.

"Will your lanterns hide me from the Scorpents, too?"

Jules shrugged. "We must stick together." He remembered how the Handoverans had seen Holden and dragged him away despite Jules's light a few feet away.

"I will get you to the bottom, so you can see the path the Scorpents take to Blood Ridge. The pits should be dotted all over. Maybe we can find a fresh trail."

"But how will I get you your fish? Is there a lake nearby?" Jules hoped to use his whistle. It was a long shot but if it summoned squirrels, maybe it worked on fish, too. He fumbled in his cloak and brought the whistle to his lips. But no sound came forth. And nothing happened. Was it destroyed when the Handoverans trampled him?

Hooks mussed Jules hair, even though Jules stood as tall as him. "Kid, don't worry about the fish. Or me, for that matter. You have more troubles than I, and that's a comforting thought to me somehow." He grinned.

Much bungling, skidding and tripping proceeded. Slippery Slide didn't earn its name for nothing. The steep grade afforded little foothold for those clambering up or down the sandy slopes. The route also failed to offer any shelter due to the scant vegetation, so Hooks and Jules stood out like two figures in a bald terrain.

One section plummeted into a ravine which eventually plunged into a watery gorge, Hooks explained between quick breaths. "So be extra careful!"

When they were partway down, Hooks heaved out, "We have to take a breather. It's too steep for my short legs."

"How will you get back up?"

"My hooks serve many purposes." He patted the bulging sack under his arm. But the glare from the lanterns, together with the reflection from moon on the sandy expanse, made it hard to see. "Maybe we can turn off the light for a few minutes."

Jules looked about and nodded. There was nothing the Scorpents could really be hidden behind or under. Several hundred yards down, the map which Hooks provided chartered a ravine. They slowed their pace, then halted.

"Maybe I can use my spider twine to guide us?" Jules said.

He tied one end of the twine around his waist and secured another end to one of the protruding roots.

Hooks held on to the line midway, slightly above Jules. Darkness enveloped the land as clouds floated across the moon, and the sallow glow over the sand dimmed.

Jules and Hooks struggled to hold on to the swaying twine. They inched their way down. Jules felt they must have been on the slope for at least one life span, but, he was thankful for Hooks's company. He realized it was a ways for Hooks to walk back home.

Then, before he knew what was happening, an unpleasant accent rattled him.

57.
OFF COURSE

TYPICALLY, SCORPENTS WERE loud and detectable with their wheezing. But this particular bunch approached silently. Before Jules even had the opportunity to turn on his dragonfly lanterns, the Scorpents spotted them.

"Elfie smell!" a guttural voice barked out. The speaker lunged at Hooks.

Hooks narrowly missed the Scorpent's grasp.

"Run, Jules!"

Very close behind Hooks, vile threats filled with filthy words rang from the Scorpents' lips.

Jules grabbed Hooks's cloak with one arm, let go the spider twine and tumbled into the darkness. Please, not the ravine, Jules thought as they continued rolling down head over heels, lanterns bashing him on the head. He landed on Hooks.

"Get off! Get off—" Hooks finally spat out his words between gritted teeth.

"Sorry, sorry," whispered Jules. "Have we reached the bottom?" He surveyed the dark grounds around him with his left foot and left hand, his mind on the ravine and gorge.

"Shh!" Hooks said. "We don't want the Scorpents knowing our location. There might be others."

"I have the lanterns on." Miraculously he'd held onto both despite the tumble.

Crunch, crunch.

"Someone's coming," Jules whispered as he edged closer to Hooks.

Loud guffawing filled the night air. "—Rage said to use fire, and that's what we'll do."

"The trader will never—"

The Scorpents must have moved fast, as their words dissipated with the night as they rounded to the other side of the hill.

When they felt sure no more Scorpents lurked by, Jules spoke. "What fire were they talking about?"

"They use fire to scare Elfies out of their hiding all the time. Maybe they located others. There was a time decades ago when they purged Elfies, but even then some still insist on coming over. Let's not get sidetracked. We need to get our bearings."

Jules thought of Ralston and his sisters. Had he done right by leaving them with an untrustworthy Handoveran? What if Starkies traded them for some antique that took his fancy? "How far away is this ravine?"

"It should not be far off." They groped about in the dimness as the darkness seemed to swallow even the light from their dragonfly lanterns.

Hooks said after a while, "I could have sworn the ravine was here."

"What do you mean?" Unlike the near-bare slope they'd rolled down from, here, tall grasses sprung out from the pebbly ground. As the breeze cut through the swaying grasses a high pitched whistle filled the night air, like someone playing a flute, a song melancholic and mournful. Now and then crickets chirped.

Hooks squinted at the map in his hand. "We've fallen off course. This is *not* the route on that map. I'm sure we're lost!"

58.
ATTACK!

THAT NIGHT THEY rested in a nook under a burnt oak tree. Better get some rest while they could, Hooks advised. He seemed to have forgotten about Mrs. Hooks and his fish. But he did tell stories of how he'd always wanted to have a son. He winked at Jules and dozed off.

While trekking the next morning, always taking the turn that led northward, something like missiles pelted toward them out of the tall wild flowers and sweeping grasses. The volley of arrows rained down in a steady stream, coming closer with each barrage.

"Get cover!" Jules cried out. An arrow narrowly grazed his arm. "We're under attack."

Quick as a flash, they shot off in different directions: Hooks to the nearest boulder, Jules behind the most convenient stump. As quickly as the aggression began, it stopped.

For a few heart pounding minutes, Jules waited breathlessly and peered from behind the stump. He spun around when someone tapped lightly on his right shoulder, and he saw it was a white rabbit. The huge bunny—a dwarf specie—persisted in scrutinizing him with its large, soft brown eyes. Its nose wiggled as it sniffed the air to determine if Jules qualified as "friend or foe."

"Nice bunny," Jules said, hesitantly. Where was Hooks?

After some minutes of silence with Jules and the bunny eyeballing each other, he peered at the long grasses that rustled up ahead. Their attackers were hiding. Scorpents wouldn't hide like this. They were evil, obnoxious, and vile. But Scorpents were never craven.

Jules decided to give it a shot. "Who's there? Friend or foe?"

The gruff answer came. "Who are *you*?"

From the cadence and inflection it was obvious the accent belonged to an Elfie, but not one native to the specific regions Jules was familiar with. Elfies from diverse districts of Reign and the surrounding areas spoke with slightly varied articulations. In some parts they even spoke with their own unique vocabulary and practiced manners Jules considered offensive.

"I am Jules Blazes, and my friend is Hooks." Where was Hooks?

"Avaline, Arnold and Aloof, here!" the nervous voice said. "We've mistaken you for foes. We'll stop shooting now. We need help. Our friend is badly hurt, and in need of urgent care."

Jules was uncertain of what to make of this. He was never exposed to any military training. But he was unconvinced he should trust them even if they were Elfies. What if they worked for enemy Handoverans? Or were Gehzurolle's spies? But what else could he do? "Come out and—and—show yourselves, first." *Where was Hooks? Did the arrow hurt him?*

The three attackers came out of their hiding place from behind a log. They were attired for war. Bits of twigs and leaves poked out of their helmets and intertwined in their dark green camo garments with the typical, but tattered, elfish cloak draped over. One appeared badly hurt. His two comrades propped him on either side.

"He's bleeding!" one of the Elfie soldiers said.

The red soaked front of the soldier's garment made Jules queasy. *Gird yourself up,* he reminded himself, not for the first time. He still had an uneasy feeling about these strangers. He focused his attention on the three as they approached, partially hidden by a swaying blade of grass.

"What happened to him?" Jules yelled from behind the stump.

"Aloof's been shot by a Handover soldier. He's lost a lot of blood. We've been running for days."

"Where from?" Jules dragged himself out of his shelter. He eyed them suspiciously from afar. *Something's odd about them, or maybe I'm becoming paranoid!*

Both Avaline and Arnold answered simultaneously, "We deserted."

"Please!" Avaline said, pleading. "Don't report us. We couldn't take the killing anymore. So we ran away when Aloof got shot, and they ordered us to carry him to the Injury House. We've been running, walking, for days."

An Injury House was a term for the hospital Elfie soldiers used. Jules didn't think Elfie regiments had invaded Handover.

"Yeah!" said Arnold, the shorter one, but he did not sound as confident.

"Yeah?" Jules said. "How did that fancy arrow propeller you used land in your lap? S'pose they handed the weapon to you before you took your vacation?"

"Oh, this?" Avaline set the weapon by his foot. "We needed to protect ourselves from the wilderness. And Handoverans. Honest."

"We've been helping Aloof stay alive," Arnold said. "We've made poultices and fed him with all the useful herbs we could get our hands on, but his bleeding won't stop."

"He's not going to heal." Hooks stepped out from behind a shrub. "What with the shuttling around. Maybe he's developed an infection."

The two soldiers unanimously conceded to finding a suitable refuge for the victim, Aloof. His face was a pale ash and dark, bluish semi-circles underlined his lower lids. His gray-tattered camo garment held deep russet stains all over.

"I may have the spot." Jules turned and eyed the white bunny several steps behind. It was scurrying into a burrow. "What infantry are you in? I wasn't aware Elfie soldiers have broken into Handover." He thought of his dad.

Avaline with the wide forehead said, "Only one Elfie force managed to maneuver the Brooke. We lost many to the storms getting here, and the beach was riddled with traps, but we came here a fortnight ago and set up camp."

"Where?" Hope surged within Jules. Maybe he could get their help.

"We're not taking you there. They'd skin us for running away."

"And what makes you think I won't do the same?" Jules grabbed the sack by Hooks's feet and snatched a giant hook from it. The blanket fell off to reveal a gleaming claw, sharp and pointed at the ends. He stepped forward and swung it at Avaline.

"Whoa!" Hooks said.

"I don't have time for games and lies. Lives are at stake, and I'm not allowing three craven Elfies to determine my fate. Tell me where the Elfie camp is."

"Up River. Three days' hike. But you'll waste your time."

"Why?"

"Because they're mostly dead—I'm sure. We were attacked. Some brown crickets devoured everything. We ran because we begged our captain to get away but he refused."

Jules ran his hand over his face. Their story didn't add up, but why lie? At least the crickets, assuming these were the locusts, made sense. They must have run away when the attack came. "Do you know a Captain Blaze?"

Avaline shook his head, but stepped toward Jules. "Please. Aloof here will join the dead if you don't help him."

"My friend will join the dead, too, if I don't come across a certain death pit soon."

"Help us, and we'll help you find your death pit."

59. VANISH

THE BURROW WAS cramped, but at least Jules felt certain Scorpents could not get to them as he considered how to proceed. He offered the rabbit some sprigs of parsley, and the rabbit hopped away peaceably to another shaft at the far end of the burrow.

After positioning the now unconscious Aloof in the burrow, Jules jetted off to forage for the herbs Hooks felt sure were growing wild nearby. This allowed Jules to scout the area on his own. He wondered where Jon Blaze's regiment might have gone to. If anyone survived the brown cricket in that camp, would they know of his father's location? And what of Cori Lacework? But his heart sank when Holden's grinning face came to mind.

The two soldiers slumped into a corner to regain their strength, whispering, while Hooks prepared the poultices and medicinal food for the patient using the herbs Jules collected. Soon Aloof regained consciousness, and his pale cheeks gained tinges of pink.

"The broth was more than satisfactory," Avaline said.

"Thanks for the poultices—" Aloof whispered.

Avaline cut in. "We can discuss how to handle tomorrow after some rest."

Jules felt he'd rested enough, so he just grunted.

"You traveling alone? Just the two of you? Aren't you afraid of Scorpents?" His eyes flickered to Jules's meager belongings of a filled pillowcase, and Hook's sack dumped in the corner.

"We have our lanterns...," Jules's voice trailed as he caught Avaline's gaze.

"Pretty lanterns." Avaline's eyes lingered on the lamps.

Jules refused to rest even as the tired soldiers started snoring.

"Hooks." He shook Hooks out of his drowsiness. "I saw something when I was scouting outside for the herbs. Come up for a bit."

When they stood outside the burrow, the sky had turned a burnished red, and the light was enough to illuminate the grassy plains. Jules pointed to a solitary redwood.

"Someone could climb up that tree so we can at least have an idea what the terrain is like," Jules suggested.

"And that someone would be…me?" Hooks squinted at Jules.

"I don't trust those soldiers—especially that Avaline. I can fight him off better than you if he tries anything funny."

Hooks shook his head at Jules and handed Jules his sack.

"You take a lantern. But I'll walk there with you, just in case."

Hooks strode towards it with sure, lengthy steps. And then, "Help! Help!"

Jules ran toward the tree. "Hooks? Hooks? Where are you?"

For Hooks had vanished. Lantern and all.

"I've fallen into a ditch of some sort," came his reply. Seconds later, his agonizing cry came. "Oh, no. No. No!" Horror resounded in Hooks's voice.

"What's wrong?" Jules rushed toward the voice. Before he could complete his question he stumbled upon the answers for himself. He almost made the same mistake as Hooks. The ditch Jules's feet tottered on the edge of was no ordinary trench. It was a death pit no longer in use. The Scorpents had filled it full. The camouflaged covering on it had rotted. But the good news was that Hooks was close to the surface.

Jules stared into the cavity and witnessed the evidence of the Scorpents' evil. The dragonfly lantern still in Hooks's clenched fist revealed the atrocities the Scorpents were guilty of under Gehzurolle's reign through the centuries. Ever since the curse. Even the Handoverans hadn't been spared.

Jules gulped and forced himself to gaze around the pit. These gnarled wretched bodies were Handoverans. His eyes locked with Hooks, and he saw tears in the old man's eyes.

"Quick. Reach out to me." Jules dropped to his knees and strained his arm out to Hooks, but still he couldn't get to him. Jules reached for his pillowcase sack, took the twine, fixed it about his waist and let the other end down to Hooks.

"Grab that, and I'll try to haul you up." He braced his legs against a nearby stone as he felt Hooks tug.

The stench of rotten vegetables and meat wafted up to Jules. Dead Handoverans. As swiftly as he could, he pulled Hooks up, but the twine slipped, and Hooks almost dragged Jules into the pit twice, instead.

"Hurry! I hear some movements in the rushes behind me."

Jules reached down and grabbed the lantern from Hooks to free his other hand. Finally, Hooks reached the edge and pulled himself out.

"You're fit for an old man."

"It's the Handoveran blood, my mamma used to say."

"What do you mean?"

"My mamma was an Elfie like you. But that was ages ago. Bless her eternal rest. She told me on her death bed, 'Me Lad, you cannot follow me now, but thanks to your Elfie blood I'll see you again, some day.' I sure miss her."

"You're a Hanfie, too! Just like those three soldiers—I knew they couldn't be pure Elfies. I can tell the slight differences now."

"I thought so, too."

"Must be your Elfie blood. That's why you could see through the lantern's light."

"Speaking of which, we better gather the lanterns and get going to the top of that tree. It's getting dark so quickly." He smelled his cloak, and crinkled his nose. "Phew! Now I really need to get to a lake. Even a Scorpent might smell me a mile away."

Jules rolled the twine into a ball. "Why do you think they killed all those Handoverans in that pit?"

Hooks shrugged and shuddered. "I don't want to know. I just want to stay away from those beasts."

"Wait! I can't find the lanterns." Jules looked about and parted the blades around him. "They were right here."

"Must be hidden behind one of these tall stalks."

But even though they located the pillowcase and the sack with Hooks's belongings, they could not find the lanterns. Jules stubbed his toe on a stone and started hopping. "Aww!"

"Who could have them?"

"Let's get back to the burrow and ask those Hanfies to help. It's the least they can do."

They trudged toward the burrow as the last of the evening light faded into the distance.

"Avaline?" Jules called out when they dropped down into the dark burrow. But all was dark and silent. The earlier snoring was gone.

Jules rushed to the corner where he knew they had slept, but all their belongings were gone, too.

Hooks laid a hand on Jules's shoulder. "They must have stolen the lanterns and split."

"I can't believe this." Jules slumped onto a stone they'd used as a seat and groped inside his cloak.

His mother *always* made them carry the light stick, which he'd *always* thought so unnecessary. Ralston made a ton of these. He snapped the light stick in two, and the chemicals mixed. Light came forth. It was dim, but at least they could see better now that darkness shrouded the land outside.

Hooks laid a hand on Jules's shoulder. "I suggest we sleep and then go up that tree with the first light. There's no reason to wallow in regret."

Jules stumbled over another stone, and yelped again.

60.
TRAITOR

HOOKS AND JULES slept in the empty burrow till the first light of day. And even though they were hungry they hurried out so Hooks could climb up the tree as agreed the night before.

"I can see for leagues and leagues," Hooks shouted as he jumped down the last few feet to the ground. "And guess what? The ravine's to the south. You should've climbed. Now I'm all stiff."

They poured over Saul's map and compared it with Hooks's.

"Let's veer right," Hooks said.

"We must look for a route with some cover in case we run into Scorpents."

Hooks said it was a good thing and a bad thing if and when they spotted Scorpents. It could mean another pit, and possibly a recent one. Scorpents won't go off their route to dig pits. That's too much work for them, Hooks explained. But if they found Holden's pit, would he even be alive? It had been three days since they kidnapped him. They didn't have to go far before they heard gruff voices.

"Stop! You're making a mistake. I work for Gehzurolle!"

Jules and Hooks stopped in their tracks and dropped to the ground. Jules motioned for Hooks to stay as he crawled on elbows and knees to check on the commotion less than a stone's throw away. That's the problem with these long grasses, you never know who's behind the next blade until they're practically running into you. There was a time of the King when the Elfies rode tall on horses and commanded even the winds to obey. A lost time, Jules thought. The mud smeared and stuck to his pants and sleeves as he inched his way to the tussle ahead.

Wheezing told him that Scorpents were there. Will they smell him?

"If Whisperer finds out, he will feed you to the Ridge."

Miranda!

The Scorpents let out a low rumble of guffaws, and soon, the scratchy rustle of twigs and leaves drifted through the air.

What is happening? Jules strained his ears to hear better. A leaf cutter ant stood in his path and looked him eyeball-to-eyeball. Jules let the ant, which reached to his knee when he was standing, scurry pass on six black legs, feelers quivering.

"No! Stop!" Miranda cried, and then silence, except for the wheezing of the Scorpents.

Their words sounded garbled, and then the same rustling of leaves and twigs. By now Jules could see what they were up to. Two Scorpents stood bent over something, then one straightened up and sniffed the air, said something garbled again, and they both roared like lions. Jules held his breath and lay flat on the muddy earth. Minutes passed and when he parted the spears of grass again, the Scorpents had left. Or so he hoped.

"What's up?" Hooks said when he found him.

"They had Miranda, but she's gone now."

"Do you want to go after them?"

"Hooks, you don't have to do this. Your wife must be ever worried for you and the fish."

"A little dieting won't hurt her." Hooks grinned despite their situation.

Jules nudged him and grinned back. “I think it’s safe to come out to see what they were bending over right there.” He pointed.

“Shh! What’s that clicking, wheezing sound?”

61.
COUNTED AS DEAD

"DOESN'T SOUND LIKE Scorpents." The sunlight streamed to the ground, but the blades of grass cast shadows and patches of darkness that swayed here and there. When Jules squinted, he realized the patches were not formed by the grasses swaying in the breeze but by moving objects. Insects. Roaches, to be precise.

Jules pulled at Hooks's cloak. "Hissing cockroaches."

"What?"

"They can force air through their breathing holes in their abdomen and make the wheezing sounds. Sounds like a Scorpent. Almost."

"Wonderful science lesson, Jules."

"They're crawling in and out of the covering over there."

"Why do you think there are so many here?"

"Let's see." He made to move toward the dense shadows that turned out to be the hard backs of roaches skittering.

"You've got to be kidding, Kid. Roaches bite."

"Only if you're very still, or very dead."

Hooks wrinkled his nose. "And they stink, too!"

"They'll camouflage our smell. Someone's crying! Hear that?" Jules walked closer to the roaches and then, *whoosh* he slipped and dropped several feet down onto something soft, mushy, and nauseating with stench. The stench reminded him of his recent experience hauling Hooks out of the pit, and he started retching.

"Jules!" Hooks was calling from above. "I guess it's your turn. I'll see how I can help." Hooks peered through the opening Jules had fallen through and coughed continuously.

"Jules?" Miranda's voice came from somewhere in the pit, muffled and strained.

In the pitch darkness, Jules felt a quivering hand grope for his arm, and as he grasped it, he quaked out a hoarse whisper, "Miranda, don't move. I think we've been dumped on top of somebody—or rather some—*bodies*."

"We're going to die like them, Jules," she said between belabored breath and sobbing. Jules didn't know if she sobbed because of remorse or because the stench made them both gag every few seconds. "Like those…bodies."

Jules grabbed about his cloak, and produced the last of his light wands. He snapped it into two, and the dim light displayed the pit they stood in. They were in a mass grave—a mountain of carcasses piled high atop one another. Living beings that once breathed, talked and walked, now lay extinguished like slaughtered animals. Only the semblance of rotting flesh and broken bones remained of them. Their essence oozed out thick. Jules tasted the decay in his mouth and gagged more. The heavy air clung to his skin like cold fingers. This pit was worse than the one Hooks stumbled into. That one held bones and skulls. This one, rotting flesh.

"Miranda? Juu-les?"

Jules was sure one of the carcasses had come back to life. A ghost awakened from a disturbed slumber? The muffled moaning flowed from somewhere underneath them. No! It came from their right side, closer to Miranda. She clutched Jules's arm and dug her nails into his skin further. Her grip was painful, but he let her cling on. He struggled to keep down what morsel of food he had left in his stomach, that bit of bite with the Hanfies who stole from him.

"Jules?" Hooks cried from above. "Find a way to pass me your twine."

Jules hugged the pillowcase with the twine to his body. It held the means for escape.

"Jules? Miranda?" the voice from the pit, grew stronger. Familiar almost.

"Holden?" Jules murmured. "Holden! Are you badly hurt?"

"I knew you'd come. I broke my leg."

Jules waved his lighted wand across the pit. A huddled form shifted on the far side against the wall. "Can you move your leg?"

"I can't stand or walk. I think I'll have to die here. But I wanted to give you something before I–"

"Don't be crazy. I came all the way for you, and I'm getting you out. You and Miranda."

"Don't trust Miranda," Holden said.

Miranda let out a gasp. "Please, Jules, I never thought it'd come to this. You don't know what it's like living with Saul."

"Don't believe a word," Holden pleaded between sobs.

"Please, Jules, I did it for my mother. I meant to right everything."

"She's a fake!"

"Shut up! Both of you. I have to think." Jules yanked his arm away from Miranda, waved his dimming light stick about and studied the wall of the pit.

Scores of hissing roaches crawling in and out on the rim of the pit became visible. Many trudged up and down the sides of the shaft waving their antennas back and forth like scraggly swords flashing above their tiny heads. Their beady eyes stared straight ahead with intense concentration. A few marched close, their feelers just above Jules's head. He cast them a glance and shuddered.

62.
ROACHES UP CLOSE

"HEY, JULES!" HOOKS called out. "We'd better hurry. The roaches are coming toward me."

"I have an idea. They're here to feast on the bodies beneath us." Jules said, quietly.

Some of the scavengers regarded Jules and Miranda with interest, as though considering if they could qualify as a tasty supper. After all, roaches devour all sorts of meat.

"When a couple comes close enough as they crawl back up the wall I will lasso them with my twine." He handed Miranda his pillowcase and rummaged through it as she held it open for him. He also took out the mirror shard and used its sharp edge to cut the twine into sections he tied together into a harness. He noosed the other end into a lasso. "My light's fading."

"Jules," Holden croaked. "The Scorpents may come again."

"I'm moving as fast as I can. Miranda, place your leg in this loop." He shoved the harness to her.

"You can't be serious." Miranda moaned. "You're *totally* insane. I detest roaches."

"Normally Blatarrias, as roaches are called scientifically, bite, but the hissing species won't attack unless provoked, or if they think you're food. Try not to qualify for either category."

Miranda snatched the harness and placed her foot through one loop. "Now what?"

Jules swung the other end round and round above his head and aimed the lasso at a Blatarria marching up. But he missed. It was too dim.

"Wait!" He fumbled within his cloak, patting here and there. Several pockets later, he fished out the firefly he'd pocketed when they first entered Heritage. It had dwindled to a semi-comatose state! "You handle this." He shoved the firefly at Miranda.

"Ee-ew! I'm not fond of insects." Miranda grudgingly grasped the firefly with both hands.

"And I'm not fond of traitors." He shot her a glare.

"What do I do with this—thing?"

"Hold it up so I can see where I'm aiming *if* you want to get out." Then Jules gestured at Hooks who appeared to be widening the opening with his hook. "When Miranda gets there, hook her to something. We don't want our prisoner escaping!"

"Prisoner? Look, I can explain everything."

"Save your sales pitch!" And he started lassoing again.

It took him many throws and careful maneuvering before he eventually fastened the flimsy silk threads to a hardy roach. Miranda's mount pulled her up the slimy wall of the pit.

Getting Holden harnessed and up the wall was harder. Several times Holden cried out in pain and told Jules to just leave him there.

Jules almost lost his temper.

"You are one of the last Keepers of Reign. Our Kingdom will forever remain cursed once all Keepers are lost. How can you only think of your pain?"

After many trials, and Hooks using his different hooks to guide the roach, Holden was finally over the mouth of the pit. In a few minutes, Jules was out, too. He felt a cool draft ruffling his hair. The air smelt lighter, more refreshing. He wriggled out of his harness and told Hooks to gather the twine.

"It stinks worse than rotten fish," Hooks said. "Disgusting,"

Jules agreed. "Leave it, then."

He rushed to Miranda and stood before her small figure huddled next to a stone. She was sitting on her haunches, hugging her knees. A giant hook secured the twine around her waist to the ground and trapped her.

"Where's my mother?" Jules said. "And don't bother lying."

"I don't know where she is."

"I said don't bother to lie."

"I'm not lying. She was there. In your house when I went to see her. And, yes, I lied and told her you needed help outside so I could search your home. Not to hurt her. I never saw her again."

"And you brought Holden's soup pot there to trick me, so we'd get to the Laceworks' and you could do what? Blow us up by lightning?"

"I—I brought the soup pot, as an excuse to visit your mother, yes, but I didn't know about the lightning."

"What did you do with Mrs. Lacework? How could you do it, Miranda? How could you sell her out like that? She was like a mother to you."

"*Like* a mother, but not my own. I need to find my mother."

"That's no excuse. Besides, your mother is dead."

"I *have* a mother. Alive. Here, in Handover. And she needs me."

"She's a Keeper's heir," Jules said. "No way she could've survived in Handover all those years. And no matter what, it doesn't give you a reason to hurt people."

"I never meant for Mrs. L to get hurt. It wasn't supposed to happen that way."

Hooks had helped Holden hobble to Miranda.

"What way?" Hooks said as he eased Holden down to sit.

"Whisperer told me if I could get the red crystal to him he'd tell me where my mother was last seen."

"Miranda, if Whisperer knows where your mother is, he'd have delivered her to Gehzurolle himself. There's a price for the head of every Keeper heir. He wants every Keeper and anyone in a Keeper household. Dead, so there'd be no heir, and no hope for Reign. Your mother's without her Book to protect her, I might add."

Miranda flicked at dirt on her soiled cloak, and brought the hood on her cloak up to cover her head. "You're wrong. You don't know anything. My mother *has* her Book! That's why they can't get her. And why she's alive, and I mean to find her not matter what."

Jules and Holden locked eyes. Impossible. He and Holden witnessed Saul read a large antique-looking tome. It had a red cover with an ancient motif and golden edges. Was that not the Turpentine Ancient Book?

63.
UNFAITHFUL SERVANTS

BUT HOW COULD Jules be sure Miranda wasn't lying, now?

"How'd you know your mother has her Book?" He stepped toward her. "Or that she's even alive?"

"Whisperer told me," Miranda said.

"Hah! Whisperer? Whisperer is Gehzurolle's agent. He'd lie for *anything*. All of Gehzurolle's agents *live* on lies. Thrive on lies. For a smart girl, you can be so blind."

Hooks laid a hand on Jules's shoulder. "We'd better leave. Maybe find a lake to wash off that stench. I heard Scorpents are attracted to foul smells."

"Let's take our cloaks off, too."

"How about the frost at night," Holden said. "We'll need our cloaks."

"Hooks has a point," Jules said. "The stench will attract the Scorpents. Better to freeze than have them upon us. We don't have our lanterns." Jules told Holden about the soldiers robbing them.

"We can wash the cloaks," Hooks said. "I know of ways to get rid of rotten smells."

Jules felt thankful for Hooks's company. But when he saw Miranda eyeing him, he scowled.

Hooks pointed to Miranda. "What to do with her?"

"Let me go. I know where my mother's house is." She rummaged in her cloak despite her wrists secured together in front of her, and brought out a folded sheet. "If I can get to Glennora I can find her."

Jules snatched the map from her. "You're coming with us, and we don't have time to go on your wild goose chase." He glanced at it quickly.

"It's no wild goose chase. They caught me because I came that close to finding her," Miranda said, making a gesture with her fingers. "If I find her, I can convince her to return to Reign with her Book."

"You're our prisoner. I don't trust you one iota. Hooks, loosen her feet, and we'll get going." Jules turned to Hooks. "I can't thank you enough for all you've done. You're not so bad for a Hanfie. Please, maybe it'll be safer for you to return home. Back to your wife."

"To be skinned alive? You're not ridding me so easily, Jules. This adventure pumps fresh blood into my veins! I've never felt so alive."

Jules shook his head. He knew Hooks worried for their safety even though the fisherman didn't say it.

Miranda told them that the trees ahead had web bridges on them. She'd traveled most of her way around Handover using them. She didn't think the Scorpents knew of them. So, after they took a dip in a large pond to wash off the smell of death, Jules decided to risk it and believe her words about the bridges. That proved to be true. He was the last to reach the branch with the web, even after the hobbling Holden, who had only sprained his ankles. The restrained Miranda kept chuckling at him.

Holden nudged him when they rested on a fork in the bridge. "Heights making you queasy still?"

"Nothing can rival the pit." He locked eyes with Miranda. "Correction. Nothing can rival betrayal." And he hopped up and slung his pillowcase sack over his shoulder.

From the arc of the sun, they determined where north lay. Hooks said this would take them to the Roaring Waterfall. It was the largest in Handover. Stories of death and despair were connected with it. Supposedly when Gehzurolle attempted to cleanse Handover of every Fairy Elf who'd migrated there centuries ago, his Scorpents urged every captured Elfie up the ridge that led to the peak, and from there, the Scorpents pushed every prisoner over the edge. Whether Falstaff's family already resided in that vicinity during this heinous crime, nobody knew.

"You don't even have the exact location of this Mosche's home?" Miranda jerked her head toward Jules, as if challenging him.

"Maybe we should shut your mouth, too."

"Tell him, Hooks," Miranda said. "He doesn't realize how huge this waterfall is. We could wander for days and never find his Mosche. And for what? What if his grandpa's not there? What if Mosche's not there? I have a better plan."

"Do we have a rag or something, Holden?"

"Don't drag me into this." Holden hurried his steps, his hobbling less awkward now, and the web bridge swung wildly as he thumped past Jules and Miranda.

"She might've gotten your mother killed, and you don't want to be dragged into this?"

"I just don't want to have anything to do with her."

"How long should we continue on the bridges, Hooks?"

"The map says to continue till Crick Hollow. That should flow further north, and it cuts Brooke Beginning almost perpendicular."

Despite the lemony scent of pine needles around him, Jules still felt nauseated, as if the smell of death clung to his pores. Or perhaps it was the wind rocking the bridge to and fro. A mountain higher than any other in Handover peeked between the foliage, spewing thick, black smoke. Palms sweaty, Jules gripped an overhang and hoisted himself up a branch.

"What's that summit over there? Looks like it's on fire." Jules pointed to the East.

"You must mean Blood Ridge. It's a volcano." Hooks didn't even climb up to see what Jules was talking about.

"How come we didn't notice it before?"

"Legend says it's always covered behind thick clouds, but on a clear day like today you can see it if you're high enough as we are now."

"Know of anyone who's been there?"

"It's not a place you want to get near, not that it's easy to get there," Hooks said. "I don't think any Handoverans have ever made it there and back alive."

"That's where Gehzurolle throws in his traitors?" Miranda said.

Jules hopped back down and shot her a glare. "And his servants." They locked eyes, and she quickly looked away.

64.
GIFT

THE BRIDGE BROUGHT them to the upper reaches, where the foliage grew densest and the crisp wind came in drifts and swayed the boughs in a rhythmic wave. On and on, they stumbled and scampered until they saw a wooden landing between two stout tree limbs.

When Jules saw the large figure perched on the branch just above the landing he drew in his breath, not believing his eyes.

"Fiesty?"

If it wasn't for a blue ribbon dangling from one of his six legs he wouldn't have thought it possible. Even Miranda's eyes were large as saucers.

The dragonfly dipped his head as Jules reached out and touched one of its wings. The fly's multi-facetted eyes glimmered in the afternoon sun. It was obvious this was not the same Feisty that Tst Tst found as a nymph and raised as their pet. His gossamer wings were bedraggled, and he had lost a leg! Yet the blue ribbon was clearly one of those used to attach Fiesty.

"What happened, Fiesty?" Jules shook his head sadly at him.

"How'd he even find us?" Miranda came up and stood next to Jules. "It's not like we're in your backyard or something."

Jules stared at Fiesty's stub where his leg was missing, then turned to Miranda. "Did you send the ravens to eat us? Did you do this to him? Did you?"

She shrank back. "Maybe if you're a little nicer, I'll tell you a secret."

Jules stared at his feet and counted to ten in his head. He even recited verses his Grandpa Leroy taught him. Grandpa told him the ancient verses could help. Could it take away the utter contempt he now felt for Miranda? How could his feelings turn against her so quickly? How could he have liked a deceiver? How could Miranda have deceived him?

Fiesty still perched on the branch. It was unlike him to not flit about. Jules turned to him and motioned with his fingers. "Tst Tst and Tippy would be glad to see you, Fiesty. How'd you find me?" He reached into his pocket and felt Abel's whistle. Could that have summoned Fiesty? Then he noticed the knot on the blue ribbon, and something white poking from within it.

Paper? Fingers trembling, he loosened the knot and slipped out the note. He recognized the swirly loops of the p's and g's. It was his mother's writing—no mistaking it. When Jules read the message, he didn't know what to do.

Dear J, any of my dear children, or any Elfie who can help:

I hope Fiesty has found you. The enemies have Mrs. L and I as prisoners, and although we are safe for now, I don't know how long we will remain here before they transport us elsewhere. The little I overheard points to Handover, possibly Euruliaf. Gehzurolle wants us. He is looking for the five Keepers and our Books. Our captors have our Books—Mrs. L's and mine. They have only allowed us possession once. They (and we don't know who they are but they are not Scorpents, maybe they're Hanfies) promise to reunite us with our Books at the end of our journey.

I don't know if I am in Reign or Handover. I was unconscious when they brought me here, as was Mrs. L, and when we regained consciousness, we found ourselves together in a dungeon under a tree with a tiny gape at the very top to let sunlight in. That's when I saw Fiesty.

J, trust no one. A traitor is in our midst. You must find his/her identity for you need to warn the other Keepers. I overheard that only three are left. Tell them to stay away and not be deceived by the charms of this traitor.

Gehzurolle plans for us five to gather together to decipher the codes within our Books to find something long lost. He is also gathering crystals to assemble the last gift. I cannot say it here, but I found out what the gift was when Mrs. L and I read our Books together last night. All these years and I knew so little.

J, hide R and the girls. They are looking for something in our home, but I don't know what. Run. Hide. And if you can, find the remaining Keepers and warn them.

Mrs. L hopes H is with you.

Find Dad, and warn him. I heard his name mentioned and worry he is in trouble. They might desire to annihilate the entire Blaze household because of me. I must stop writing now. I hear them coming.

No matter what happens, I love you all.

Mom (E B–L)

E B–L is Erin Blaze-Leroy.

Jules stared at the paper for a few moments. *Gift?*

Different rumors had circulated about what it could have been, but when the ancient Keeper Falstaff left Reign centuries ago, he brought the gift with him, and the secret died with him.

Jules slumped his shoulders and wondered about the other Keepers. One must be Saul. Mosche could be the fourth. But who was the fifth? And how could Jules find out?

Holden nudged him. "What is it?" He peered over at the open note still in Jules's grasp.

"Read it aloud!" Jules shoved the note at Holden and cast a glance at Miranda. Was she the traitor his mother was referring to? She betrayed Mrs. L to whatever force it was that kidnapped her. And whoever it was also kidnapped his mother. Was it Whisperer? Would Miranda even tell the truth if asked? His heart sank.

His mother must not be with Mosche. Unless Mosche was in it, too. Did Mosche lure Grandpa Leroy as well? But if Mosche was a Keeper he'd never make a pact with the Enemy. Or would he? Miranda did, and maybe even her mother before her, if she'd survived this long in Handover without her Book. Was the captor a Hanfie—a half-breed?

Miranda touched his arm, and Jules jerked back.

"I'm not the traitor," she said.

"And I'm not a fool."

"This *gift*—I know something that can help," Miranda said. "It's a chest in my mother's house. I think it has pieces of the gift. Help me find it. Her cottage is in the pomegranate grove. You're wasting your time looking for this Mosche."

They locked eyes for a long moment. Her blue eyes turned green and sparkled like emeralds. Her soft hair flopped over one eye, and Jules almost brushed it aside for her as he'd done so many times when they talked by the tree stump in his backyard.

Jules pressed his lips together and swallowed. "This grove—is it near the waterfall?"

"It's in Glennora. Let me see your map. I can say if we're close." She smiled and edged toward him.

Jules looked up and noticed Hooks studying him. He thought Hooks shook his head slightly.

"What chest?" Jules handed her the map.

"My mother carried our family heirloom to Handover. Grandpa Saul said she stole some ancient pieces from him when she snuck away a long time ago. I think this must be it."

"How can this chest, or this gift, whatever it is, help *me*?"

Miranda glanced at the foliage above and drew closer to Jules. "The forest has ears. But," she leaned towards Jules's ear. "Gehzurolle would be willing to trade the gift for anything. For your mother's life and mine and Mrs. L's."

"And you know this because?"

"I overheard, when I snuck into Euruliaf. I almost got away, too, but they caught up in Heritage and caught me, and said I knew too much."

Hooks stepped toward them and coughed. "I've heard of Glennora. I don't think we want to go there. It's too close to Euruliaf, and if the Scorpents want to ambush us that would be a perfect place to overcome us."

"Precisely. That's why my mother chose it. They'd never guess she lived so close," Miranda said. "It's a day's walk to Euruliaf. I've never been to Glenorra, but I heard it's beautiful."

Hooks cleared his throat loudly. "And if the Scorpents want to trap us, Glennora has numerous ideal spots for a surprise attack. I have heard stories of Scorpents boasting of the area."

"Jules, Hooks has a point," Holden said.

Jules ran his hand through his blonde hair that had grown shaggy during the past few weeks. It felt sticky with sweat and grime. The dip in the pond hadn't been sufficient. A long bath infused with lavender and heather flowers might take away the smell.

"Let's get to Roaring Falls first. I need to think this through," Jules said.

Miranda stood up, kicked at a stone and skulked away. She turned and looked at Jules. "If you think you'll find your Grandpa Leroy with Mosche, you'll be sorely disappointed."

65.
FATAL FALL

IT TOOK ALL of him to not slap her. Jules held his breath and spun Miranda around. "What d'ya mean by 'sorely disappointed?'"

"Leave her be, Jules," Holden said. "She's upset she's not getting her way as she's used to."

"Think what you like," Miranda said. "But you'll be sorry you ignored me."

"What do you mean, Miranda?" Hooks said.

"His grandparents are dead! Dead! Drowned. Happy?"

Jules dashed toward her and shoved her shoulder so hard she fell backwards.

"Enough!" Hooks rushed to Miranda and gave her a helping hand. "You sure understand the art of provoking, Elfie girl. These are your friends."

"Friends? They are no friends."

"You are blind, girl," Hooks said, softly. "You don't know the value of a friend. How can you be so cold about it—even if it's true?"

"It *is* true." Miranda was crying, now. "And I would have said it sooner, but I couldn't bring myself to say it because I knew it would hurt him."

Jules grabbed his sack. "Don't believe a liar. Let's go, Holden." But his heart felt like it had been torn out of his chest. The broken lantern, the water-stained letter in Starkies' drawer, they must speak of Grandpa's doom. Jules stalked to Miranda and tightened the bind around her wrists.

"Ouch! It's hurting me."

"A stone heart cannot feel pain."

"Jules, look!" Holden pulled himself up to the branch and stood next to Fiesty. "Fire!"

Fiesty took off from his perch and flitted above Holden's head.

"How far is it?" Jules asked.

"Can't tell. Lots of black smoke."

"Is it coming this way?" Hooks, too, hauled himself and stood next to Holden. "It's east of us. Could be from Heritage. I hope it's not near my place. Doesn't look like it's coming our way."

"Where's Fiesty?" Jules looked about.

But Fiesty was gone.

"The last time Fiesty acted strange, ravens attacked us."

Holden and Hooks slid and jumped down from the branch.

"You don't say," Holden said.

"We'd better get going," Jules said.

But a buzz of wings alerted him and he scanned the upper reaches. Just as he motioned for Miranda to start walking, a dark cloud overshadowed the platform they stood on and Fiesty landed next to them. But not just Fiesty. He arrived with four of the largest dragonflies Jules had ever seen. What could this mean? Fiesty hobbled toward Jules on his five legs, his gait unsteady.

"If I didn't know better I'd say he wants us to ride his friends," Miranda spoke for the first time since her fight with Jules.

"We can't ride them!" Jules said. "It's safer to walk the bridges. Don't think I'll loosen your bindings even *if* we're riding them." To Fiesty, he said, "Follow us with your friends."

But Fiesty nudged him just like he did on that afternoon before the ravens appeared. Back then they thought Fiesty was insane.

Now Jules and the others trudged a few steps, but Fiesty didn't make an effort to follow. His winged friends stood erect on the platform, too, as though waiting for instructions. Their bluish-green wings caught the rays.

Jules turned and motioned to Fiesty.

"Maybe he's warning you, like the last time," Miranda said.

"If I wanted your opinion, I'd ask," Jules said. "Thank you very much."

"If my life wasn't at stake, I wouldn't suggest it. But I don't want to end up dead on account of your stupidity."

Hooks hurried to catch up with the boys and said, "Maybe we should look into Miranda's suggestion."

"I'm grateful for your help so far," Jules said to Hooks. "But this is our burden—mine and Holden's." He pointed to Miranda. "She's the reason our families' lives are at stake, so I'll handle this *my* way." He stalked off, shoving the small of Miranda's back. "Let's go!"

What happened next went so fast nobody had time to react. The web bridge shook violently, and the branch the bridge was secured to gave way with a loud *crack! Whack!*

Jules grabbed for the railing of the bridge, but that gave way, too, and he found himself free falling, one hand grasping his sack, the other grasping the severed railing. Where was Holden? He turned and saw Holden, further up, clinging to the railing like himself. But Miranda and Hooks must have fallen all the way down. He saw no trace of them. The thrust of the falling branch broke the web bridge in half. Jules and Holden were on the upper half still connected to the platform they'd been on. But Miranda and Hooks, who'd stood a little ahead, dropped with the branch to the forest below.

66.
GIVE UP

"HOOKS! MIRANDA!" JULES transferred the sack to his teeth. With his now free hand, he grasped the twine, realizing that the only way to safety for him and Holden was to make their way up the swaying twine back toward the platform between the branches that were still secured to the tree.

Holden already started the slow climb using his knees to clench the rope and pulling himself up using the knots on the web twine as footholds.

Jules followed suit. He didn't think he'd ever make it to the platform but, after what felt like hours, he heaved himself up and, sitting on the platform, he panted and peered at the ground. Beside him, Holden rubbed his red knees and rope-burnt hands.

"I slipped a few times," Holden confessed.

"Me too."

"Do you think Hooks and Miranda made it down safely?'

Jules gulped and avoided Holden's eyes. "I don't know."

"What should we do?"

"I don't know." He wished Holden would stop asking. He didn't want to be the leader anymore. Didn't want the mission. Didn't want to think. He sat there like a stone.

"Hey, don't space out on me."

Jules didn't answer.

"Jules! You can't do this."

"It's my fault they fell." Jules's voice was flat and barely above a whisper.

"Look!" Holden pointed.

When Jules looked up he saw Fiesty hovering above him. Fiesty's four friends flitted about between the foliage. But Jules still didn't respond.

"Let see if they'll come to us. We can ride them."

"Don't remind me."

"If you're not going to say or do anything, I have no choice but to act for the both of us."

"Whatever."

"Jules, grow up. Stop thinking about yourself. Isn't that what you told me? This is not about you. Or me. Our moms' lives are at stake. Maybe even Ralston's and Tippy's and Tst Tst's and Bitha's. Maybe even Mosche's. Reign needs us. We should act like Keepers—not just say we are."

"I never asked to be born a Keeper."

"Well, me neither. But facts are facts."

"You go, Holden. You ride Fiesty. Or his friend. I just want to sit here and wait."

"For what? For Gehzurolle and his forces to get you? That's it? Give up?"

"Miranda was right. My grandparents are dead. I guess I sorta knew. But I didn't want to accept it. Why are we going to Mosche? What good can we do?"

"Didn't you read your mother's letter? If he's a Keeper we need to warn him—even if your mom or mine are not there."

"Mosche's lived decades without our help. His family lived centuries without our help—"

"But he wrote to your Grandpa. Don't let your Grandpa die in vain. Something good must surely come of all this!" Holden waved his hand at the foliage above. Fiesty swooped down and landed next to Jules, wings spread open.

Jules stroked the dragonfly's wing. Delicate like lace. What possessed the King to breed this giant specie? He'd tried riding Fiesty before. In their backyard. In secret, of course. He'd straddled Fiesty, his legs on either side as he sat right behind his pet's head. They'd flown high enough to know it could be done. He turned to Holden.

"I'd known my grandpa must have drowned since Abel told me about the sardius. That red crystal Tippy found—that flash I saw that night—they were related. Grandpa Leroy was the important Elfie who died. And I was a fool not to put two and two together."

"You'd be a bigger fool to sit here and rot. Miranda was right about you."

"What she say?"

"Forget it. We're wasting time. I'm looking for Miranda and Hooks, and leaving you to weep like the willows."

"Hey!"

But Holden had already grabbed his meager belongings in his satchel and approached a dragonfly perched next to Fiesty. He touched the dragonfly's back, the part just behind its bulbous head.

"It's too bristly," Jules said. "You'd need to lay something on it or you'd scratch your thighs bad."

Holden cast him a sidewise glance.

"I rode Fiesty before," Jules said.

"I thought you were afraid of heights."

"We didn't get high. In fact, we're a lot higher on these trees now."

Holden pulled a spare pillowcase from his sack and laid it on the spot he planned to sit on.

"Wait!" Jules said.

"If I don't go now they could die, or maybe I'm already too late." Holden heaved himself onto the dragonfly's neck.

"What did Miranda say about me?"

"That you're too in love with yourself to notice her." And he shoved his heel into the dragonfly's flank. "I'll call you Bristles." He patted his ride's head between its green-blue eyes.

Jules wrapped his palms over the crown of his head. *Too in love with myself to notice her? What could possess her to say that?* A tear dripped from the tip of his nose, and he wiped it with the back of his hand. *What's the point of crying? I'm probably too late. For Miranda, for Hooks, for Mother, and definitely, for Grandpa and Grandma. And who knew how Dad was faring?*

"It's never too late, Jules." a melodic voice said.

Jules swiveled his head left and right. *Who said that?* The voice seemed vaguely familiar. But no one was there. Even Holden had taken off with all the dragonflies.

"Who's there?"

But only the wind answered as it whistled through the leaves in the upper reaches. Jules laid prostrate on the platform, resting his weight on his elbows and leaning over the platform to look for Holden.

It was a long way down. The sunlight filtered through the leaves and flickered like golden ballerinas twirling all about him. Even if Holden was in his line of sight, he'd never be able to discern him with how the light played tricks on his eyes. If one of the dragonflies returned, would he even dare to ride it all the way down?

Jules could see why Miranda preferred Holden to him. For all of Holden's plainness he'd proved himself reliable and trustworthy. And brave. Jules tried to make the right choices, the difficult choices. But Miranda's words cut too deep. He should have listened to her. They should have left on those dragonflies, instead of relying on his pigheadedness. And now Miranda and Hooks had to pay the price for his poor decision. His pride.

Jules leaned over the platform and squinted. Surely he must be able to sight the glint of a dragonfly wing or something. But the sunlight dazzled his eyes, and the glitter neither confirmed nor denied that Holden was still flying on his dragonfly steed.

Jules sat back up and hugged his knees to his chest. In a million years, he never imagined he'd sit alone in the middle of a forest—in Handover, no less—bereft of family, friends, and even a pet.

A cold wind blew and a chill ran up his spine. Jules wrapped his still stinky cloak tightly about him, and that was when he felt the lump in his pocket. He drew it out. The whistle Abel gave him. The soundless one that didn't even squeak.

He blew into it since there was nothing left to lose and nothing to do but blow his rage into the useless piece of wood. Blow and blow until his lungs felt like deflated balloons and the muscles in his cheeks ached. Blow until there was no breath left in him. He clutched the whistle so hard it left grooves in his fingers.

And he would have gone on blowing until he passed out except a violent gust shook the platform, rattled it and almost swept Jules off. Alarmed, Jules looked up. It looked like night had suddenly cloaked the land, and he was plunged into darkness.

67.
KING STAR

HAD A RAIN cloud propelled itself toward this part of the forest? Jules looked about. It was suddenly dark. Was this a natural occurrence? Was it a storm? But more than gusts, the flapping of a million wings, or so it seemed, resounded all about Jules.

He squinted and saw what looked like butterflies, by the thousands, storming into his midst, their wings, even in the dimness, shimmering like magic. Jules gasped. Dust from their wings swirled about him.

The largest butterfly he'd ever seen swooped and landed next to him, wings pumping. That was when Jules remembered the wooden whistle still clutched tightly in his fist.

He studied it and shifted his gaze to the butterfly. Could it have summoned this cloud of butterflies? And maybe even Fiesty and his friends when he'd blown it when he was with Hooks? Winged animals of giant species? Was that what this whistle called forth?

Jules cautiously slipped the whistle into his pocket and grabbed his sack. From it he drew out a twine and, amidst the batting of wings circling above, he edged toward the sole butterfly eyeing him with large bulbous eyes of green and black pattern, fringed with short feathery protrusions. He'd never seen a butterfly so up close. From the markings, he gathered this was a monarch, albeit a giant one. Monarchs were known for their ability to fly hundreds of miles without stopping.

He expected the monarch to jerk back or maybe even dip its head ferociously toward him as he inched his arm out slowly to it, but the insect remained as still as marble. He wasn't sure how he was to harness the butterfly's spindly body with his web twine but figured if he didn't secure himself to it he might fall to his doom once they flew. For now Jules was certain he must fly. But if his experience of maneuvering a dragonfly was slim, his expertise with butterflies ran even slimmer.

When he determined he couldn't quite reach around its neck, or what seemed like a neck, he placed a firm hand on its bodice and hitched himself up onto the crook between the head and the body where the forewings attached. Just as he leaned forward to secure the twine, one hand grasping his sack, the butterfly thrust its wings upward and Jules toppled backward. Before he knew it, they were airborne. And all the other butterflies were swarming behind them.

How to steer this thing?

Jules balanced himself as best he could and shut his lids tight, until he realized it wouldn't matter if he fell with his eyes closed or opened. A fall was a fall. At least butterflies didn't flit as speedily as dragonflies would have done. Jules's eyes adjusted to the dimness of the forest as evening came, and he leaned forward and scoured the forest floor as the butterfly dipped and glided over the lower bushes and undergrowth. Behind them, trailing in a single file, the butterflies of varied hues and sizes aligned themselves as they flapped their colorful wings.

If Jules hadn't been so worried he'd have enjoyed the sight. Where was Holden? Had he located Miranda and Hooks? If only he'd insisted on Hooks returning to his wife.

Night was fast approaching. Between the foliage the stars above twinkled happily as though no trouble existed in the world. How could they be so cheerful?

His mind flitted to the story of the King and the star. It seemed a long time ago when Grandpa Leroy read about the King who'd created their Race. And of how, when the King had completed his Book with his own blood that late night, he'd returned to his home in the sky and was birthed into a star.

Early that morning their Kingdom's astronomers detected that star and named it "King Star." It twinkled brighter than all others. Was that why the King never returned?

Lost travelers used that prominent King Star as a guide to find their way. It always appeared west of the moon. Jules rummaged in his cloak and took out Abel's crude map. If he couldn't locate Holden maybe he could still find Mosche. If he could identify his location using the stars maybe he'd know where the waterfall lay.

The other butterflies must have flown away as he found himself alone with his ride who insisted on soaring higher now instead of taking them aground. Jules studied the sky and identified the different constellations—the Lion, the Eagle, the Bear, the Woman—easily enough, but not that bright star that could guide him.

Where was the King Star? Jules had wondered how the King Star was related to the red crystal. Now he knew. And it made sense. All the pieces fitted together. At least he understood the flash-in-the-sky mystery—the King Star had given birth to the red crystal as a token to commemorate the passing of a Keeper. And Gehzurolle found it satisfying to gloat on this, hence his insatiable desire to collect each token as a memento of his hatred of Elfies. Particularly Keepers. Ever since the King entrusted them with the Books, and especially, the gift.

As he kept looking up Jules thought he saw a shooting star but wasn't sure—was this a good omen? Of hope? When there seemed to be none?

In the quiet, the bubbling of a river jolted him. Jules craned his neck and twisted his torso to identify the gurgling source. A silver patch peeked between a few lone cypresses ahead.

Brooke Beginning? Or was this some other river? Crick Hollow? Or River Run? Although those were supposed to snake deeper into Handover, encroaching Euruliaf, Gehzurolle's capital.

If I landed I might get a reference point.

A rustling of leaves made him swivel his head at the boughs behind him, but nothing became apparent. Was someone following him?

Eventually, he managed to persuade the monarch to fly him to the river's edge and to sail down onto a log on the bank.

Where to now?

But a nagging uneasiness bugged him. He slipped off the monarch and stood on the log, his hand gripping the map.

If the River was Brooke Beginning he could follow it north and find the rivulet to the waterfall. He might even be able to hear its roar.

To his horror, when he turned to climb back onto the monarch he found the butterfly gone.

I'm in the middle of nowhere.

Jules was just about to jump off the log when the log moved.

Oh, no! Not again. He wanted to slap himself for not having learnt his lesson. An alligator. And a speedy one at that. Something must have scared the reptile as it burst into the water with a ferocious spurt and submerged its head. Jules clung with all his might to the rough scaly back but he lost his grip and toppled into the fast flowing water.

68.
UNDER WATER

WHEN JULES WAS absolutely certain he was dead, he opened his eyes underwater. It was dark and murky, filled with lots of woody pieces floating here and there.

I need to breathe!

His lungs felt like bursting but even with all the kicking he couldn't rise to gulp air. He looked up and saw the underbelly of the alligator. Maybe he stood a better chance staying below. His mind flitted to his grandparents.

When he thought of them he forgot he was afraid of the Brooke.

The current bore him to the far right, where a pinpoint of light shone. He scissor-kicked his legs as best he could and used his arms to push the water to get to the top. He never thought he could swim, but he actually made some progress. But the current, too strong, sucked him in another direction.

When his head smacked into something hard, he groped about hoping to grab something he could use to pull himself up and out of the water, his sense of direction gone haywire. Soon his fingers found a ledge above the waterline. He thought about the possibility of some evil waiting for him there, but by now his lungs felt like bursting. He grabbed the ledge and hauled his weight up with all his strength. After the scramble up he lay on the ledge, flat on his back, chest heaving. He held his sides and took measured breaths. His lungs ached. His head felt light.

When he sat up and glanced about, he noticed two torches enclosed in an onion shaped crystal cover lighting the cave. Were these the lights he'd spotted? What was this cave? He sloshed toward a torch, his boots wet and heavy, and on tiptoes tried to reach for the torch but it was too high up the wall. The underwater cave was damp, but at least it wasn't submerged. Did someone live here?

I can't stay here forever like a river rat!

Something about the light reminded him of Arnett, the nymph of the Brooke, and what she'd showed him. Was this *that* underwater cave? He recognized the onion shape of the torch covers. Made of hexagonal-cut crystals, like miniature honeycombs, the covers threw light in a hundred different directions in the cave. Each torch turned out to be a single taper burning bright. When Jules stepped farther into the cave he noticed more taper torches hung at intervals and leading into a dim tunnel.

Had Arnett created this tunnel? Was this a dream? Slowly he walked up the dim passage, following the lighted path, until the gurgling of rushing water attracted him. Minutes later, the dimly lit tunnel dead ended at an underground channel of water.

Now what? How did I get myself into this?

Water flowed from one side of the opening on the cave wall into another in the opposite side. The water, some kind of underwater spring, must be coming from a source high in the mountain and flowing down to this cave.

Jules bent his knees and poked his head into one of the openings of the underwater stream but the crawlspace on both sides wasn't big enough for him to crouch or squeeze into. Only a small gap spanned the rapid current and the ceiling of both tunnels.

Sharp stones will shred me to pieces if I swam in there. I was lucky I didn't drown the first time.

He sighed and slumped onto the stone floor, except the stony ground didn't feel hard and wet the way stone floors should. Something soft and springy lay beneath him. He rolled the springy substance to the nearest torch, stared at the padded object, and scratched his head.

It was a large cocoon; intact, except for a hole at the very tip. And not just any cocoon either. If his entomological studies proved correct, this was an abandoned overwinter cocoon, which meant one thing about its casing. It should be waterproof. But there would be only one way to prove this.

Rummaging about his soaked cloak he found the mirror shard with the '—ook within' message. He slit the cocoon lengthwise near the top. It was light. He hoisted it to the edge of the swift waters of the underground stream, slithered, feet first, into the opening he'd made, and with eyes squeezed shut, sank deeper into the casing. Once inside, he pulled the opening closed and wiggled the cocoon closer to the water's edge. The rushing water was right next to him now. He rolled off the edge and splashed into the stream. In the water, the cocoon bobbed before hurtling down stream.

I hope I don't drown!

69.
SURPRISE VISIT

FAR AWAY, NEAR the bank of Brooke Beginning, Tennesson lingered over his freshly brewed tea—ground chrysanthemum petals steeped in boiling water. Scalding, just the way he liked it. He hoped it would take away the migraine. Where were those kids?

"Enjoying it piping hot, even after so many years?" The voice was soft, melodious, yet Tennesson jerked up as though an arrow had pierced his heart.

He squinted at the figure by his doorway and blinked a few times. His breathing slowed until he forgot to breathe altogether.

"How did you?" He heard his voice, hollow. "Who are you?" A million other questions stabbed him, but he just gaped at the slender figure in the gray green cloak by his door, standing as still as alabaster with a face almost as pale.

"I'd imagined this meeting a thousand times over but it never quite went this way. I guess life always has an extra something that can throw one off course."

"Are you real?" Tennesson sucked in his breath and started breathing again. How had he not heard the warning bells?

As though reading his mind, the visitor said, "I've known about your bell system for a while. Each time I get close I wonder if seeing you again was best. But I have no choice now and desperately need your help."

Tennesson rubbed his eyes. Something he felt he should have done from the beginning. Ghosts were not real.

Again, as though knowing his every wave of thought, "You think I'm an apparition?" The figure reached out her pale arm, lithe but sinewy, from beneath the gray cloak. "Touch and see. Although I realize once you find the truth you might never forgive me. Or want to see me."

Tennesson took three steps forward and touched the pale limb. He gasped. "But it cannot be."

"I'm sorry." She nodded. "I did it for you and for our baby."

"Baby?"

"I have much to explain, but we don't have time. Our baby—she, she's sixteen actually, and she's in terrible danger."

"Wait. Sixteen? Who? We have a child together?" Tennesson's voice grew harder with each word. "Luella, I thought you were dead."

"And in some ways I have been. I had to make them, and you, believe I was dead. It was for your own good."

"Don't tell me what's for my own good. Living in misery was for my own good? Why did you leave me? Deceive me?"

Luella glided to the dining chair, still the same one she was used to before she had up and left, and made it seem the Scorpents had whisked her away. She sat on its edge. She patted the dining table top lightly. "Sit for a bit. I cannot excuse my deception, but if you'll give me five minutes, I'll explain why I left."

Tennesson eyed her hands and noticed the ring still on her fourth finger. He sat opposite her.

"Remember the day Gehzurolle sent the edict for Scorpents to get us?"

"I couldn't forget if I tried. And I've tried."

70.
WHAT HAPPENED

"I WAS TENDING the butterflies in our garden when I overheard Scorpents lurking. I guess I have feelers for them or something. I meant to leave you a message, but I didn't have time, so I thought I'd return later. But I must have passed out in the hole I was hiding in.

"When I came to, someone had moved me to his home. An elderly Elfie who lived in a tree. He made me look at his candles and it cured me, at least temporarily, until I started to feel queasy again and again. Even watching the candle all day and all night didn't help. I didn't know I was going to have a baby."

"Our baby?" Tennesson straightened in his chair.

Luella nodded and wrung her hands. "By that time I knew our baby would never be safe in Handover. The Elfie—Abel's his name—helped me with the baby till she was strong enough for me to take her to my childhood home in Reign. I meant to leave her there and return home to you, except...." She looked at her fingernails as though studying them with care. "I have a secret that could endanger you by my coming home."

"Yet it's all right to lie to me?"

She shook her head slightly and avoided his eyes. "There's something I should have told you from the beginning. When I left Reign, it wasn't just my father I was running from. I was running away from my inheritance."

"Most people run *toward* their inheritance."

"Not this one. At least that was what I felt then. But things are different now. It's been different for a while, and I'm trying to right my wrongs." She reached out and grasped Tennesson's wrist on the table. "My father is a Keeper. Which makes me his heir."

Tennesson shifted in his seat. Suddenly, he felt inundated with Keepers. "And is that so bad? Being a Keeper?"

"Bad—that was what I felt. Scorpents killed my mother because she wasn't careful and had roamed to Handover looking for herbs. If she wasn't from a Keeper family she wouldn't have been such a target."

"Is that why you roamed to Handover too? To become a target?"

"I came here for a better life. I thought I'd be safer here if nobody knew I was Keeper material. But you can never really escape who you are, you know. My mother shouldn't have come here, especially without the Book."

"But *you* came without your—Book?"

"Yes, but when I delivered my daughter, our daughter, to my father for safekeeping, I stole his Book and returned to Handover. I figured he was smart enough not to leave Reign without it. Anyway, the Book's why I was able to survive all these years. The Book and a lot of hiding kept me alive."

"So, you came back to Handover to return to me except you had to wait sixteen years to do so?" Tennesson sipped his cooled tea.

"I have my reasons for leaving Reign."

"And so why is our daughter in danger now? Gehzurolle found out she's Book-less, so to speak?"

"Worse. She's in Handover—searching for me. Or so Abel said. And Scorpents have sent her to a death pit. You know what that means?" Her voice broke.

"Everyone with a brain knows what those pits mean. But are you sure?"

Luella reached into her cloak and brought out a paper. She unfolded it and laid it on the table. "Abel drew me this map. His *friends* told him the possible sites."

"If Abel has so many friends, why didn't you ask them for help?"

"They're not Elfies, or even Hanfies—"

"Handoverans? He can't trust them? So, maybe they lied—"

"Not even Handoverans. They didn't lie—couldn't lie. They're squirrels."

Tennesson's eyes grew wide, and he pushed the map back toward Luella. "Perhaps your life of deception has affected you more than you realize."

"Just because you can't understand doesn't mean it's not real, or true, Tene. Abel talks with them with whistles—I don't comprehend it all, my-self. " She looked about the room. "There's something else I lied about."

Tennesson swiveled his head and glanced at the front flap door. "Don't tell me—you're working for Gehzurolle."

She stood and stuffed the map back into her cloak. "I guess it was a mistake coming here, hoping you'd help. I don't blame you, but, no, I would never work for Gehzurolle."

"Luella?" He locked eyes with her.

She chewed her lower lip. "That's just it. I'm not Luella."

Tennesson's eyes narrowed.

"Ahh, you're an imposter? I could live better with that."

"Luella's not my real name. I'm Chrystle, daughter of Saul Turpentine, whom you know is a Keeper."

"Saul? Saul Turpentine?" Tennesson said the name as if he was in a trance. "I know that name!" He stood and his chair almost toppled. "Those Elfie kids who were here." He stared at Chrystle as though she'd gone mad. Before she could interrupt he told her of Jules and his siblings. "I was just thinking, worrying, for them, when I saw you at the door."

"Tene, we must help them. Abel said she could be with them. Maybe they're caught, too. Help her, our daughter."

"What—what's her name?"

"I thought you'd never ask. Miranda."

Tennesson stared at the ground for a long time. "Miranda," he muttered.

"You know the terrain better than anyone. If anyone can find the pits it's you. The Scorpents threw her in there yesterday, or the day before. Please."

"I'm too old for traipsing around, Lu—I mean, Chrystle, or whatever your name is."

"If you can't do it for me, do it for her. Because if you don't…."

"Where would we even start, assuming you're telling the truth?"

"I know the Scorpents who took her. I heard where they're heading. If we catch up with them they might clue us in—maybe I can spy on them. But I can't do this alone. And I have no one else. Abel refuses to leave his drey."

"Show me that map." Tennesson reached his arms toward her. "I can't promise anything. But I'd like to help those Elfie kids, too. They asked me before, but for some reason I felt I should stay here." He looked at Chrystle.

71.
SCORPENT VISIT

BACK AT STARKIES'S home, Ralston pulled Bitha aside and whispered, "We better hide. I overheard something awful."

With eyes round like the moon she'd just been staring at, Bitha turned to Ralston. "You're scaring me."

"Shh!" Ralston pointed to Tst Tst and Tippy playing with two strange wooden toys that looked like life-sized dolls with yellow yarn hair. Tippy even dressed one with her cloak pretending it was her twin. Starkies had passed the toys to them to keep them quiet as Ralston worked on his drawing for Starkies, and Bitha dusted the furniture. "Let's move so Starkies can't hear."

They sidled to a long counter in the corner filled with antiques and artifacts Ralston couldn't put names to and squatted behind the counter, Ralston always turning his head to eye Starkies.

"Those visitors Starkies had, well, they weren't traders or even customers. They were informers, maybe spies."

"What do you mean?"

Ralston pulled Bitha closer to him and into her ear said, "They were warning Starkies that soldiers or Scorpents are on their way here. That's why Starkies shouted at Tippy. I think he's scared, too."

"Did he mention us to them?"

"They talked in low voices. The only reason I heard was because I was fiddling with Grandpa's broken lamp and I must have turned it on and was walking by, but Starkies didn't see me. Neither did his informers."

"You fixed it?"

"I guess so. And there's something else. Something terrible."

Bitha stared at him with big eyes. "What?"

"The spies, they had two dragonfly lanterns with them—looked just like ours."

"You mean?" She stared at him with knowing eyes.

Ralston nodded. "Jules's. But let's not tell the girls." Ralston jerked his head to where Tippy and Tst Tst sat playing. "I hid the lantern I'd mended in the cellar."

"That's stealing!" She wagged her finger at him.

"It's self protection. We don't know that Starkies won't sell us off to Scorpents if he's threatened. Sure, he wants the crystal Jules promised, but surely not at the expense of his life."

Bitha's brows twisted with worry lines. "You think Jules got to Mosche's safely? I had a bad dream about him."

"It doesn't look good if they'd lost the lanterns. We must make a plan in case Jules gets delayed or if he's—"

A loud rap on the counter jolted Bitha and Ralston.

"Where," Starkies said, "are you, Ralston? Am I keeping a free boarding house here, with no one bothering with expenses? Where's that portrait I need?"

Ralston held his breath and wondered if they should just pop out from behind the counter. He scanned the long surface cluttered with items and noticed some artwork lying against a wall at the one end of the counter. If he could crawl there alone he could pretend he was in deep thought gazing at the art. It wouldn't do to raise Starkies's suspicion that he was plotting anything with Bitha. Desperate times call for desperate measures, he pacified himself. He brought his finger to his lip and gestured for Bitha to stay while he crawled quietly to the stacks of artwork.

"Ralston!" Starkies boomed out.

Tippy and Tst Tst shrieked and jerked their heads toward the angry Starkies. He turned to them. "Do you know where your brother is?"

They shook their heads, but then Tippy said, "There!" She pointed to Ralston, who'd stood up near the end of the counter, away from Bitha.

"Why didn't you answer, boy?"

"I was—" Ralston brought out a framed portrait of a woman by his side. She looked familiar. "Who's this?" he blurted before he could stop himself.

"Never mind that. I need you kids to stay in the cellar this evening. I'm expecting company, and it wouldn't do to have Elfie smells around."

Ralston nodded.

After a quick dinner of dried bread and even drier fruit pieces that tasted bitter and a cup of thin soup that tasted like dishwater, at least in Tst Tst's opinion, Starkies rushed them downstairs. "Hurry!"

"How long will your guests be here?" Ralston said.

But then loud knocks were heard.

"Stay here," Starkies hissed and took three steps at a time back up to the living area before they could even say yes. A loud click told them he'd locked them in.

Bitha tugged at Ralston's cloak. "What if he brings the Scorpents down here?"

72.
TRICKED

THE SECRET CELL was still as miserable as ever, smelling even stronger of mothballs and mold, but somehow Ralston felt hopeful. Of course, Starkies mustn't come back down or his scheme would be ruined.

"I have a plan. Where's Tippy?" Ralston glanced at Tst Tst.

"It's as you instructed, mi-lord!" Tst Tst bowed deeply.

Bitha gave Ralston a glare. "What exactly is your plan? Where is Tippy?"

Tst Tst held up the wooden life sized doll, still wearing Tippy's cloak.

Bitha shrieked.

"Shh!" Tst Tst said.

"We," Ralston began, "didn't have a chance to explain, but Tippy's upstairs, probably behind the counter, still."

"Ralston, are you insane?" Bitha stalked to the doll, yanked the cloak off its wooden shoulder, and, gripping the cloak in one hand, trudged to the top of the stairs and jiggled the door knob with her other. "Scorpents could be coming to this house, and they could take Tippy away. They can smell her. That's why Starkies placed us down here!"

Ralston had never seen Bitha's face so flushed. "She has the lantern I fixed. And she's going to let us out." He climbed the stairs and bent to speak into the keyhole. "Tippy, are you there?"

But even after several minutes no reply came.

Bitha pushed him aside and tried to coax Tippy. Still no reply. She faced Ralston. "Now you really bungled things."

"I don't get it," Ralston said. "She's *supposed* to come to the door and let us out. I need to hear what those *visitors* are up to. I don't trust Starkies."

"And so you kindly left Tippy to him? To the Scorpents?"

"Tippy!" he whispered again and jiggled the doorknob some more.

But no reply came.

73.
FIRE

BEHIND THE COUNTER Tippy fell asleep with the lantern lighted and still in her grasp. And she would have gone on sleeping except a shout startled her. Someone was quarreling. Who? It sounded like Mr. Starkies with some others with rough voices. And wheezing breaths. Stuffy noses?

Tippy stood and stretched her legs. Her knees gave a crack. That was an uncomfortable position to sleep in. And cold, without her cloak. At least the doll was feeling warm. The top of her head reached just the top of the counter, so she tiptoed to see where Starkies was. Three bulky forms had their backs to her and Starkies faced them, small and not his usual fierce self at all. The bulky guests didn't smell very good, like rotten fish, or something.

Suddenly, Tippy remembered she was supposed to get to the door to the cellar and let Ralston out. She dug into her pants pockets and finally found the key Ralston had given her. He'd made it himself. Her brother was good at those sorts of things.

The shouting grew louder.

"—you promised," one of the bulky guests said.

Starkies coughed. "The elder one is away, but once he returns I promise to deliver them all to the master at once."

"Tell us where they are now, and you will not be penalized."

"Penalized? You promised payments, first for the crystal, then for the hostages."

Tippy wondered what "hostages" meant. She dug one hand deep into a pocket and felt the smooth red crystal she'd buried right at the bottom of that pocket. It gave her comfort. It reminded her of Jules and the troubles he'd helped them through. It also reminded her of Grandpa and his old smell. She missed that smell: like tweed and the peppermint her grandpa loved to suck on. Must get to Ralston. He might scold her. Or worse, hurt her doll.

Lantern in hand she sidled toward the door, the wall to her back.

"—why do you have Elfie smell in your home if you claim they're not here?"

"It's an old smell, my Lord Lucius," Starkies said."From when the boy was here. I told you, he'd gone to the waterfall. Roaring Falls. But he'll be back and then I can—"

Tippy kept watch of the bulky forms as she edged her way, the wall cold on her back. She could still hear them quarreling, but less clearly now that she'd rounded the corner and entered the room with the dining table. The cellar door lay behind that tapestry hanging of a cottage set on a tree stump with boughs heavy with red fruits. Tippy halted and cocked her head to one side. Only bits of words from the smelly guests reached her ears.

"—tie him up—"

"—light the fire."

Tippy heard Ralston from the other side of the door and whispered to him.

"Hello! How's my doll?"

"Where were you?" Ralston asked.

She started to tell him of the quarrel.

"Never mind what you heard, just use the key and open the door."

She jiggled the wiry key Ralston had created and moved it around in the keyhole, but nothing happened. "It's broken."

"It can't be," Ralston hissed at her.

"Oh-oh," she whispered.

"What is it?"

"Some steps."

Tippy slipped out from behind the tapestry and crawled to hide under the dining table.

Three pairs of black boots trudged back and forth before her. And belabored wheezing.

"Nobody's here."

A gruff voice said, "Sure smells suspicious."

Tippy thought they smelled suspicious all right.

"What do we do with the traitor?"

"Burn him! Burn the whole house. He lied to us."

A body was dumped right in front of Tippy and she clapped her palm to her mouth. Mustn't scream. It was Starkies. They must have been carrying him! His eyes were closed, his skin pale, and his wrists were tied behind his back, but what struck Tippy was the way his neck was bent at a strange angle. She wanted to touch him, open his eyes for him, but stopped herself.

One pair of legs trudged toward the kitchen door and Tippy caught another smell besides the rotting fish scent as the guest walked by. A strong pungent smell not unlike when her mother poured liquid fire into the clay pot she used as a stove. Then just like that the three pairs of legs stormed past her table and out the room. Tippy crawled to Starkies and held her forefinger under his nose. She'd seen Jules do this to test if some mouse they'd found lying stiff near their house was still alive. She then laid her ears on Starkies's chest. Nothing. But she couldn't be sure. A whoosh caught her attention and she felt the house quite hot suddenly. A glow came from the kitchen area.

Perhaps Ralston would know what to do. But if she went back to the cellar door he was sure to scold her for not trying hard enough to open it.

But she really couldn't and she'd tried so hard. Then an idea struck her. She reached into Starkies's cloak pockets, first one then the other. And she felt it. A ring with about twenty different keys. She didn't know there were that many locks in the house. She flew to the cellar door and banged on it.

"Where have you been?" Ralston asked.

"I found keys." She proceeded to try one after another. She decided to start with the smallest.

"Tippy, where are the guests?" Ralston said.

"They left."

"Where's Starkies?"

"Resting."

"Hurry. It's growing hot down here."

"It's hot here, too."

"Tippy, how'd—"

But the lock clicked and Tippy pulled it open.

Ralston felt a gush of hot breeze whoosh past him into the cellar, and he heard the crackling of things. What?

"Girls, hurry!" He pulled Tst Tst and Tippy in each hand, while Bitha grabbed the mended lantern. "Where's Starkies?" He turned to Tippy. But bits of the roof caved in before them and a piece hit Tippy's head. She fell backward and Ralston was able to lurch her away right before she hit her face on a table corner.

The doorway was already ablaze.

"Over there!" Tst Tst pointed to a window still open and unblocked by falling debris.

"But," Tippy said, "we must help Mr. Starkies."

74.
STAR GAZER

JULES GULPED AS water seeped in through the top of the cocoon. Like a leaf borne by currents the cocoon skiffed and dipped into the icy underground river. The waterway must have coursed a journey under the mountain as it emerged on the other side of the slope into a swift river. Few trees and vegetation lined the bank.

By the time Jules climbed out of his dwindling cocoon after his underground rapids ride, he'd swallowed gallons of water—he'd swear by it. Soaking and trembling from cold, he collapsed by the bank and checked his arms and legs. He must be alive since his limbs ached with cuts and bruises and his head throbbed as if about to explode with a constant thump of what seemed like a war drum. And his stomach churned with river water.

Shivering, he sat on his haunches and tilted his head to the side. With his right hand he pummeled the ear above. But the water in his ear canal refused to flow out. He gave up after a while and decided to tolerate the constant gushing sound.

What should he do next? Where was he?

If he followed the course of the water, where would it lead him? The night sky was filled with a million stars and provided some light. He'd lost Abel's map. He searched his pockets and found Saul's soaking one—practically useless now since he had no bearing. Still he looked at it with the dim light of the stars. He reread his mother's note and the letter Mosche had sent Leroy—both also drenched. Perhaps he should seek shelter. How would he even get back to Starkies's to retrieve his siblings? He crawled on cut hands and knees slowly to the nearest bramble. Afraid he might fall asleep and freeze to death, Jules kept rubbing his cheeks and arms to keep his blood circulating.

Then he heard it.

Muffled and gruff voices of individuals arguing came from his far right. His ears felt so blocked by water he couldn't make any words out. A constant roar persisted in his head, even after he tried to drain the water out by shaking his head vigorously.

He crawled closer toward the voices and hid behind a boulder, careful not to snap a twig, even though his frozen brains warned him he was on the verge of hypothermia.

Were those Scorpent voices?

On bruised knees he crawled until he saw the shadows when he peered between two large oak leaves. The light of the full moon outlined a band of what looked like Handoveran soldiers with their crested helmets fraternizing with Scorpents, heavily garbed for war. Someone mentioned "attack," and maybe even the name "Mosche" and "Keeper," but he couldn't be sure.

If only his ears would stop roaring like a lion. What were they searching for? Or maybe *who* were they searching for, since it looked like they were searching for someone. He hoped it wasn't him.

Had someone alerted Gehzurolle he was on his way to Mosche's area? He could have been sighted. And the web bridge may not have broken accidentally. How did a branch just crack and drop like that? Where were his friends?

Jules shuddered as a chill ran up his spine. *Mustn't sneeze*, he reminded himself.

One of the Scorpents hauled a sack from behind a bush. It was wriggling like a jumping bean. The Scorpent dumped the sack on the ground and the wriggling stopped.

Who was in there? Was it Mosche? And were they ready to take him to the same place they kept his mother and Mrs. L captive? Would the Scorpents lead him to his mother?

If he tried to free the captive he might get caught. But Jules didn't ponder much longer for a cold hand clamped over his mouth.

"Shout and you're dead," the voice whispered in his ear.

75.
CHAOS

THE HEAT WAS getting to Ralston as the fire blazed within the rooms. Starkies lay unconscious near the counter.

"He's too heavy to move." Ralston pulled one leg as Tst Tst and Bitha pulled the other foot so hard Starkies's boot came off.

Tst Tst, sweat pouring down her chin, heaved again and pulled. "I don't think we can move him."

A beam crashed behind her, and she coughed and slumped on the floor.

Bitha said, "Look at Tippy!"

Tippy had collapsed next to Starkies, her body a rag.

"But we can't leave him," Ralston said, his arm over his mouth.

Bitha dropped Starkies's leg. "We don't even know if he's alive." Eyes tearing, she covered her face with a sleeve and edged toward Tippy. "I'm taking her out." She cradled Tippy's head and jerked her own chin to the window.

Tst Tst helped her carry Tippy to a window.

"Where's Ralston?" Bitha turned to Tst Tst.

"There!" Tst Tst pointed to Ralston, who was doubled over behind them and carrying three lanterns and heaving. He'd found Jules's lanterns.

The girls dropped out the window and limped away from the black smoke and the crackling of burning wood.

"Hurry, Ralston!" Tst Tst turned to Ralston and sighed when she saw him sprint away just as the blaze licked out the front door. He held the lanterns in front of him and tossed two to Tst Tst and Bitha. The fire consumed the home faster and faster until the whole tree stump it rested on burst into flames.

"We need to go farther away. Remember Holden's house?"

The sisters nodded and pulled Tippy, who limped along. Several onlookers, Handoverans in night clothes and disheveled hair, had gathered about gawking at the disaster. None came forward to help.

Ralston said, "There could be Scorpents about. Turn the lanterns on."

And true enough three Scorpents lunged out of the shadows of nearby trees and grabbed Ralston before he could turn his on.

"Run, girls!" Ralston shouted.

The Scorpents lifted their noses toward the starry night sky and one sniffed the ground by Ralston's feet. He shoved Ralston to his companion, who picked up the boy between his forefinger and his thumb as if he was a bug. "What girls?" it wheezed out. Even with their thick accent and gruff voice their words were plain as day. It was the same voice Ralston had heard at Starkies's.

Ralston fumbled with his lantern but accidentally dropped it. Too late. He shut his eyes and cringed as the iron grip released him into a dank, mold-smelling sack. He hoped the girls made their escape.

****

By the time Tst Tst and Bitha had pulled Tippy sufficiently away from the blazing house a crowd milled about the front lawn. Tst Tst couldn't stop crying and kept blaming herself.

"I should have carried the lanterns for Ralston, then he wouldn't have been so slow."

"Crying won't help." Bitha didn't sound any happier either.

"What are we going to do now?" Tst Tst wailed.

"If you don't stop the ruckus, even the lanterns won't shield us."

The three sisters sat under an oak tree, one of the few they'd seen nearby. It reminded them of home.

"I wanna go home." Tippy tugged at Bitha's cloak, which by now stank and looked gray and had holes.

"Stop it, Tippy. We don't even know where home lies."

Tippy pointed at the stars.

Tst Tst remembered the story of lost Elfie travelers who used the King Star to find their way. If she could find it, then she'd know where west lay, for the star always appeared on the west side of the moon. Could Tippy somehow have heard of the legend, too?

"You see the King Star?"

Tippy nodded and pointed to a bright twinkle.

Bitha squinted at the night sky, too. "We don't know if it's the real King Star. The moon's not out."

But as Tippy insisted at pointing, they kept staring at the sky until a white line zipped across, tearing the black expanse as the dazzling line ripped from the supposed King Star toward the direction away from where they stood.

"Was that a meteor?" Tst Tst enjoyed all things science and learned more than was required. She glanced at Tippy, who tugged at her sleeve and showed her the sardius. "What? Your red gem, again?"

Tippy said, "It's another one, another present from the King Star." Tippy shoved the red crystal at Tst Tst. "I saw it come that night. Jules ran away and I followed him, and I saw the flash from my bedroom window."

Tst Tst said, "What are you talking about?"

"The present!" And Tippy shoved the crystal back into her cloak pocket.

Bitha said, "We can't hang around. We might as well go in that direction. Maybe it's where west lies."

"And if we don't hear the river that means we're lost?"

"You have a better solution?" Bitha asked.

"I'm just *say-ing*. No need to get upset, Bitha."

Bitha sighed. "I'm sorry. It's just that if the present must mean an important Elfie just died, as Jules said, maybe a Keeper, then which other Keeper just died? Again?"

"There's Saul Turpentine, and he has his daughter, Chrystle, and there's Miranda—we don't even know if she's alive. Then there's Holden and his mother, Mrs. L. Then there's possibly Mosche…."

And Bitha said, "And there's us—Mom, and us, and possibly Dad because he's married to Mom. We don't know but there could be another fifth family."

Tst Tst sobbed. "I don't want to think about it."

Bitha gripped her arm. "But if that's really the present from the King Star, then the direction it took must be toward Reign." She pointed to her right.

"What's the point of going home? No one's there!"

"We can ask Mr. Saul for help."

Tst Tst stopped sniffling. "Okay, let's go toward that meteor. I don't even know how we're going to cross Brooke Beginning."

"Maybe we can find Tennesson."

76.
NO ESCAPE

THE STRANGER GRIPPED the top of Jules's cloak and pulled him backward as they both edged away from the congregation of Scorpents and their guttural, hoarse grumblings. The stranger seemed to know exactly where to maneuver both himself and Jules in the underbrush in order to avoid the cracking of twigs.

Finally, he yanked Jules's cloak even harder, and Jules stumbled back into a hole in the ground with rocks all about him.

"Don't think you're safe yet," the stranger whispered again into his ear. "They can hear even with their ears sliced off."

Jules often meant to ask why Gehzurolle had sliced off the ears of his servants, but for now he meant to know who his captor was. Except he couldn't see the face. It hid behind the cowls of a hood pulled far over the stranger's brows. The roaring in Jules's ears grew worse, and it shook the insides of his head as if his skull was going to split into two.

"Mind each step or you'll fall and be dashed to pieces." This time the stranger spoke louder.

It was already dark before, with only the light of the stars twinkling, but now in this rocky depression in the ground, Jules had to rely on his sense of touch to ease farther down the crevice. Where were they going? Below them a dim light glowed. The stranger was just below Jules and appeared to wait for him at intervals. He didn't seem worried that Jules might try to escape.

Where would Jules escape to anyway?

77.
DEEP, DEEP

AS THE ROCKY tunnel widened the light coming through from somewhere below made it easier for Jules to know where next to place his foot. The slightly balding patch of the stranger's head poked through his reddish hair, for he'd thrown his hood back. He was an Elfie, possibly a Hanfie. When the stranger stopped and looked up, Jules noticed his ebony eyes and bushy brows.

"You want to tie this over and around your waist." He reached upward toward Jules and handed him a thick hemp. "Double knot it or it might come loose." He pointed to the rope about his own waist.

With fumbling fingers Jules secured the rope, cinching it tightly. "Who are you?"

"This is no tea party, boy. The Scorpents may soon find our entrance. So, follow me."

The stranger pushed off with his feet, expertly stepped between the openings in the crevices, and finally disappeared below Jules. Where'd he vanished to?

"Hur—rry!" a voice echoed from below.

When Jules slipped farther down to where the stranger sat, he realized what he'd have to do, and he gasped. A bell shaped cavern was under his feet and only air lay between him and solid ground a hundred redwood tree lengths below. This was farther than anything he'd tried before. His head spun.

Once I follow him there won't be any turning back. Should I try to get back up the crevice? He gazed upward. Darkness greeted his eyes. And what if a Scorpent lay waiting at the entrance?

The figure of the stranger rappelling down made Jules's stomach churn, but he gulped down the bitter taste in his mouth and let go of the rope in his grasp an inch at a time. At times, it helped to shut his eyes and clear his mind. The lighted, dome-shaped cavern was well lit, and for once Jules wished it wasn't so bright.

"I was wondering," the stranger said, "when you'd get down."

"Who are you?"

"Mosche's the name. I trust you are Jules Blaze?"

Jules had expected Mosche to be older with more creases on his face, maybe with wiry white hair, but this youthful looking Elfie with shoulder-length hair curled at the sides and his deep-set eyes wasn't the picture he'd imagined. Also, the roar in his ears had lessened tremendously. He hit his temple to test his ears.

"What's wrong with your ears?"

"I got water in them—there's a constant roar, but it's better now."

"The roar's from the waterfall. But we're deep in the mountain now and that mutes the noise somewhat. It'll get louder once we get to my place. But you'll get used to it. Sometimes I hardly hear it." He guffawed as if he'd cracked a joke.

78.
MOSCHE, FINALLY

"SO, YOU'RE REALLY Mosche?" Jules stumbled as he hurried to keep up with the older man's brisk pace.

"Last I checked in the mirror. And I apologize if I startled you, but we shouldn't dawdle with Scorpents hunting for me. They have a scout in that sack of theirs. At least that's what I overheard. So it's a matter of time."

"Do you know who it is? The one in the sack?"

Mosche shrugged. "They never let him out, at least not yet. But I pity the fella. Scorpent style is to get rid of their helper as soon as he becomes of no help."

"You and your family've been here ages. Why would they find you now?"

"I'm not saying he'd find me this instant. But eventually, perhaps. We still have a ways to go, so let's talk and walk." He must have sensed Jules's weariness, for he said, "It's all flat terrain from here."

During the brisk trudge Jules told of his grandpa and the letter.

"I'm sorry but Leroy never came here, and I never sent him a letter."

Jules halted and stared at the ground. "Are you sure?" He groped about his pockets and showed Mosche the soggy letter. Some of the words had blurred due to the soaking but still, it was readable.

"I never wrote this."

"Then who gave it to my grandpa?"

"Good question. Who knew about there being five children in your household?"

"All our neighbors. It was no secret."

"I certainly never knew it. Although this is good news for me."

"That there are five of us?"

Mosche handed the note back. "My wife passed away and left me no heir. Which, as you know, is crucial for us Keepers, especially since only the child of a Keeper can qualify."

"I'm sorry to hear about your wife."

"Not as sorry as I when it happened three years back. But maybe you or one of your siblings can take over from me when the time comes."

But Mosche still looked so young. Why the rush?

"I'm not as young as I look, but youth is a side effect of studying the word in the Ancient Book, as you already know."

No, Jules didn't know. "I always wondered why Keeper families only have one child."

"Part of the curse. Which makes me wonder why there are five of you? Only one condition exists for this oddity. Perhaps we should wait until my home before we talk more."

"But how did you find out about this 'oddity?'" What was this one condition? Jules was sure he couldn't take any more bad news.

"It wasn't easy but I pieced the information together as I was trying to find answers to *my* problem—how I'd have to resolve my lack of an heir. But tell me, why *is* Gehzurolle seeking you?"

Jules took a deep breath and told about the red crystal Tippy had found.

Mosche stayed his hand upon Jules's shoulder. "It could very well mean your grandparents lost their lives in the Brooke. The timing of the flash and the red crystal seemed too coincidental. And where is Tippy now?"

"With Starkies. They're waiting for my return after I locate you and hopefully find news of our grandparents, or our mother. We have no one else to turn to. Our father's a general with a regiment that roams about, and we haven't received any news for ages."

"You mustn't lose hope. We *will* find her. And Holden's mother, too."

"But I don't even know where Holden is!"

By now they had approached a faint outline of a rectangle, as high as Jules was tall, etched in the wall. When Mosche pushed at it with both hands the rectangular slab creaked open into a large room, lit with torches secured to the walls. The room was decorated sparsely with a round table and chairs surrounding it. Once again the roaring sound vibrated in Jules's head. He cupped his ears.

"That's the waterfall behind my other entry." Mosche gestured.

After the relative quiet of the tunnel Jules understood why he'd thought the roaring sounded from his ears. The Roaring Waterfall lived up to its name.

One side of the dining room wall was covered by a bookcase with a few books, and on the opposite side two doors led to different rooms. But all this was not what shocked Jules. Mosche, it appeared, had failed to mention an important detail, and as Jules stepped into the brightly lit room, the wavering gleam from the wall torches too bright after the dimly lit tunnels, he gaped.

"Oh, yes." Mosche motioned to the figures seated in the room. "My friends have been awaiting you. We spoke about such mind boggling issues I forgot about them."

"Jules!" It was Holden.

And so they exchanged stories of their adventures since their last plight. Holden's dragonfly had brought him to Miranda, who was hanging for her life as she clung to broken bark of the tree their web was attached to. And after, with the help of Fiesty, they even located Hooks. But nothing could be done for poor Hooks, who'd broken his neck in the fall.

Jules stared glumly into space, and hung his head. *I should have insisted he go home! I should have, I should have.* He pressed the heels of his palms into his eyes. He'd never see Hooks again. Hooks who had been so kind, and selfless. And who'd been a true friend. Even if they'd just met, and had led such different lives, Hooks was more trustworthy than Miranda ever was.

Mosche said, "Are you okay, Jules?"

"You never know when you might see someone for the last time."

"Wisely said."

Jules remembered Hooks mentioning his own Elfie mother who'd died years before and how he'd hoped he might see her one day. Perhaps Hooks was even now speaking with his mother. Would he, Jules, ever see his mother, or even father, again?

"To continue the tale," Mosche said, as he laid four cups of steaming hot tea on the table before his guests, "the dragonflies brought Holden and Miranda to the only Elfie they've been working with for years—right to my doorstep, not that I have steps before my door."

He gestured for Jules to follow him to one of the doors on the other side of the room. "Come and see."

Jules locked eyes with Miranda for an instant. How'd she still have those ridiculous ear clips attached he didn't know. He turned to follow, tea mug warming his freezing palms as he cupped the walnut. He'd glanced at the dried bread and chunky soup Mosche had set before him but his appetite had shrunk considerably since Arnett's dream. Or maybe it was due to poor Hooks. He still didn't want to believe it.

"There!" Mosche pointed to the opening with the cascading waterfall acting as a drape before it. Icy sprays strayed into the room and gave it a damp feel.

On both sides of the door stood wooden shelves filled with odd-shaped objects. As Jules peered at these, their irregular shapes almost familiar, he saw what they were. Lanterns. Wing touching wing, the lanterns were in varied sizes. Their shapes were obvious now.

Mosche took one and presented it to Jules. "My family has been crafting these for generations since we moved to Handover. Great way to escape Scorpents. Especially needful if one lives in Handover."

"So *you* are the master craftsman they talked about, who lives in the hills of Handover?"

79.
FORGOTTEN PROMISES

UPON THE SHELVES stood rows and rows of dragonfly lanterns each similar to but not exactly like the replica next to it.

"Yes. Our lantern making is about the only thing that remained constant since the time of the King. Except, perhaps why Gehzurolle's after your family."

"What do you mean?"

"Gehzurolle's always hated Keepers. But now he seems more bent on annihilating us."

"I guess it helps that he has Elfie traitors working for him." Jules shot a glance at Miranda, who sat quietly sipping her tea. She hadn't acknowledged Jules one bit since he had stepped into the room. Her eyes looked glazed and her lids looked puffy.

"That aside. Take a seat, Jules, this will unsettle you."

After all I've been through? "I seriously doubt it." But Jules stalked to the dining chairs nonetheless and sat next to Holden and avoided looking at Miranda again.

"Let's start at the beginning. Before the King left he gave Eleazer a set of Books written with his blood. Books that contained all the wisdom the Elfies needed to reign over Reign. Eleazer was to keep the Books safe *but*, worried, he himself being old and capable of dying before the King's return, distributed these Tomes among his five children—two sons and three daughters: not unlike how you have your four siblings, Jules. To the eldest, Falstaff, he also bequeathed the King's gift, also dubbed as Petra, and which until recently every Elfie could only guess at."

"Why was that?"

"Let's not get ahead of ourselves. The gift was handed to Falstaff—my ancestor. But a horrible thing happened."

Here Miranda interrupted. "If I'm no longer a prisoner, I'd like to take my leave. I have no time for history lessons."

"But," Mosche said, "Scorpents are everywhere outside. They'll smell you out." He tapped his nose.

"I can handle Scorpents better than you think."

"Why the rush?"

"I have reasons. You speak here of the gift, but I already know more than you think."

"It's unwise to tempt fate. And what *do* you know of the gift?"

"That it's not lost, as you fear."

"I fear nothing but foolishness such as yours. It was foolishness that brought the curse upon our Kingdom, and only wisdom can reverse the curse we've been under."

Miranda scoffed. "I told Jules before—we need to get to my mother's home. She has a chest and the gift lies in it."

"And who told you this?"

"My sources. My mother stole it from my grandpa."

"Impossible. The gift has been lost for centuries."

"Lies are everywhere."

Jules interrupted. "Of course, your specialty. You should know."

Miranda glared at Jules, closed her eyes, and sat as still as a rock.

Jules said, "Please, Mosche, ignore her. The gift could be related to the problems my family faced these past weeks."

"It is the reason Reign has been cursed these past *centuries*," Mosche said. "If we don't reclaim or find the gift, we will forever remain small. And perhaps for some it is a worthy stature, but the Book tells me I was created for bigger things. Pardon the pun." He chuckled to himself, as if he'd said something that had amused him times before.

Jules leaned forward. "So, if we find this gift we'll all turn back to our size as before the curse?"

"If we get it to the Point. But the problem lies even *after* we get it to the Point. How do we transport all the Elfies there? The Book says only those who look upon the gift will be transformed back to our ancestor's former glory. That is a promise, and a warning."

Jules said, "A warning?"

Mosche shrugged. "I don't claim to have all the answers, but that's what my Book says."

Holden said, "But why did Falstaff run away to Handover?"

"Ironies of ironies, to keep the gift safe! My Book says, he ran away in the middle of the night, with the gift wrapped in his cloak. But that was not the worst of it. In his cunning he found his home behind the veil of the waterfall, and thought here he could settle as Keeper of the gift, at least until the King's return, and since he, son of Eleazer, was a lantern crafter, and was the most skilled of the children, he figured he could escape Scorpents well enough with the dragonfly lanterns.

"But his brother, Flamethrower, had secretly followed Falstaff and in a heated struggle Flamethrower fell to his doom here at the falls. But not before he'd grabbed the gift.

"Falstaff, too, didn't escape unscathed. In the fight, he'd hit his head and fallen onto a ledge. When he came to he remembered neither Flamethrower, the gift, nor knew what had happened except that he was soaked and lying by a waterfall ledge.

"And he never even realized he'd shrunk to inches of what he was before: for in losing the gift, he triggered the curse. Only later did the truth come to him from others who'd suffered the fate and told him—for even Scorpents and Handoverans reduced in size. Of course, none knew Falstaff was the cause of the curse. And neither did he himself realize this for he never regained his lost memory."

Holden leaned toward Mosche, "So, how did you find this out?"

Mosche said, "When my wife died I had way too much time and regret, so I buried myself in studying my Book. Flamethrower's Book, which had shrunk and later was found. Night and day I meditated on the words."

"Your Book prophesied all this?" Jules asked.

"Each Book has different prophesies. It's the Keeper's job to seek these out." Mosche said.

Holden scratched his brow. "So to reverse the curse we find the gift?"

"And take it to the Point," Mosche said. "The gift was the main reason why Gehzurolle has hated Elfies all these centuries."

Jules said, "It could still be *in* the waterfall. Does your Book say *where* in the waterfall?" Jules thought of the underground tunnel. Who'd laid those onion shaped candle lanterns? Arnett? Why?

80.
SHATTERED HOPE

MOSCHE SHOOK HIS head. "The gift shattered when it fell and its pieces scattered. That's the only explanation I can come up with."

"What *was* the gift?" Jules cast a glance at Miranda to see her reaction, but her face remained impassive and her eyes flickered away from him when he looked.

"Until recently none knew, but—" Mosche pulled his Book from a shelf behind him, dropped it on the table with a loud *thunk* and turned the crinkled pages. He pointed to a verse in it, and read, "'When shattered the crystal will shatter the lives of all whom the King created.' The King created us—Elfies, and also Handoverans, and even Scorpents."

"What does that mean?' Jules asked.

"By itself, anything. But then I paired it with another verse," Mosche said, and he flipped the leaves of the Ancient Book. "With his crown shattered the King could not return."

"A crown? A crystal crown? Why didn't other Keepers put the puzzle together before?"

"Keepers like *yourselves* who never studied your Books?"

"Well, you did it easily enough."

When Mosche slammed the Book shut even Miranda drew in her breath sharply.

"You have no idea the hours I've poured into finding this gem of information. You forget no one knew what to look for—Eleazer died instantly of a broken heart when he discovered his two sons missing, and the gift beside. All was considered lost. When Eleazer died, even *before* everyone shrank, the mystery of the gift died with him. No one but he and his two sons knew of the gift's existence. He hadn't even trusted his daughters, nor his wife, enough to tell them.

"No, young Jules, my ancestors and yours never thought to put two unrelated verses together as part of the same context. And I wouldn't have, too. Except I overheard of Gehzurolle seeking a red crystal and recalled a red crystal mentioned before in another section. Here." He flipped the pages again and the rustle of the paper-thin sheets seemed louder even than the waterfall's roaring. Mosche's guests waited.

He read, "'For the Lord of Shadows collects crystals: red, blue, green and purple, to spite the King.' So I asked myself, why would crystals matter so much?"

Jules said, "Tippy's red crystal!"

"Excuse me," Miranda cleared her throat. "Could this prisoner use the restroom?"

Everyone turned to her, and Mosche nodded to the door by the room with the lanterns. "In there."

She stretched her legs and walked to the door.

"Not that one, the other." Mosche pointed to the opening next to the lantern room.

Mosche said, "I'd remembered reading about the King Star giving off crystals of different colors when a Keeper passed away. The crown was crystal. Is that a coincidence, or does it mean something more significant?"

Holden said, "Is Gehzurolle collecting the crystals to make his own crown?"

"That I cannot confirm. But if we can get all the Keepers together with our Books, we would be able to fit more pieces together and maybe even locate the crown. For I believe each book holds a portion of the answer."

Jules said, "That may be the reason Gehzurolle is doing the same. He already has my mother, and Mrs. L. Maybe he has Saul, too. Miranda said Saul doesn't have his Book, although I could've sworn he was reading it in his home."

Holden nodded.

"It could very well be that Miranda's mother stole the Book, and that's what kept her alive in Handover. And it could explain Saul's refusal to accompany you here. Without his Book, a sworn Keeper is an easy target for Gehzurolle's forces in Handover."

Was that why his grandpa died? Because he left Reign without the protection of his Book? And who wrote that note urging Grandpa to leave? Jules felt his pockets and brought the soggy papers out. He straightened the crumpled map Saul had drawn and gave it to Mosche.

"Saul seemed to know where you might be hiding. Look. It's not precise but accurate enough."

Mosche stood and walked to the lantern room where the light was brighter. Standing by the door, Mosche stared at the rough map. "It was no secret that Falstaff lived at the waterfalls. But this is curious that Saul knew which one—he must have his ears tuned to the whispers of Handover. But something more disturbing has occurred."

"What?" Holden and Jules both said.

Mosche pointed to Saul's scribbling. "Notice the lettering? Looks like the writing of that note you said I wrote."

Jules had thought the writing on his grandpa's letter looked familiar, but realized now the capital letters "Ds" and "Ps" on both documents were identical. "Saul wanted my grandpa to find you! But I can't believe he'd want Grandpa harmed by sending him to Handover—they were buddies."

"It was strange that Leroy left during a bad storm. Seemed almost unwise. Unless he was urged. Tricked by someone he trusted. A friend?"

Jules sighed. "What should we do?"

"With my dragonfly lanterns we can sneak among the Scorpents to seek further news." He walked into the lantern room but halted. He turned back to face the boys, his expression grave. "It appears two of my lanterns are missing."

81.
INHERITANCE

"MIRANDA!" JULES SHOT to his feet and rushed to the door that led to the restroom area. "I wondered why she took so long." But searched as they did, Miranda remained missing.

"She was in a hurry," Mosche said.

Holden kept pushing his thumb into the bridge of his nose. "I hope it's not to help the Scorpents find us."

"She wouldn't have taken the lanterns if that be the case," Mosche said.

Jules slammed his fist on the doorpost. "She's gone to the cottage she mentioned before—where she thinks her mother lived—in Glennora or something."

Holden said, "Should we run after her?"

Mosche said, "She might not have gone far."

Holden jerked his chin at the opening at the end of the lantern room, with only the waterfall acting as a curtain to the outside world. "She left by the entrance we came in. The one by the waterfall. If she loses her footing on that slippery ledge she'd—shouldn't we stop her?" He rushed to the open doorway and peered out, sprays from the waterfall striking his face and clothes.

Jules shook his head. "But what about our mothers? And Ralston and the girls? And we need Mosche to hide."

"I've hidden all my life, and I intend to change that."

Jules said, "But there's one more thing you promised to explain."

Mosche strode back to his dining table and patted the surface for Jules, gesturing for him to come over. "Yes, your family. Perhaps you'd better sit for this one."

What could shock Jules further? "So, why are there five children in the Blaze household?"

"Historical fact shows Keepers to possess only one heir. And this has been true except on one condition—when *two* Keepers marry. When that occurs the Book says that the couple will be blessed with five—the number of the King's grace."

"That may be so, but only my mother is heir to a Book. My father comes from a line of soldiers."

"Remember Flamethrower? His son, Cedric, took over as his heir, but even so Flamethrower never swore Cedric in before he fell to his death. In fact, before Flamethrower secretly followed Falstaff, he *hid* his Book, so Cedric never found it. To save his family from being a 'Bookless' target of Gehzurolle, Cedric changed his last name."

Holden said, "So no one knows where that fifth Book is?"

"Or who that fifth Keeper was. Only that the fifth Book was hidden among the King's other books in the King's library. But today, even the library is lost."

Jules leaned forward, eyes wide. "So what did Cedric change his name to?"

"To still honor his father, he changed the family name from Flamethrower to Blaze."

"Blaze?" Holden and Jules said together.

Jules said, "So the library was an inheritance."

"The family passed the entire library to Cedric to make up for the loss that was not really his fault. But still, without his Book, Cedric was technically not a Keeper, so he removed himself from the circle of Keepers and, as you know these days, Keepers tend to live by themselves. Pity."

Jules slumped into his chair. "That explains the secret library in our cellar."

Holden gaped at Jules.

Mosche said, "In your cellar? That must be the inheritance Cedric received as Keeper since he never found his Book."

"So, is my father safe without his Book?"

"As long as he remains in Reign."

As General of the Elfie army his father, Jon Blaze, tended to protect the borders that were most attacked by Handoverans hoping to gain foothold into Reign. But still, didn't the three Hanfies who stole his lanterns say an Elfie regiment had broken into Handover? That the Elfie camp was destroyed by fire? Had another crystal fallen from the King Star he hadn't known about? A shiver ran up his spine. How could he even hope to find his father to warn him of this fate? He wrapped his fingers about his temples and dropped his head farther into his palms.

Then an idea hit him.

"Mosche, if we look into your Book it might say where my dad might be, or even what we should do. I can't imagine where we could start to solve our troubles. My troubles." How could he find anybody at this rate? How could he return to his siblings without his mother, or his grandparents?

Mosche opened the Book again and peered at the words, eyes squinting. "The Book has never lacked wisdom, that's for sure."

After some moments of argument, Mosche read a verse they all finally agreed upon. "Be a light to the darkness and a help to the helpless."

Jules agreed. "What about that prisoner in the sack? We can sneak up on the Scorpents and even if he's of no particular help at least we'd have done some good."

Holden said, "But what if he's a spy, or a Handoveran who doesn't like Elfies? He might spiel on us. Just because the Scorpents have him doesn't mean he's pro-Elfies."

Jules shook his head. "You forget our lanterns? If he's Handoveran and against us the lantern will keep us invisible."

"But what if he's an Elfie traitor?" Holden sounded defeated.

Jules shot him a glare.

Holden said, "I'm in—let's get him out."

They agreed to rest till daylight, for Scorpents are known to be most active in the night, but lethargic in the sunlight. This would avoid a Scorpent confrontation in case the lantern didn't shield the escaping prisoner, for he could very well be a Handoveran.

Once early light dawned, they returned to the Scorpent camp via the slippery ledge of the waterfall and Jules wondered if Miranda was already making her way undetected to her mother's cottage. He wished her well even though thoughts of her left a bitter taste in his mouth. A traitor to the end!

82.
GLASS TWINE

ALL WAS STILL at the Scorpent camp and the early light of dawn rained down upon the lumps of Scorpents interspersed here and there. Shrill breathing that ebbed and flowed like the rhythm of the waves pierced the constant roar of the waterfalls.

At least I don't have to worry if I sneezed.

"Where was the sack with the prisoner?" Holden whispered into Jules's ear.

They crawled on cut elbows and scraped knees to get closer. Some Scorpents slept around a bonfire they'd created in a clearing, where swaying grasses in the background bended back and forth with the gentle breeze.

"My bet is," Mosche said, not bothering to whisper now, "they've buried him."

"Alive?" Jules said.

"Hopefully—if they still have use for him. And seeing that they haven't found my place that's what's going for him. Unless they've given up on him being of any use."

Jules pointed. "Look at that pile of leaves there—could be a possible site they'd hid him under."

They crawled to the leaf mound behind a group of three snoring Scorpents. When Jules shoved his arm into the leaves his hand hit a burlap sack, rough in texture and hard as if housing something. He groped it and it shifted.

"Someone's definitely in there," Jules whispered.

The sack lay in a ditch scooped out and carelessly covered back again with leaves. He parted the leaves to make a tunnel for Mosche to poke his head into. Mosche reached in and loosed the tie at the top of the sack.

"Be still," Mosche said to the sack's opening as the sack wobbled.

"Help!" The voice from the sack was rough and weak. "Water…."

The Scorpents must have tried their dehydration tactics on the prisoner.

"We will free you—but promise to be quiet."

"Yes!"

One of the Scorpent guards stirred in his sleep and stopped snoring. He shifted about as if seeking for a comfortable position and grunted. The knot was a work of intricacy. Mosche ceased the untying. He motioned to Jules to give it a try.

For having bulbous looking fingers Jules was impressed, and annoyed, by the Scorpent skills of such delicate magnitude. It was almost impossible to untie.

"Use my blade." Holden offered his dagger to Jules who now tugged at the loosened tie and sawed at it. Holden had won the dagger at the local wood-cutting competition months ago.

"Hurry!" Holden whispered.

Somewhere in the forest behind them feet scampered about and Jules drew in a sharp breath. "This thing won't cut!"

"I didn't think it would, but I was hoping," Mosche said. "Glass twines. Only a diamond edge can cut through these."

"How do *they* undo this?" Jules gestured with his chin at the sleeping Scorpents.

"They use their hooked claws. Something we sorely need now." Mosche continued tugging at the twine, careful not to cut his fingers on the glass coating.

83.
DIAMOND-TIPPED CLAWS

JULES WONDERED ABOUT his friend, Hooks, and how he'd broken his neck. If only he'd listened to Miranda that one time. They would have been on the dragonflies when the bridge fell. Mosche didn't think it was an accident. Some force had worked to break that tree limb so that web bridge would fall.

"Holden," Jules said, "hand me your dagger. I have an idea."

Jules took the blade handle and gestured with it to Holden. "Cover me with the light."

"What are you up to?"

"Just make sure you shine it bright." Jules crept up to the Scorpent guard lying on his side, arms flailed above his head. With the blade he sawed at a hooked nail on the guard's forefinger. It twitched as he sawed it.

"You're going to wake him," Holden said.

Jules turned, glared at his friend and placed his finger on his lips.

The Scorpent's hand quivered and his fingers opened and closed as if his palm itched. Jules and Holden locked eyes and they stared at the other two guards to the left of their victim. One of them sat up on his haunches and rubbed his eyes. The beady eyes behind hooded scales turned toward Jules and Holden and blinked three lids, one closing after another, then opening again each successive lid wider than the one closest to the eyeball. Jules had never seen such dead eyes, bereft of feelings, of hope, of love; filled only with hate and suspicion.

Could he feel pity for these creatures of the night, servants of evil who pledged their allegiance to their master, Gehzurolle? Jules held himself still and dared not even breathe. Would the Scorpent smell him? Already it lifted up its nose as if sniffing the day. It swiveled its head, its thick neck the same width as its head, toward the pile of leaves. Mosche must have hidden himself in the leaves for a glow appeared under one side of the mound.

The awoken Scorpent shifted his weight toward its chum having the manicure. It leaned toward its chum's face and peered at its chum's mouth, a gaping hole, four fang-like teeth on its upper jaw. Did it notice the dangling claw on that twitching forefinger? Seconds stretched to minutes, and it seemed like hours for Jules.

After blinking some more, the Scorpent turned to face its sleeping companion on the other side and slumped down on its back and closed its triple lidded eyes.

Sunlight bearing down through the sparse canopy above made the cutting job more tedious than it should have been. They must have been at this for awhile. Sweat streamed down Jules's temples, particularly since the dragonfly lanterns also produced significant heat. He worked fast and furious until two claws were sawed off. Hard as iron rods, and curled at one end, Jules thought the curved claws would make great fishing hooks. They bore some similarities to the fishhooks his friend Hooks had borne with him. Could Hooks have killed Scorpents, or at least collected their claws, somehow?

Mosche grinned at the boys when Jules handed one claw to him. "I almost suffocated under these leaves."

"How's the prisoner?"

"Not a squeak. We better hurry though—he was already dehydrated, and we didn't bring water."

With amazing nimbleness, Mosche hooked and unhooked the glass twine knot, maneuvering it so the knot slowly unraveled. Jules carefully wound the portion of twine already loosened so the glass would not slice Mosche's fingers. When the knot came undone, and the sack opened, they slowly let the huddled figure out, which was when Jules stepped back and gasped.

"You're one of the thieves," Jules cried.

Holden prodded the Hanfie's shoulder. "Why are you here?"

"Having a party," the Hanfie thief Aloof said, as his knees buckled and he slumped to the ground next to Jules's feet.

Mosche hushed them. "Regardless of what he did we must help him."

Jules said, "We did that *before* and he ran off with our lanterns."

"It's not how you think," Aloof said, softly.

Mosche instructed Jules and Holden to gather twigs and stuff these into the sack. Deftly, Mosche re-tied the twine, of course not with the same tightness as the Scorpents did. But still they thought this sufficient to buy time for when the Scorpents awoke, closer to evening. "Save the greetings for later," he warned when the boys tried to get Aloof to explain himself.

Before they left the Scorpent camp, Jules tugged at Mosche's cloak. "I noticed they have more of that glass twine next to the guards."

"So?"

"We should take it."

"It'll shred you."

"Not if I wrap it up."

"They could awaken any moment. We need to hustle out of here."

But Jules said, "It'll just take a moment." And quickly he left and managed to slide the coil of glass twine out of the burlap sack next to the guard. But something else slid out with it. Jules held the pouch in his palm and gazed at it long. His pouch!

84.
CONFESSION

HOW DID THE Scorpents come upon his pouch of stones? They must have met up with Starkies, which meant his younger siblings could be in danger. Jules felt like kicking himself for leaving them. But the alternative had seemed worse, and when he thought of Hooks he felt he must have done right leaving them. He pocketed the pouch and resolved to look at its contents when they reached Mosche's home.

Lumbering, Holden and Jules, on both sides of Aloof, transported the Hanfie toward Mosche's. But leading him across the slick ledge of the entrance was a near impossibility. Aloof was barely conscious during some of the way. Jules had a good mind to shove him to a watery grave.

"We can't take him the other way, either." Mosche scratched his temple.

The thundering waterfalls roared in their ears. Strange how even the roar of the falls didn't seem so thunderous now that Jules was used to it

They slumped Aloof to the ground. What to do next?

"Leave me," Aloof said.

"He's delirious," Jules said.

Aloof stretched his arm. "I'm not. They have your brother."

"Who?"

"Those Scorpents."

"Ralston?"

"You have another one?" Aloof reached for Jules's cloak and drew him close. "They were taking us to the Keepers. They think your brother knows where the Book is."

"An Ancient Book?"

He coughed. "I don't know. They want me to kill your brother once we find the Book. Scorpents can't kill Elfies in Reign, remember?"

Scorpents were not supposed to kill Elfies directly, especially Keeper descendants, and especially not in Reign. Only agents of Gehzurolle who could summon the elements of the air or nature or other creatures could directly murder a Fairy Elf. At least that was what the Book said.

Jules bent over Aloof's face. "Where's my mother?"

"I swear I don't know. And I couldn't stop Alvin from stealing the lanterns. I was shot, too weak, remember?"

"Did you see Ralston?"

"Just a glimpse—I heard yelling."

"How about the girls?"

"The Scorpents burned the house, burned Starkies."

"Burned Starkies? What about my sisters? Did they escape?"

Mosche stayed Jules from shaking Aloof. "We need to stay quiet, boy."

Jules got up and beckoned to Holden. "I'm going to find Ralston."

"Wait," Mosche said. "Aloof's too weak. We'll hide him under leaves and come help you."

They crept back to the Scorpent camp even as the day waned. Things were taking longer than expected. What happened to Bitha, Tst Tst and Tippy? Jules's stomach churned and knotted. Under which pile of leaves had the Scorpents hid Ralston? He realized that the first sack he'd seen wiggled vigorously. There was no way Aloof could have had the energy to move so.

"I saw that wiggly sack back there." He pointed for Saul.

"If we hurry we can do it."

"I have a confession," Jules said.

Both Mosche and Holden stared at him.

"What?"

"I tied up the three guards by Aloof. So when they awake they'd know, at least that someone pulled that on them."

Mosche smacked his forehead. "They'd think it was me, and look even harder to find my home."

"I'm sorry. It just took me a minute, and they deserved worse."

Mosche glared at him. "Water under the bridge, I suppose." But he still shook his head at Jules. "Scorpents hate each others' company, so they'd only sleep close together for a reason."

"Like guarding someone?"

Mosche nodded.

Jules jerked with his chin. "How about those three huddled under that oak."

"Good eyes," Mosche said. "But there's another threesome to my left, too."

"Let's try mine, first. Holden, where's that hook you used?"

After making their way to the huddled three, they found a mound covered with leaves with a burlap sack within. They proceeded to undo the twine as they'd done for Aloof.

"Piece of cupcake," Holden whispered, when he'd sawed through the last knot with the hook. Mosche had explained that the tips of Scorpent nails were dipped in liquid diamond and can tear open practically any material. "Works better than my dagger."

"Hey!" A voice behind Jules startled him. He swiveled and came face to face with a woman with a strangely familiar face. "Shh!" she said and nodded to Holden and Mosche as well.

Clearly she was an Elfie, petite with a strong profile, and the bluest eyes. But who was she?

85.
THE SWITCH

WHERE HAVE I seen her before? Jules wondered. But she answered before he posed the question.

"I'm Chrystle—Saul's daughter. Shh! I'm here to help."

"How do we know you speak the truth?"

She rummaged and shoved a stone in Jules's hand. "From Tippy. She said to be sure you bring it back to her. Personally. Oh, and Tst Tst said, 'XYZ'. Got it?"

Jules opened his mouth, but someone tapped him on his shoulder and he turned to face Tennesson. They hugged quickly.

"Tell me how my sisters are."

"Your sisters are safe. But they have Ralston." He jerked his chin at the Scorpents.

Jules stared at the red gem in his palm and felt its smooth coolness within his fingers. This could be the token to confirm Grandpa's death. He put the sardius to his lips and then pocketed it. But before he could ask more someone spoke from the now wobbling sack.

"Who's there?" The person's muffled voice came through the thick burlap weave.

"Ralston!" Jules said as he opened the mouth of the sack.

"Jules!" Ralston cried a little too loudly.

One of the slumbering guards yawned loudly and sat up.

Jules clapped his hand over Ralston's mouth. Into his brother's ear he said, "Quiet."

Ralston, eyes wide, shook his head. "I'm sorry about the girls." He mumbled as his eyes strayed toward the sleeping guards.

Jules said, "We'll explain later." He turned to Chrystle, but she brought her finger to her lips. "Ralston, leave your cloak in the sack so they think you're in there."

Jules shrugged his cloak off his shoulders and offered it to Ralston. "Here, give me yours. I'm taking your place." With Ralston's cloak on, for they were the same size, Jules made to get into the sack.

Ralston said, "No! What are you doing?"

"They're going to take you to Mom. I intend to get there—it's the only way I can save them."

Ralston held onto Jules's arm. "No!"

"Mosche, take him away, quick. Ralston, the girls are safe."

Mosche said, "Are you sure you want to do this?" He handed Jules two lanterns.

Jules nodded. And to Holden he said, "Keep my sisters safe, or I'll come after you."

Chrystle helped Jules into the sack. "Your sisters came back to Tene's place and we've hidden them. But before I go, tell me, where's Miranda? I felt sure these Scorpents had her."

Jules stared into her blue eyes so much like Miranda's and swallowed a lump. "Ask Mosche. He'll tell you. Get away before they awake." He jerked his chin at the Scorpents. Dusk was already there.

Chrystle's gaze flitted to the sleeping Scorpents, as if she hoped to see Miranda nearby, then she started to secure the top of the sack. "Be careful—especially if you see my father. Don't trust him."

Jules said, "I know. And tell Tippy I'll keep her gem safe."

And they said good-bye after they cinched the top tightly with the glass twine.

Alone, quietly, Jules said, "Goodbye," to no one in particular.

86.
FLAMETHROWER'S BOOK

HOW LONG THEY must have traveled Jules couldn't tell. The Scorpents opened the top twice and dropped bread rolls hard as stones both times, and a satchel of water once. They must have not suspected anything although Jules had heard the ruckus caused due to the Scorpents he had tied together with the glass twine.

Afterward, when they found the sack with Aloof filled with brush, they had even punched Jules's sack and he balled up in pain in the crammed quarters even though he was already bunched up. He was just glad they didn't hit his lanterns; they were his only hope for escape. He did his best to protect the lanterns from damage.

The Scorpents carried him on swift feet and he imagined he must be on a shoulder, although sometimes they dragged him and jagged stones bruised him here and there. For the most part it seemed like they wanted him alive. No doubt to find the Book for them. He guessed it must be his father's Book. Flamethrower's long-lost Book. How they were going to cross Brooke Beginning he had no idea, although soon enough he felt his sack heaved onto the back of some insect, its bristles poking into the sack in some parts, and cutting his legs.

Once airborne, the wind currents pierced through even the thick waft of the burlap sack and sent a chill through his bones for it must already be the end of fall, and soon winter would come upon them. With the diamond tipped claw he'd stolen he made a hole in the sack. A river wound below them, dark like a stream of black ink amidst the verdant tops of trees. It was late in the day, or maybe it was early in the morning. Jules couldn't tell. He dozed on and off and didn't know day from night in the sack or how much time passed. They were going to Reign, he was sure. But where or when would they descend?

He planned for his next steps, and wondered about his father's Ancient Book. Where was it? When Flamethrower left he had not known he was never to return. He must have hidden it in the library amidst the King's other books. But which ones? It would be too numerous to go through each title and surely his Blaze ancestors must have already scoured through everything ages ago. Who knows, maybe they'd even taken all the books down although it would take some feat given the largeness of some of the tomes compared to the Elfies' shrunk size.

The books were filed alphabetically, so neatly, as though the original librarian had kept the order and no one had disturbed this. But what if Grandpa had stumbled upon it? Surely he must want Jules or his mother to know, or at least have an inkling to its whereabouts.

The next time Jules peeped out the hole in the sack the entire world had darkened. Black cone shapes took form in the distance. Conifers? Redwoods? He must have shifted about too much as he peeked for next thing he knew the Scorpent rider grunted something foul and thumped him on his head, hard. So hard, Jules lost consciousness.

87.
WHERE WAS MIRANDA?

RALSTON WAS SURE he'd lost half his weight, so when Mosche offered him a dinner of poached quail eggs and a buttery cream sauce served on a large dinner plate with tiny blue flowers, Ralston ate as though he was preparing for a yearlong fast.

Chrystle told him of how his sisters had stumbled upon a squirrel and having little option had ridden on it. It brought them to Abel's drey for it appeared that Abel was a King to them. He'd fed them and bundled them off to Tennesson, and they'd arrived not too soon, for Tennesson was about to leave with Chrystle to search for Miranda.

Once Mosche updated Chrystle on Miranda, she felt sure she could find her daughter in Glennora. The plan was to convince Miranda to return with Chrystle to Reign, and Tennesson would take Ralston and Holden to the girls. If things went as planned, they would meet at Tennesson's and Chrystle would take them back to Reign.

Ralston couldn't understand the fuss about a Hanfie they'd hidden in the leaves and had disappeared.

"He's Aloof—the same Hanfie," Holden explained, "who stole from Jules. Question is, where is he? He's gone! And where are his two cronies? What if he leads them to Mosche?"

Ralston said, "The three Hanfies brought the Scorpents to Starkies. When we saw the lanterns they brought, the girls and I suspected Jules must be in trouble and we planned our escape."

In any case, Tennesson would take Ralston and Holden back to his home to meet the girls, and then he'd show them the way back to Reign. Of course they would get there days after Jules, provided the Scorpents took him straight to Reign.

"I know where the kids can cross the Brooke." Tennesson turned to his wife and smiled. "Chrystle used to commute back and forth to Reign by a secret course to conduct her trade. It's a safe route up in the trees. I call it the treetop highway, so there're no mines or traps to be concerned with. The route leads to the Big Rock where the Brooke runs the smoothest, and we will use the hidden pulley to get down. I'll accompany them to the edge of the River, where the boulders span across."

Chrystle insisted she'd get to Glennora safely on her own to find Miranda. She told Ralston and Holden, "Once you're in Reign, follow the river south until you get to the area near my dad's place. You'll see the weeping willow half submerged in water there."

Holden said, "That should be easy. And I can find my way to the tunnel we fell into near my place. It'll be a safe hiding spot."

"Just," Chrystle said, "be careful my dad doesn't spot you. The lanterns will hide you from the Scorpents, but not from Saul."

Both Holden and Ralston nodded vigorously.

Tennesson hugged Chrystle before they left, and said, "Mosche, you take care that Hanfie doesn't follow you back here." His eyes roamed to the room with the lanterns. "Pity we can't carry more of the lanterns to Reign."

Mosche said, "Everything in its time." He turned to Chrystle. "Come by with Miranda on your way back and we can proceed."

88.
SCREAMING

WHEN JULES REGAINED consciousness, he found his hands bound behind his back, but he was still in the same sack since he could feel with his feet that the lanterns still lay under his calves. The Scorpents must not have seen them and, better still, they hadn't realized that he had switched places with Ralston. That's what happened to those who relied only on their sense of smell.

But even as he thought about scents he detected a strange odor. Something was burning. In fact, the crackling of twigs or leaves being burnt became apparent. Were they trying to burn him?

Jules sat up and struggled in the sack until his hand reached his pocket with the mirror shard. Careful not to slice his fingers, he retrieved it from its velvet wrap and sawed at the twine that bound him, for these were the ordinary hemp sort and not the glass twine used to secure the sacks.

Once loosed of the bindings, Jules cut at the hole he'd begun at the bottom of the sack. The crackling of the twigs sounded louder, and worse, someone was screaming.

Who were they trying to burn alive? Could it be his mom, or Mrs. L? Jules worked with more vigor, attacking the hole with the diamond tipped Scorpent nail since it was sharper than the shard, which he'd pocketed.

"No—oo!" It was definitely a female voice. And it was definitely familiar. But the pitch was too high to determine who it was. Was it his mother?

Jules's eyes scoured the dark forest when he'd freed himself from the sack. Night again! Between the underbrush ahead, the flames from the fire burning orange brightened the area. He threw one lantern down, and turned the other on. Lantern swinging from his left hand, he half-stumbled, half-ran toward the flames.

Would Saul see him with the lantern if he went close to the victim to save her?

Saul must not be around, or at least Jules couldn't imagine that Saul would watch this horror, for who'd bear to sit and witness a fellow Elfie being burned at the stake?

"No—oo!" The voice again.

Jules took another step, but something crunched beneath his booted foot. He picked up the object: it was about the size of his pinky, made of metal, with intricate floral design etched on it. Miranda's ear clip!

The wail continued, more frenzied than before. "Ahhh!" Definitely Miranda.

Through the gaps in the brush, Jules saw her. Miranda, the traitor. The one who sold his mother to the Scorpents. He watched, transfixed.

The flames crackled, flickered, like tongues. They licked more and more of the twigs and brush surrounding her. Miranda wriggled and thrust her head back and forth, obviously trying to free herself from the rope that bound her to the stake. A few Scorpents mingled about, not even bothering to look at her, as if burning Elfies was a normal practice. And maybe it was to them.

The flames devoured with ardor from the outside in, like a circle closing in on Miranda, and she screamed and sobbed on and off.

How had she gotten caught? Why wasn't she in Glennora? And why hadn't the lanterns she'd taken from Mosche hidden her from the Scorpents?

With Miranda, Jules just never knew where she stood. One minute she would be off to find a crown in a chest but supposedly smashed to smithereens and lost for centuries; next, she would be patronizing with Scorpents, although she obviously wasn't on friendly terms with them now.

To run into the flames would be tantamount to suicide, for surely the fire would kill him before he got to her. An open burlap sack, similar to the one they'd transported him in, lay crumpled nearby. Was she caught and then taken prisoner in that? A lantern in one hand, he draped the burlap sack upon his shoulders and darted into the flames. If the Scorpents had seen a walking burlap sack it must have not registered, for they went on their business with loud grunts and mocking.

The smoke rose thick around Miranda, and she must have passed out, for her body remained still and slumped to one side. Jules was surprised the flames were still some feet away. In typical Scorpent style the best way to kill was to take the utmost advantage of torture first. With one upward jerk of the hook on the hemp twine securing Miranda to the stake, Jules freed her.

Her limp body almost slid to the ground, but he caught her and slung her over his shoulder. The smoke rose thick and black about him, and he coughed uncontrollably, and so loudly he was sure the Scorpents heard him.

But then again the crackling of the fire rose almost deafeningly about him, and the Scorpents' garrulous laughter was enough to mask any coughs. Sweat poured down his temple, and he wiped at his stinging eyes. With the sack draped over her body across his shoulders and his head, and one hand still clinging onto his lantern, he dashed into a section with the tamest flames.

As he broke through the fire and leaped across the last of the ashen ground, Jules stumbled and Miranda fell with a heavy thud next to him. When Jules pulled her arm toward him, her limb felt strangely cold after the heat of the flames. Even in the dim lighting of the lantern he saw that her lips, cracked, held a bluish tinge.

"Miranda, wake up!" he whispered. He shook her shoulder.

Was he too late? He slapped her cheeks.

89.
SHIELD

WHEN HE GLANCED up he noticed that four or five Scorpents surrounded him and Miranda. Their broad faces bore down at Jules even as he clutched Miranda's arm, but their eyes seemed vacant, as if they were looking right through him.

The lantern!

Jules brought the lantern closer and waited. Could they hear him breathe?

One of the Scorpents bent his head toward Jules and stretched out his arm as if to touch him. Jules flinched. The large hands with the spoon-like fingertips and diamond-tipped nails reached past Jules and snagged the burlap sack by his side.

The Scorpent tossed the sack to his mate standing beside him, and they dispersed with a garish laughter.

Though the fire hadn't burnt them, Jules noticed blisters on his arm, and he smelled of singed hair. That and fumes from the burning pyre itself must have confused the Scorpent sense of smell. Regardless, it wasn't the time to speculate. If Whisperer or Rage showed up, would they see Jules and Miranda? Or smell them? And what about Saul? Was he around? Did he allow Miranda to be burnt?

Once Jules managed to hide Miranda behind a rock, he patted her cheek, this time gently, to revive her. Her eyelids fluttered. She coughed a few times.

Jules stared into her sky-blue eyes as they opened. "I'm sorry I don't have water to offer you," he said, holding her hand. Her wrists were bruised and cut.

She shook her head vigorously a few times, pulled her hand away from Jules and covered her face with both of them. "No, *I'm* sorry."

"It wasn't your fault you got caught."

Her voice was muffled, but Jules still made out her words. "I didn't get caught."

Jules crinkled his eyebrows involuntarily.

She said, "I gave myself up."

"But why?"

Miranda sighed and stared into space. "Because I wanted them to take me to your mom. I overheard they were going to get her, and I thought I'd prove myself to you by saving her. Then you'd know for sure I'd changed and I was telling the truth about the chest."

Jules locked eyes with her.

"I told them I could take them to your dad's Book. I thought they'd just let me ride like one of them, but they must already know where your dad's Book is, or maybe they already have their hands on it, since they didn't think I was worth anything. And I almost died for nothing."

"Not for nothing." He reached for her hand and pulled her up. "Great minds think alike."

Jules told her his reasons for switching places with Ralston. "C'mon, we still have work. My mom always said, 'A Keeper's work is never done.' I wondered how the Scorpents were able to stake you like that. That was brave of you to offer yourself for my mom."

"I forgot about them having the right to kill me if I offered myself."

Before long a raucous fight broke out among the Scorpents and the branches swayed as if a hurricane played havoc with the trees. Jules held Miranda by her shoulders, and they slid farther into the crevice between the rock and the hard earth.

"What's happening?" Miranda said.

"I heard Gehzurolle's paying a visit to Reign." He shrugged. "We'd better hide. Do you know where we're at?"

90.
SINISTER MEETING

MIRANDA EXPLAINED THAT before they'd tied her to the stakes she'd recognized some of the odd growths of willows by the Brooke. Jules didn't even know they were near the Brooke.

"Didn't you try to peek out when they brought you here?"

"I was unconscious."

"Oh?"

"I'll tell you later. So, is Saul's place close by?"

Miranda's eyes flitted to the branches. "They weren't taking us there. Your mom's somewhere under the Brooke. That's what I heard."

"Under? How's that possible?" Jules didn't want to think of the implications of being under the river. It hit too close to his grandparents' drowning.

"Those tunnels you mentioned before near Holden's place? They run all over. Most were created by Handoverans who wanted to escape to live here in Reign centuries ago. Supposedly they'd dug one that runs from Handover to here."

Jules remembered the rusty rungs that went up the walls in some of the tunnels.

Miranda jerked her chin at the Scorpent ruckus. "Looks like they just discovered that the Hanfie they caught is gone."

"He's the very one who stole my lantern."

"Really?"

"I hope he was telling the truth when he said he'd changed and doesn't mean Elfies harm. I left him with Mosche and your mother."

"My mother?" She shook his shoulders.

Jules clued her in about Chrystle and Tennesson and how he'd convinced them Miranda had left for Glennora. "I had no clue you were in the camp. Look!"

Before them leaves and debris swirled and a gray mist snaked across the forest floor like a serpent slithering and searching for someone to devour. When the mist stopped, it formed a figure with a hooked beak and dark eyes. It stood not a stone's throw from Jules and Miranda, but the rock seemed to protect them for now.

Jules thought the apparition was speaking to him but saw that an Elfie stood to his right, partially hidden by the rock. But he recognized the voice.

"I just need to verify one last issue in the Book, and then I can take you to that library."

"You'd betterrr be right thisss time."

Jules cupped his hand over Miranda's mouth, for she'd looked like she was about to shriek. They must stay hidden or they would lose their chance to spy on Saul's activities.

91.
THE REAL TRAITOR

WHISPERER SAID, "GEHZUROLLE left specific instructions about the Books. So you read speedily."

Jules edged his way out of his hidden position and peered to spy on the scene.

Saul said, "What did you burn over yonder?"

Whisperer said, "A traitor you needn't worry yourself over. Although it must have been a weakling, after all."

"What?"

"The traitor," Whisperer went on, "doesn't smell as intense as I predicted."

"It's not the Hanfie who tried to escape? Or did I hear you also got that boy, Ralston?"

"My Scorpents say we no longer have need for the boy, although it would have been nice to have him as a bargaining chip—just in case the mothers try to trick us."

By now Jules couldn't hear Saul's reply. He motioned to Miranda and whispered in her ear. "Do you know the entrance to that tunnel?"

"It's near Holden's house," she said.

That tunnel near Holden's home was the meeting point for his siblings. What it they met up with Scorpents? Or enemy Handoverans? Jules could only hope the lanterns stayed true.

"I need to find Flamethrower's Book before Saul does. Can you find my mom on your own?"

"I can do better—I know where to hide them."

"Here—take the lantern."

She took it from him and kissed him lightly on the cheek. "For luck."

Jules stepped backward and almost fell.

She said, "What about you?"

"What?" Jules thought she sounded worried.

"Do *you* have a lantern?"

"I brought two and have another hidden over there." He pointed to a bush some steps away.

"When they're safe, I'll come find you."

"No. Stay there. I'll find—" But it was too late. Miranda had already slid away from the rock hideout and, quick as flash, she was gone. Jules didn't have time to worry; he cast one glance at Saul and crept away in the opposite direction toward the hidden lantern.

92.
SECRET LIBRARY

JULES COULDN'T BELIEVE all he'd gone through as he stepped into the dark spiral steps that wound deep under his home to the cellar library. When he reached the door into the cellar he found it bolted. Saul or one of his agents must have locked it the last time he was here, for Jules recalled he had not closed the door then.

With difficulty Jules slid the latch open inch by inch, careful not to make the rusty slider creak. Still, it squeaked. He took a deep breath and waited. Surely no one was in the library unless they were trapped within. Once the bolt was closed, the solid door was impenetrable. Jules took the diamond-tipped Scorpent nail from his pocket, slipped the hook-like portion between the latch and door, and shaved off a small portion from the bolt itself. With the rust shaven off, the latch slid back silently. Better than oiling it, he thought.

An idea hit him.

Once inside the cellar he placed his lantern on the floor, rummaged for the thin glass twine from his pocket, careful not to cut himself, made a loop with the twine, and hooked the loop over the handle of the latch. Holding onto the twine carefully, he closed the door and pulled the twine so it re-bolted the door from the inside.

With the diamond-tipped hook he sawed off the twine. If Saul and the Scorpents got there before Jules had a chance to escape then at least they wouldn't think he was hidden in the cellar and hopefully they wouldn't think to bolt the door again if they left before him. It would be impossible to open the door from the inside.

Having accomplished this task Jules held his lantern high and scanned the cellar with its high ceiling. He gazed at the books with different eyes from when he had last been there.

Was this the very library the King had once sat in while penning the Books? It was possible the whole library had sunk and a tree had grown over it, since that had been centuries ago. And the ceiling was incredibly high. Every other item of furniture must have been taken away. Only the bookcases and books were left.

The books in the shelves looked just as big and formidable as when Jules had last seen them. They lined the four walls of the cellar with the dozen or so middle bookcases spaced back to back reaching to the ceiling.

Old books sat there by the thousands, some stacked on the shelves, most arranged by height next to one another, spine to dusty spine, on the bookshelves. Some of the books had interesting spines made of shells or bound with lace, now almost tattered. Most of the tomes loomed tall—several times taller than Jules, and many considered him tall for an Elfie.

Much had happened since he and his siblings had hidden in there.

If I tried to think like Flamethrower I might find his Ancient Book.

Lantern in hand, Jules walked past the first row of books, soldiers at attention, standing guard, still and stately. Coated with a thick layer of powdery dust, the volumes looked like they'd been untouched, let alone read. Which was a good sign.

If the Ancient Book had been slipped between one of these it would have left a gap because these books had stayed the same size but the

Ancient Book had shrunk. Furthermore, the spines of the Ancient Books were different from these bound tomes. The double X's made of coppery wire on the spine would have surely stood out, which meant that sticking them between any two books wouldn't have been enough to conceal them.

Grandpa Leroy must not have found the Book, for surely he'd have brought it to his mother. Yet he'd written that cryptic message '—ook within.' Look within? Book within? Hook within? Crook within? Grandpa must have found clues about its whereabouts from his own Book. But that by itself had not been enough to get him the exact location.

Saul, at least according to Miranda, did not possess his own Book, and Grandpa didn't know of Jessie Lacework being a Keeper, or he might have asked to research hers. Which meant only one option remained—to visit Mosche.

Grandpa must have shared his suspicions of the Book in the library with Saul, who connived to take advantage of Grandpa's desire to locate Mosche and sent him that fake letter.

Perhaps Saul did want Grandpa to find Mosche and bring him back so Saul could also get his hands on the fifth Book and sell that to Gehzurolle to get his prize—the crown or Chrystle, or both. Or maybe Saul just wanted Grandpa out of the way so he could capture his mother and Mrs. L. and get their Books.

Regardless, how could Jules locate Flamethrower's lost Book with only a scrap of a clue, and even that a dubious one? Grandpa must not have told Saul, or surely with '—ook within' and with the kidnapped Books, Saul would have deciphered things, and he'd have his hands on the Book by then.

Jules wiped off some of the dust on the spine next to him. AOG Sigrid, or *Art of Games* by Sigrid. He took another step and cleaned the next spine, AOW Thoryn, *Art of War* by Thoryn. Systematically, Jules wiped with his cloak and read the spine. And then it hit him.

Since Flamethrower was still tall *before* he left Reign and the curse hit the Kingdom, the books at Flamethrower's eye level would have been several shelves up. Unreachable for Jules presently unless he had hours to climb.

But if the Book was up there and it left a gap, no one Jules's size (which included everyone in Reign and beyond,) would even know. But, if Flamethrower wanted to hide it somewhere inconspicuous he must not have used a shelf that was eye level and obvious at the time of the hiding. He'd have hidden it either behind something or placed it on a lower shelf. But not spine outward, not even with the Book's leaves facing out, as again it would have stuck out from the others. But where was it?

93.
"—OOK WITHIN"

"—OOK WITHIN," TRULY meant "Look within," and also, "Book within." Because the Book was hidden within another Book and Jules thought he knew where now. He kept on reading the titles, but not each one as before. He skipped every five or ten books.

The books were arranged in alphabetical order, and he quickly realized this was not the correct row.

How long had he been reading and searching? Mustn't lose track of time, he reminded himself.

The dust proved to slow things as he constantly had to rub his nose so as not to consistently sneeze. When he was on to the fifth bookcase, his heart thumped so loudly he was sure anyone lurking above in the main house would hear it. The book was titled, *Only One King* by Eleazer, and before it, the letters "OOK Eleazer." This must have been the Eleazer of old that stories associated with the King who left and could not return due to the lost crown. If he could pry the book loose from its tight fit between the two that stood guard on its left and right, Jules felt sure the Ancient Book lay inside.

But try as he might the "OOK" book wouldn't budge.

And worse, footsteps thudded near the doorway into the cellar. They must have slid the latch open without Jules hearing it. What if Saul was there? He'd see the lantern. Jules turned it off.

Gruff voices with a shrill wheeze at the end of each breathy sentence floated into the room, followed by an altogether familiar voice. Saul's. The gall of him to bring Scorpents into this cellar. Would they stumble upon the broken glass twine he'd looped over the latch or had that fallen and perhaps in the darkness been overlooked?

Jules hoisted himself up the OOK book. Thank goodness for all that practice scaling up the barks of redwoods and whatnot. The gap between the top of the book and the bottom of the shelf above him was not much—about the width of his shoulders—but it was enough for him and his lantern to squeeze into. The bookcase was one of ten that backed onto another. Once perched on top Jules wiggled his legs toward the back of the bookcase and he lay prone, head overhanging the top of the book's spine.

Hurry! Jules told himself. He rummaged inside his cloak pocket and cut his finger on the diamond tipped hook but bit his lip to stop the pain. What it Scorpents smelled him? Better squeeze farther back. He wiggled like an earthworm toward the back of the bookcase even more.

The voices were clearer now and the shadows of the visitors made huge shapes here and there as the torches they carried brightened the library.

"The Book," Saul's voice boomed in the high ceiling of the cellar, "should be in one of the middle cases. Look for the title, *Only One King.* Let's divide. I hope you lot are literate."

So, Saul had figured out the location using the two Books in his hold.

"What," a Scorpent voice said, "do we do with them?"

Who were they referring to? Surely Miranda had reached his mother and Mrs. L and taken them to safety?

"Take the women back to the hideout and watch them. Once we get the Book we can transport the whole lot to the Master," Saul said. Feet trudged across the stone floor.

How could Saul, a Keeper, call Gehzurolle his Master? Jules felt contempt and pity for Saul for having sold himself.

Then Saul said something that startled Jules, and he drew in his breath sharply. "And if the Master queries about Jon Blaze's death you must support my claim that I was not to blame. Besides, his son, that Ralston boy, can take over as Keeper and translate, so all's not lost."

"So let's hope the Scorpents find the boy," a voice hissed, almost inaudibly.

94.
FOUND AGAIN

JULES HELD HIS breath for so long he almost passed out. He never thought he would lose his dad. When did this tragedy happen? How? Saul, it seemed, was to blame.

His stomach churned and his throat constricted. How could Saul betray them so? Jules lay there paralyzed. If he jumped onto Saul he could strangle him. Cut his throat with the diamond tipped hook. After all, the lantern would hide him from the Scorpents.

But what could that accomplish? And what about his mother? And Mrs. L? Who'd save *them* if he was caught? And his dad's Book? Strange, he never considered Flamethrower's Book as his dad's. Without the Book the Keeper could be so easily defeated.

A familiar voice broke through Jules's grief.

"Rage will release the locusts once we find the boy. They should be arriving any minute."

Locusts? In Reign? Jules had heard they were trained to devour Elfies whole. Were these the same ones he'd run into in Handover? So, why were they brought here?

"Of course," Saul muttered. "What do we have here? *No Turning Back* by Llewellyn. NTB. We are already at the 'N' series. Let's hope the 'OOK' book isn't on the upper shelves."

So Saul hadn't figured Eleazer's book sat on a bottom shelf. Jules squeezed himself farther in, toward the back of the bookcase. His feet found a gap behind the *Only One King* book. He slid down with a soft thud and pressed his back against the back board of the bookcase.

Dust flew up and tickled his nostrils when he landed. He cupped his nose with one hand.

"Did you hear that?" Saul sounded very close.

"Maybe the boy sneaked in here." The same familiar whisper sounded.

Whisperer!

Saul, again. "Can't be. The cellar door was locked from the outside. You float to the upper shelves and see if the title's up there."

A whoosh sounded and the bookcase shivered as though Whisperer's presence between the shelves sent shivers up the spines of the books as they stood guarding the Ancient Book.

"Try," Saul shouted, "not to bring the entire bookcase down, Whisperer."

Jules thought it excellent that the bookcase had shifted as another idea struck him and he brought the diamond-tipped hook out again. Who'd have thought he'd have so many uses for a Scorpent claw.

Several minutes passed and, between the wheezing of the Scorpents and Saul's muttering as he read the titles, the cellar library teemed with activity and noise until Saul said, "Ahh! I got it. I found it. *Only One King.* Help me take this volume out, you useless lot. It's stuck tight."

Scorpent feet trudged toward the book, and Eleazer's book shook as they tried some method to loosen the hold. They managed to slide another book next to it out first and this fell with a thump, barely missing Saul, who cursed.

"You almost crushed me, you oaf!" Saul said, "Hurry. It should be within this one."

Four Scorpents held onto the spine of the "OOK" book.

Saul went on: "Flamethrower cut out the pages inside and hid the Book within this one. I'd never have guessed that 'OOK' referred to both 'book' and 'look' within and also the call number of the book, of the *only* book Eleazer ever wrote, too. "

Another thump resounded as *Only One King* dropped to the floor, having been successfully maneuvered out of its slot.

"Once we open the cover, the Book will be within—of course it wouldn't occupy the entire cut-out as it had shrunk—" Saul stopped short when the cover was thrown open by four Scorpents. "How can that be?" Saul said.

"Where isss i-it?" Whisperer hissed out.

But even as Saul, with the help of two Scorpents, flipped the cut-out pages, the Blaze Ancient Book remained amiss.

Whisperer said, "The Master will be upset, most upset. Essspecially since I urged him to visit Reign for thisss most auspiciousss time. I will blame you, Saul. I will tell the Master *you* tricked me, tricked usss all into wasting the Master's time. Where isss the Book? Do you not wish to see your daughter and granddaughter again?"

"Maybe it was the boy! He must have stolen it. Got here before we did. If we hurry we'll find him before the Master gets here. He couldn't have gone far."

Whisperer swirled and turned back into his dark density of smoke self and floated toward the cellar entry. "Who shut thisss door?"

Jules on the other side of the bolted door, lantern in hand, crept back up the steps thankful he was able to see with the light, especially since he had to grope with one hand when finding his way to the door of the library, and then slide the bolt shut in the dark. His other hand clutched at his chest, the Blaze Ancient Book within his grasp.

The diamond-tipped hook had served its purpose in more ways than he could've imagined, for he had cut a hole through the pages of Eleazer's book with it, easy enough due to the age of the papers, crawled in through the opening, and taken the Book even whilst Whisperer was busy rattling the shelves and Saul was muttering his grumbles.

But how long could the bolt hold the Scorpents in? And could Whisperer slide through the gaps between the door and the jamb?

95.
BUZZING

IN THE CLOSET Jules placed his ear to the door, afraid more Scorpents lurked outside. But no sound came through.

He stepped into the living room and gazed around. Was Gehzurolle truly on his way to Reign? Was it another of Whisperer's bluffs, for Gehzurolle's agents had no qualms about using any means to get their way?

The house felt cold and lonely without the usual chatter and quarrels of his siblings and his mother's usual banter. But maybe it felt especially lonesome because his father would never walk in again. Nor his grandpa and grandma.

Behind him, deep under the closet, a faint rumble came through. It was a matter of time before Whisperer figured a way out of the cellar.

Jules knew he must get to the hideout Miranda mentioned and make sure his mother and Mrs. L were safe, but he felt paralyzed by the news of his dad. He clutched the Book to his chest and rocked back and forth, trying to stop himself from sobbing. He pushed thoughts of his father away from his mind, happy times, scolding times, misunderstandings. It was such a long time ago his father had left them to go ward off the Handoveran soldiers.

Did Dad realize he was a Keeper? Was that why *his* parents, too, had died prematurely when his father was a teenager? At least the Blaze Book would tell. But now was not the time to speculate, Jules chided himself. Not the time to reminisce. And regret. And what of the locusts? That was when Jules noticed a buzzing, droning, and grating on his nerves. What was that annoyance?

When Jules peeped through the shutters he found his answers. Right before his home, several steps away in the clearing between the oak trees, was a gathering of thousands, perhaps millions of locusts, brown with feelers that sang a song of war. They stood at attention, hard-shelled body lined next to hard-shelled body, with only their gangly feelers rubbing against each other as if in impatience, as if awaiting instructions.

Then the front door burst open and unlikely visitors stumbled through it.

"Jules!" It was Miranda.

"What are you doing here? I told you to stay with Mom."

"They're fine. Mrs. L was ill but your mom's taking care of her. We heard a loud buzzing and your mother told me to check on you."

Behind her, Holden, Ralston, and his sisters followed her in, stumbling.

"What," Jules continued, "are you all doing here?" He turned again to Miranda. "Did you bring them here?"

Miranda said, "We only met seconds ago around the bend."

Holden said, "Abel helped us. And Tennesson showed us the way."

Ralston said, "We came to warn you. The locusts are here to eat any Elfies left behind in Reign. Some force is keeping them calm, but we heard they'll begin their feasting once Whisperer passes instructions."

Jules pressed his knuckles against his temple. "Did Fiesty bring you here?"

"With his friends," Holden cut in. "They met us by the river. But they left in a frenzy when they saw the locusts out there."

Ralston added, "They're too many. Millions. Gazillions. And not just here, too. We saw them on the way."

96.
BLOWN AWAY

A DEEPER RUMBLE escaped from the closet.

"What," Bitha said, "is that?"

"Whisperer. Too much to explain. We must leave now."

"But what about the locusts?"

Jules slipped the Book into one of his deeper pockets and patted about looking for something. He brought out Abel's whistle and turned to Ralston and his sisters. "Do you have one?"

They nodded. "Abel gave us one each," Ralston said.

"We're going to blow them away."

Ralston said, "What?" His eyes widened.

Jules stepped through the front door and the rest followed suit. When he started blowing into the whistle, no sound issued forth, but he remembered that was what had happened before and how help had come in the form of Fiesty. And then another time, the butterflies.

After a few minutes, Holden jabbed Jules on his side. "How long do we keep blowing?"

"Until something happens."

But the locusts remained, still focused on rubbing their gangly feelers, still unmovable. Will they up and leave? Or will they only obey Whisperer's call? Or maybe Gehzurolle's? Was Gehzurolle already on his way?

Stop worrying, Jules.

A breeze shook the boughs directly above him, and the afternoon sky must have darkened, for suddenly the light faded. When Jules took a step off the porch, an acorn dropped in front of him.

Whoa!

Then another and another came down. Was it raining acorns? He glanced up. Eyes were watching him. And beaks poked out of the leaves on the branches here and there. He thought to stop blowing but didn't. When a bird swooped toward him, Jules jerked back. He recalled the black birds that had attacked them on that evening so many weeks ago. Ravens had tried to eat them. But the birds that swooped toward him, toward them at the porch, weren't black.

They were white. Doves!

Jules had read of them, but had never seen them before in Reign. And here they were.

A handful of doves dove toward Jules and his companions, but the rest, in the hundreds, maybe thousands, flapped toward the waiting locusts and began to peck at them as feed.

"Quick, we must leave before Whisperer escapes." Jules shoved the whistle back into his pocket, grabbed Tippy's arm and pushed her toward a dove that had alighted directly before them. But she twisted herself free and held her hand out.

"My sardius, Jules."

Jules ruffled her hair and, having found the red stone, dropped it into her open palm. "I told you I'd take care of it. Now, c'mon."

She hugged him as he placed her on the dove.

Holden said, "I can ride with Tst Tst."

And Ralston rode with Bitha.

As Miranda swung her leg to get onto her dove, Jules reached for her arm. "Take my place and ride with Tippy. I need to return to the cellar."

"Are you insane?"

"Your grandpa's in there—they'll kill him for sure for losing the Book. Here, take this, and hand me the lantern." He handed her Flamethrower's Book, which he knew was really a Blaze Book.

"Let me talk to him," Miranda said, her eyes tearing.

"Later. I need to ask him some things. Just take them to my mom, and this time, please, wait for me there."

"But—"

But Jules already took off, lantern high above his head. Would Saul listen to reason?

97.
CRUSHED

HE'D EXPECTED WHISPERER to have broken through the cellar door and to be waiting in the house with his Scorpents. But when he entered stealthily all remained quiet. Ominously quiet. He was about to step into the closet when a moaning stopped him.

Behind an overturned dining table a pair of boots stuck out. Jules tiptoed and peeked behind the furniture. Saul lay on his back, eyes closed, as if asleep, except for the moaning. The Scorpents must have hurt him. When Jules went on his knees to check his hands, he landed on a sticky mass on the floor.

Blood! That was when he saw the blade sticking out of Saul's chest.

"Oh, no! Saul!" He touched the old Keeper's forehead and cheek to revive him, but Saul's eyes remained closed. "Mr. Saul. It's me, Jules." And felt stupid for saying it. Why would Saul even care about him at the moment? "What can I do?" he whispered to Saul.

"It's too late."

"I don't get it. They're not supposed to be able to kill Elfies here. In Reign."

"That's right. But I gave myself to them, remember?" Saul sounded resigned. He held out his hand as if in surrender, and smiled weakly. "Where's Miranda?"

"She's safe, with my mom."

"They told me they burned her. You saw her? Sure she's safe?"

"She's fine."

"Miranda must leave Reign. Gehzurolle's locusts will eat every Elfie on sight, and there is no hiding."

"What do you mean?"

"He has found the crown and will place it on the Point. I know it. You realize what that means, boy?"

"What our people have been waiting for centuries to see. We'll regain our height. Just like before the curse."

"You don't get it? You think it such a great thing to reverse the curse? To grow back to the size we were? Don't you see—where one curse ends, another begins."

"What do you mean?"

"When the crown is placed on the Point, *everyone* will grow. Even those hiding under the earth and the trees. They'll all be crushed."

Jules remembered what Mosche had warned. So that's why the Book said Elfies had to gather to watch the crown at the Point. It was for their safety. "We can rally everyone to come out."

Saul smirked. "Everyone? Gehzurolle has the Elfie-eating insects everywhere: locusts, mantises, ghost insects. And Rage has ordered them to consume every Elfie on sight. This will force Elfies to hide underground or in trees. And what happens when they regain their size then? Leave me, boy. It's time for me to wither."

Jules moved to drag Saul by the arms, but the old Keeper slapped his helping hands away as if he was swatting at mites.

"Stop! Go save yourself and my Miranda. And my Chrystle, too—*if* you can find her. And tell her I did it all for her. To save her before Gehzurolle gets to her. It's too late for me."

"We don't know if Gehzurolle got the crown."

"Will you be a fool till the end? Messengers just spoke of Gehzurolle's victory. Gehzurolle would win in the end—always knew that, always felt in these bones of mine."

"You shouldn't have—felt that. Whisperer's a liar. And so's Gehzurolle. I refuse to believe it. I *won't* believe it."

Saul closed his eyes and sighed deeply. "Your faith never failed to amuse me. That was the one thing that prevented me from killing you when I had the chance, boy. The whole lot of you."

"Killing me? When?"

"When you came asking about your mother. Thought I'd gotten rid of you for sure sending you off to Handover."

Jules swallowed hard a few times. "Saul, tell me about my father. What happened? Where is he?"

But Saul didn't open his eyes, and his breathing lessened until it ceased.

98.
LIGHTNING SPEED

JULES SHOOK THE old man's shoulder violently and sobbed. He hadn't told his siblings about his dad, for he'd hoped that what he'd heard wasn't true. His father couldn't have died. Shouldn't have died.

But it was too late for Saul to answer now. Wiping his face with his sleeve, Jules stood and glanced about the room.

He stalked over to a partially destroyed armoire, one door tottering on its hinge, and he groped within the scattered papers in its drawers till his fingers found something soft and silky. He took it out and unfolded the square of silk. It was his grandmother's scarf Saul had brought back that early hour when he'd brought the news of the capsize. In it lay his Grandpa's pocket watch and the old man's felt hat. He'd give them to his mother. Maybe they'd give her some comfort.

Jules groped again within the drawers and found a broken mirror: the one his dad always used when he shaved. That was when he saw that the glass shard with the "OOK within" message came from a part of this mirror. He still had the shard, carefully wrapped, and hidden in his cloak. He'd fix it to the looking glass and give it to his mother as a memento.

When a thud-thud came from the closed shutters, Jules froze. He ducked behind the overturned dining table, slipped the items into his pockets and crawled to the window. He peeked between the slats and breathed a long sigh. It was Fiesty pecking at the window in a frenzy. Far in the distance between the bulky trunks of oaks, the doves were still pecking at their feed. It wouldn't do for a dove to take Fiesty as food.

Swiftly, Jules got out to check on his pet. But when he strode to the door again a roar above stopped him from knocking. Thunder? He hadn't noticed any lightning through the window slots due to the canopy. Was this like the solitary flash last night, a single warning of a pending storm?

The hair on Jules's arms stood on ends. Static electricity. Just like when the lightning destroyed Holden's place.

Jules rushed out the front door and hoisted himself onto Fiesty, and with one hand on its neck and another hanging on to the lantern he said, "Quick—"

Just as they airlifted a gush of hot air shot past him like a fiery arrow and the oak tree that held his home burst into flames. How they escaped the fire Jules couldn't say, for the instant they took off his tree home exploded like firecrackers. He forced himself not to think of Saul, who was lying in there, nor the things he'd grown up with and were tied to his grandparents and his family. A lifetime of childhood memories evaporated in seconds. Would the fire consume the books deep in the cellar?

Fiesty must have sensed the danger, too, for he darted in and out of the tall grasses, higher and higher, and away from the burning tree. Amidst the black smoke and wailing of doves flapping to get away, Jules saw a trail of gray puff swirling upward. Whisperer?

"Faster, Fiesty." Jules knew he was no match for the powers Whisperer could harness against him. The heat from the fire turned his face red and the smell of singed leaves and smoke made his eyes tear.

From the gray swirl something like silver arrows shot out and pierced the clouds that hung low, and the sky growled as if in pain. More and more thunderous crashes sounded as lightning struck tree after tree. The ground vibrated and rattled as though giants were stomping everywhere. Several of the conifers blasted into flames as the bolts shot down upon the forest with greater speed. Each affected tree instantly burst into flames and burned black before toppling with deafening booms. The lightning consumed some trees whole.

Whisperer was destroying everything Jules loved.

Before long Jules's backyard resembled a graveyard for dead trees. Some of the conifers rested on top of toppled trunks; a few tottered between unscathed neighbors like unpredictable see-saws.

Jules let go of Fiesty's neck and groped deep into his cloak until he found it. It felt heavy and the soft leather supple in his hand. He hefted the weight in his palm and with his teeth cinched the leather strap of his Grandpa's leather pouch even tighter. He'd be sad to lose it, too, but his Grandpa must surely approve of his plan if he succeeded.

One hand still grasping the lantern and Fiesty's neck the best he could, he jerked Fiesty around and headed toward the mass of gray swirling by an unharmed tree. Jules, holding onto the leather thong, slung the pouch filled with the gem stones upward over his head and twirled it round and round, lassoing it faster and faster till the pouch became a whirring blur over him.

When he flew as close to Whisperer as he dared, he let go the leather thong and the pouch of stones rocketed toward the dark mass. Jules didn't hang around to see its effect until he was a few trees away. The pouch must have come loose when it hit Whisperer, for its contents tumbled in the air, a hundred different hues that caught the dazzle of the fire and lightning. But that was not what amazed him.

Instead of falling to the ground, the gems spun about their own axis, practically at lightning speed and, having gained such speed, each stone flashed across the empty space and raced toward the sky leaving a trail of silver in its wake, not unlike the flash he'd seen whizzing across the sky that night.

What had he and Grandpa collected all those years? When another tree crashed close to where he and Fiesty were hovering Jules knew it was time to escape.

99.
TRUTH

JULES JERKED FIESTY here and there to avoid the lightning bolts and the crashing trees. Perhaps Whisperer was still at it. Was his family safe in that tunnel near Holden's already-destroyed home?

When they got there Jules alighted and raced to the hole near the rock. Someone had piled stones on top of each other around the hole so it was even better hidden than before.

The moment he slid in and landed at the bottom a hand reached out and grabbed him.

"Jules!" the voice was familiar, but it was dark, too dark to decipher features and faces, and it had been a terribly long time since the speaker greeted him. But when someone brought a lantern up close, Jules leaned over, and hugged his greeter with all the strength left in him.

"Dad! Saul said you were dead."

"I'm sorry he scared you." Jon Blaze ruffled his hair, even though Jules stood taller than his dad by at least a hand's width. "You went through some awful stuff. I came back as soon as I'd heard about the locusts. We saw them fly here. Holden and Ralston saw my troop when we were on our way to the house and they told me everything. I'm sorry we came too late to help you, but I'm more than glad you're safe."

"But we can't stay here. Saul said Gehzurolle's found the crown and means to use it to destroy Elfies."

Miranda led them toward the cave she'd brought Erin, Jessie, and the rest of the children to hide in. As they hiked deeper into the tunnel Jules informed his father of all he'd learned.

Jules said, "If Gehzurolle brings the Crown to the point, all of us still underground will be crushed when we turn bigger."

As it turned out Gehzurolle had not found the crown and that it was just another lie, John pacified him.

"Still," Jules said, "we should help Chrystle get it, or hide it, until we're all ready."

Jon Blaze agreed. He had his regiment ready for redeployment.

"Mom!" Jules rushed forward and gave his mother a long hug. Even Holden was seated by his own mother, as she lay on some blankets with her head resting on a bundle as a pillow. John Blaze had brought enough supplies to last a few days.

"I'm glad we're all safe." Jules reached into his different pockets and brought out the gifts he'd brought for his mother. "I'm sorry about Grandpa and Grandma. And I even brought you Dad's looking glass." He told them about how he'd figured out the location of Flamethrower's Book and all agreed they should pool their thoughts to figure out what to do next. They agreed it was of utmost importance to hide the three Ancient Books. Gehzurolle must not get his hands on these at all cost.

Later when alone with Miranda, Jules said, "I'm sorry about Saul."

"Me, too. More than I care to admit. I know it's going to hit me hard later—that he's gone. He was a father and a mother to me all my life. But I could always tell he lied to me, here and there. He was so bitter about my grandmother's death, and then, my own mother ran away. I still can't believe it—what he tried to do."

"I guess your mother had reasons to leave him."

"And to take his Book away." The rim of Miranda's eyes were red. "But still, he loved me. And I was blinded by my desire to find my mother, no matter what. I guess, seeing you, and Holden," she glanced at Holden, "with your mothers always close by, made me jealous. I let that feeling take over me. That jealousy." She shook her head and looked at the ground.

"I know about jealousy. I saw you and Holden sharing secrets, and I felt that was unfair. How come I don't have a best friend. But it's hard losing a grandparent. I know."

She locked eyes with him. "Do you think Saul knew your grandpa might lose his life when he sent him to Handover?"

"It's any body's guess what went through Saul's mind."

Miranda twirled the stray hair by her cheeks with her fingers. "He was consumed by trying to find my mother, just like me. We were both blinded. But he was also consumed by anger, too—that my grandmother died so prematurely. He wanted to blame someone for it, so, he blamed the King, he blamed the Ancient Books, and the laws the King laid down. He never saw that his anger would cause him more harm than good."

"What's good is that once we get all the Books together we'd know for sure how to proceed. I miss Mosche and even Abel. Him and his crazy whistles."

"I wondered about those. He must have some diagrams to follow."

"He has his secrets, but he's a good guy."

"Like you." Miranda wrapped her golden hair into a low knot and slid it under her cloak.

"I always *wanted* to believe you. I'm glad Gehzurolle hasn't found the crown. It'd be awful if we were to change back to our normal size suddenly while some of us were still in the trees or underground." Jules's eyes wandered to Holden. He was talking to Mrs. L who seemed pale and weak. How were they going to find Mr. L?

Even Jon Blaze didn't have a clue where their infantry went.

Miranda said, "Still, I intend to leave for Handover to find my mother when dawn breaks. Just to be sure Gehzurolle's forces aren't really going to the Point with the crown. Care to join me?"

Jules looked at his siblings. They lay huddled in the corner, and his parents, sitting on the floor cross-legged beside them, were quietly talking.

"Let me enjoy my family a bit. When I started out I wanted to find the truth about what happened to my grandpa. I never thought my mother could be kidnapped, or that I'd lose some of my siblings along the way! I need to appreciate them for a bit. I understand your need to find Chrystle. And, you know I met your dad?"

She laughed. "I can hardly believe it, myself. He's supposed to be dead!"

"Rals didn't tell you the details?" So, Jules told about Tennesson and how he'd helped them willingly, even though he was a Handoveran. "I can show you how to get to his place on my map. He's waiting for your mother. There must have been a change of plans. I thought they were to take Ralston and the girls here."

"I better talk to Rals, then." She made as if she was going toward Ralston who sat next to Jon Blaze but turned to face Jules again. A wisp of hair fell across her high forehead. "Sure you don't want to follow me tomorrow morning?"

"I'm not sure about anything. The Books might very well point me to follow you. That's the other thing, I never thought I'd hear myself say that about the Books." He smiled, brushed the golden wisps from her eyes and pushed the strands away from her face. He brought his other hand up and fastened the metal clip he'd stepped on earlier, to the tip of her ear.

"You're not alone on that. I never saw the need for the Ancient Books before, too. Who'd have thought?"

"Just don't take off without saying goodbye." Jules yawned.

Miranda laughed. "I'm going to talk to Rals, and then I'm going to catch some shut-eye. You look like you haven't slept in ten years!"

"Sure feels like it. I have a feeling that once I sleep, a million buzzing mosquitoes couldn't wake me."

So, that evening, after a quick supper, they all settled down for the night. Jessie Lacework's condition had deteriorated and she had slipped into a coma. Holden had to drag his mat to sleep next to her. Another neighbor, a Mr. Knapp, had appeared looking distraught, and so the Blazes had invited him to spend the night in that cave.

That night, Jules tossed and turned, hardly sleeping at all. When he woke up with a start he heard a whisper and in the doorway of the underground chamber he saw Saul beckoning to him. Was it a dream? He rubbed his eyes and stared at the tunnel but the vision was gone.

To be continued...

DEAD DREAMS

A YOUNG ADULT PSYCHOLOGICAL THRILLER MYSTERY

Prologue

THEY SAY EACH dead body, a human corpse, has a scent all of its own, a sweet-sour smell. A cadaver dog picks up the odor as clearly as a mother recognizes a photo of her child. Of course, I wouldn't know, for I am no dog. I might as well have been, the way I'd stooped to yield to my basic instincts. My mind wandered to her, what her unique smell would be when, and if, they ever were to find her.

****

After what happened, I decided to write out the events that led to that day and details in case I'd missed something, or might need it for defense, or in case they found me dead. My relatives might need to piece together the things that had spiraled out of control, if they wanted to put me to rest, to forget me altogether. That would be least painful for them. I nodded to myself as I sat in the car. I thought of my most favorite girl in the world: Lilly. At least Lilly'd have my dog, Holly, to remember me by.

My friends used to call me Brie, short for Brianna. But, I could hardly count anyone a friend any more. I'd have to resort to back-watching if I wanted to survive.

Chapter One

IT STARTED ON a warm April afternoon. Gusts of wind blew against the oak tree right outside my kitchen balcony, in my tiny apartment in Atherton, California. Sometimes the branches that touched the side of the building made scraping noises. The yellow huckleberry flowers twining their way across my apartment balcony infused the air with sweetness.

My mother had insisted, as was her tendency on most things, I take the pot of wild huckleberry, her housewarming gift, to my new two-bedroom apartment. It wasn't really new, just new to me, as was the entire experience of living separately, away from my family, and the prospect of having a roommate, someone who could be a best friend, something I'd dreamed of since I finished high school and debuted into adulthood.

"Wait for me by the curb," my mother said, her voice blaring from the phone even though I didn't set her on speaker. "You need to eat better." Her usual punctuation at the end of her orders.

So, I skipped down three flights of steps and headed toward the side of the apartment building to await my mother's gift of the evening, salad in an á la chicken style, her insistent recipe to cure me of bad eating habits. At least it wasn't chicken soup double-boiled till the bones melted, I consoled myself.

I hadn't waited long when a vehicle careened round the corner. I heard it first, that high-pitched screech of brakes wearing thin when the driver rammed his foot against it. From the corner of my eye, even before I turned to face it, I saw the blue truck. It rounded the bend where Emerson Street met Ravenswood, tottered before it righted itself and headed straight at me.

I took three steps back, fell and scrambled to get back up as the vehicle like a giant bullet struck the sidewalk I had only seconds ago stood on. The driver must have lost control, but when he hit the sidewalk it slowed the vehicle enough so he could bridle his speed and manage the truck as he continued to careen down the street.

My mother arrived a half minute later but she had seen it all. Like superwoman, she leaped out of her twenty-year-old Mercedes and rushed toward me, all breathless and blonde hair disheveled.

"Are you all right?" She reached out to help me up.

"Yes, yes," I said, brushing the dirt off my yoga pants.

"Crazy driver. Brie, I just don't know about this business of you staying alone here like this." She walked back to her white Mercedes, leaned in the open window, and brought out a casserole dish piled high with something green. Make that several shades of green.

I followed her, admittedly winded. "Seriously, Mom. It's just one of those things. Mad drivers could happen anywhere I live."

She gave me no end of grief as to what a bad idea it was for me to live alone like this even though she knew I was going to get a roommate.

"Mom, stop worrying," I said.

"You're asking me to stop being your mother, I hope you realize this."

"I'll find someone dependable by the end of the week, I promise." No way I was going back to live at home. Not that I came from a bad home environment. But I had my reasons.

I had advertised on Craig's List, despite my mother's protests that only scum would answer "those kinds of ads."

Perhaps there was some truth to Mother's biases, but I wouldn't exactly call Sarah McIntyre scum. If she was, what would that make me?

Sarah's father had inherited the family "coal" money. Their ancestors had emigrated from Scotland (where else, with a name like McIntyre, right?) in the early 1800s and bought an entire mountain (I kid you not) in West Virginia. It was a one-hit wonder in that the mountain hid a coal fortune under it, and hence the McIntyre Coal Rights Company was born. This was the McIntyre claim to wealth, and also a source of remorse and guilt for Sarah, for supposedly dozens of miners working for them had lost their lives due to the business, most to lung cancer or black lung, as it was commonly called. Hazards of the occupation.

And then there were cave-ins, which presented another set of drama altogether, Sarah said.

I sat across from her, the coffee table between us, in the small living room during our first meeting. "So, that's why you're not on talking terms with your family? Because of abuses of the coal company? " I asked.

We sipped hot cocoa and sat cross-legged in the crammed living room, which also doubled as the dining space. I'd never interviewed anyone before, although I'd read tips on the Internet.

"I just don't want to be reminded anymore," she said, twirling her dark ringlets round and round on her pointer finger.

"But, it's not entirely your dad's fault those people died of lung problems."

"I guess, but I just want to get away, you understand? Anyway, I'm almost twenty-one now. That's three years too late for moving out and establishing my own space." She took tiny sips of the cocoa, both hands cupping the mug as if she were cold.

I walked to the thermostat and upped the temperature. A slight draft still stole in from a gap in the balcony sliding door I always kept open a crack to let the air circulate.

"So, your family's okay with you living here? In California? In this apartment that's probably smaller than your bathroom? With a stranger?"

"First off, it's none of their business. Secondly, you and I won't *stay* strangers." Sarah flashed me a grin. "Besides, I'm tired of big houses with too many rooms to get lost in. And, have you lived in West Virginia?"

I shook my head. The farthest I'd been was Nevada when we went for our family annual ski vacation. "I heard it's pretty."

"If you like hot, humid summers and bitter cold winters. So, do I pass? As a roommate?"

She looked about at the ceiling. I wondered if she noticed the dark web in the corner and the lack of cornices and crown moldings. I was sure I smelled mold in the living room, too. But I wasn't in a position to choose. Sarah was.

"As long as you're not a psychopath and can pay rent." I returned her smile.

"I don't know about the psychopath part." She shrugged and displayed her white, evenly-spaced teeth. "But here's my bank account." She tossed me a navy blue booklet with gilded edges and with golden words "Bank of America" on the cover.

I fumbled as I caught it and was unsure what to do. "Should I peek?"

"Go on." She gestured, flicking her fingers at me as if I were a stray cat afraid to take a morsel of her offering. "No secrets. I can well afford to pay rent. And, I'm a stable individual."

I flipped the first few pages and saw the numerous transactions in lumps my parents, who were by no means poor, would have gasped at. The last page registered the numbers: under deposits,

$38,000. My eyes scanned the row of numbers and realized that the sum $38,000 came up every sixth of the month.

My mouth must have been open for she said, "You can stop gawking. It's only my trust fund. It comes to me regardless of where I am, or where I stay. So, do I make the cut?"

I handed the bank book back. We discussed the house rules: no smoking; no drugs, and that included pot; no boyfriend sleepovers or wild parties, which was a clause in my landlord's lease; and Sarah was to hand me her share of the rent, a mere $800 a month, on the twenty-eighth of every month, since I was the main renter and she the sub-letter. She didn't want anything down on paper—no checks, no contracts, and no way of tracing things back to her, she'd stressed a few times.

She fished in her Louis Vuitton and handed me a brown paper bag, the kind kids carry their school lunches in. I peeked inside and took out a stash of what looked like a wad of papers bundled together with a rubber band. Her three-month share of the deposit, a total of twenty-four crisp hundred-dollar bills. They had that distinct new-bank-notes-smell that spoke of luxury.

I gulped down my hot chocolate. "Why all the secrecy?" I asked as I wrapped up the interview. I could understand not wanting parents breathing down her neck, but as long as they didn't insist on posting a guard at the door, what was the harm of them knowing where she lived?

Sarah glanced about the room as if afraid the neighbors might have their ears pinned to the walls, listening. She leaned forward and, her face expressionless, said softly, "My parents are dead."

Watch out for Book 2 coming out early 2014 as Jules's adventure continues. Sign up for the newsletter to get updates and contests information.

***

Key of Reign, Reign Fantasy Book 2
out Spring 2014

Other Books by Emma Right

Dead Dreams Book 1 now on Amazon

A young adult contemporary psychological thriller and suspense mystery.

Eighteen-year-old Brie O'Mara has so much going for her: a loving family on the sidelines, an heiress for a roommate, and dreams that might just come true. Big dreams—of going to acting school, finishing college and making a name for herself. What more could she hope for? Except her dreams are about to lead her down the road to nightmares. Nightmares that could turn into a deadly reality.

If you have enjoyed this book please leave your short review at your e-retailer, or leave your comments at emmaright.com

Made in the USA
San Bernardino, CA
21 February 2015